CLOWNFLESH

TIM CURRAN

Crystal Lake Publishing
Where Stories Come Alive!

www.crystallakepub.com

First published by Bloodshot Books in 2019

Current version copyright © 2025 Tim Curran

Join the Crystal Lake community today
on our newsletter and Patreon!
https://linktr.ee/CrystalLakePublishing

Download our latest catalog here:
https://geni.us/CLPCatalog

All Rights Reserved

ISBN: 978-1-964398-27-3

Cover Art: Alex McVey | alexmcvey@gmail.com

Layout: Jacque Day | jacqueday.com

Follow us on Amazon:

WELCOME
TO ANOTHER

CRYSTAL LAKE PUBLISHING
CREATION

Join today at www.crystallakepub.com & www.patreon.com/CLP

1

Tonight, a blizzard has come, a raging monster of a blizzard with screaming subzero winds, its belly choked thick with snow and freezing rain, and Craw Falls—a very unexceptional little town in the southeastern corner of the state—is directly in its path. All of that's bad enough, but what's even worse is that which has come with the storm, using it as a sort of camouflage as it hunts its human prey.

But that's for later.

For now, out on Crow Lake, a scant mile from the town, Milford Zeiss sits in his little ice shack jigging for perch with a dropper rig. He hates the idea of calling it a day because the jumbos are really running and they're taking his waxworms as soon as he gets them in the water. His bucket is filling up and he can see a perch fry in his future of the sort he hasn't known in years.

But that storm...

Oh boy, she's a good 'un, Mil thinks, dropping his line in one last time. Twenty seconds later, he pulls out another big fat-bellied perch and into the bucket it goes.

By then, the shack is shaking in the wind and even Mil—who's fished Crow Lake since 1954 when he was eight years old—is starting to get a little concerned. Sighing, angry at Mother Nature for kicking up her heels on a night when the fishing was not just good but spectacular, he packs away his gear and closes the damper on his woodstove to starve the fire.

Under his breath, he says, "There's always tomorrow," but this does little to cheer him. He knows how damn finicky the fish are out on the Crow and a night like this could not come again for weeks or months or even years. That's the real kick in the ass of it.

Defeated, Mil opens the catch on the door and the wind yanks it out of his hands. Damn. Some kind of blow. In the light from the lantern in the shack, the snow is a funneling maelstrom of pure wrath. He has to hunker down against the frigid gales as he steps the few feet to his 1976 Polaris Colt and turns it over. He lets her run a few moments to warm up.

Back in the shack, after wrestling the door from the fingers of the storm, Mil shoves a Winston in his mouth and shows it some flame with his Zippo. Helluva night, he thinks. A real shitpot. But he's seen worse (or so he tells himself). As he draws off his cigarette, he knows he'll find shore all right. He's only a quarter-mile out and the depression of the ice trail will be easy enough to follow. Besides, that old Polaris of his is like a horse that knows its way home even if its rider doesn't.

Mil figures he's probably the last one out on the ice tonight with that storm kicking up its heels. A die-hard. That's what he is. But when the fish are biting it takes a real act of God to shake a Zeiss off the ice. His old man used to say the town puppies call it a day at sunset and that's when the real men do their fishing. Mil smiles at that. Still, he knows a blizzard out on the ice isn't something to take lightly. He's lived through enough winters in the far north to have respect for them.

One last drag off his weed and he tosses it into the stove and calls it a night. He turns off the gas lantern and pulls on his wool mittens. Taking his fish bucket, he opens the door and lets the wind take it so it doesn't wrench his arm out of its socket. He stows the bucket on the back of the Polaris and gets ready for the ride back in. He locks the door of the shack and goes over to his snow machine. There, he pauses.

Hell is that?

Despite the near-perpetual drone of the wind, he hears something like tinkling bells out there in the darkness. That's insane. Then he hears it again and it sounds a little closer. Funny. Way out here. But who knows, some fool might have tied some wind chimes or something to his shack and the storm pulled them loose. A few years back, he recalls, Johnny Pallanpa bolted a six-foot flagpole to the top of his shack to fly the stars and stripes in support of the troops in Iraq. One night during a storm like this, the wind found it and ripped it free along with a section of the roof it was bolted to. By the time old

Johnny was done patching it, grunting and griping the whole while, he didn't feel like such a good American anymore.

Mil smiles at this.

Then he hears the jingling even closer and the smile fades. Something about it just isn't right. Not out here. Not in the storm and the darkness way out on the frozen lake. He isn't afraid exactly—hell, he survived the Battle of Ia Drang back in '65 with the 1st Air Cav and after that, not much has ever rattled him—just concerned. As he climbs on his sled, he hears the jingling bells and they're closer still.

That's enough.

2

Mil guns her and takes off across the hardpack at a respectable clip, finding the depression of the ice trail easy enough and following it steadily. He'll make shore in ten minutes. It would have been quicker if he could've jammed the Polaris full throttle, but no sense taking the chance of losing the trail in this blow. It's coming on strong, the wind trying to peel him off the seat, visibility down to fifteen feet. The storm is worse out here on the ice, he knows, because there's nothing to slow it down—no trees, no hills, nothing. It rolls on full force, gaining momentum.

He hears the jingling bells again and goddamn if they don't sound like they're practically right next to his ear. Still, Mil's not scared. Inside his snowsuit, he's sweating now, and his heart is pounding, his jaws locked tight so his teeth won't chatter, but still, he's not afraid. He knows what fear will do to a man. He saw it firsthand at LZ X-Ray back in November '65 when the fighting got real thick and the NVA threw everything at them but their boots and rice bags. Fear could make you think funny and make mistakes.

Not far now, not too far.

Mil keeps this in mind, mentally reaching out for the shore as the snow cycles around him in an unending vortex. He keeps going, pushing the sled a little harder now. With a shard of ice in his heart, he sees a form standing on the side of the ice trail. What he sees cannot be. Not out here. The form waves to him as he passes and grins.

Faster now, cracking open the throttle. He's got to make that shore. If nothing else, he's got to get there. His mind is filled with stark imagery of LZ X-Ray and he remembers back then, so many years past now, how he kept telling himself if he could only make it to daylight things would be okay. Now he needs to reach that shore. Because if he does, then everything—

Jesus H. Christ.

That figure is ahead of him again. Just standing there with opens arms, waiting for him. By this point, Mil knows that there's no way it could have gotten ahead of him. Not on the ice. In the dark. In the storm. Whatever that thing is, it's certainly not human. He can see its grim, grinning face, its teeth grown long and sharp. He opens up the throttle. He's going to run it down, roll right over it. Here it comes, here it comes. God, look at its eyes.

At the last moment, the figure steps aside and Mil feels something like a steel cable encircle his neck, yanking him off the sled. He hits the ice. He hits it hard, something in his shoulder giving with a bolt of white pain. The sled careens into the snowbank, rides up it, then flips back over, coming to rest treads up.

Mil fights to his feet despite the agony.

He has a lock-blade knife at his belt and he pulls it now, flicking the five-inch blade open. The storm rams into him, throwing snow in his face. Freezing winds try to push him back down. Some of the 1st Air Cav's piss and vinegar still boiling in his veins, he thinks, show yourself, you fucking freak! You want a piss-up, you're going to get one! Then the figure is right there next to him. Its teeth are like icicles, its hands like the talons of a bear reaching for him. With a cry, Mil stabs the knife into it and it makes a wild, strident yelping sound and then one of its paws comes at him. His throat is torn out before he can even think of moving.

Gasping, blood filling his mouth and gurgling out of his torn neck, he falls to the ice, his life steaming from him. The figure watches him die and only when he stops moving, does it fall on him to feed.

Although he's been sheriff of Clay County for ten years now, Will Teague knows he's still considered the new guy by a lot of the old timers. He, like his predecessor, stands very much in the shadow of Lester Pease, who was either the best cop that ever lived or the biggest asshole ever to wear a badge. It depends on who's doing the asking and who's doing the telling.

Lester retired in 1993, after an astounding record of forty years as county sheriff. He was replaced by Benny Lacks who held office until Teague ousted him in 2005. But twenty odd years has hardly dulled the edge of Lester's reign and his shadow has only grown that much longer. To the old timers of Craw Falls, Lester Pease was the following: the biggest, baddest cop they'd ever known, equal parts Dirty Harry and John Wayne, one diligent, dutiful, hard-assed sonofabitch and nothing ever went down in those parts that old Les did not know about. When shit happened, he was there with a shovel to scoop it up long before it left the asshole of Fate and soiled the pristine ground of his beloved Clay County.

This was how some of the old timers remember Les. How much of it was truth and how much was invented and how much was simply Lester's own propaganda making the rounds is anyone's guess.

As the blizzard worsens, Teague cruises the byroads of the town and thinks about those things that he knows about old Lester that no one else does—the embezzling, the fabricated statistics, the planted evidence, half a dozen other unsavory items that he learned about as a deputy sheriff serving under old Les. Benny Lacks never figured any of it out because if he had, he would've put Les in handcuffs. Teague, of course, could have done the same but he let it ride because, ultimately, no one was hurt, and no one had to do any hard time because of Lester's botched/manufactured investigations. Les was gone now, so it was best to forget the past regardless of how sordid it was. But up until his dying day, Les knew that Teague knew all about him and whenever they crossed paths, Les had trouble meeting his eyes. The long shadow he cast had a way of shrinking to nothingness.

It's an odd thing to be thinking of on this night of blowing snow and raging winds, but sometimes the past comes back to a man in the strangest of ways.

As he drives, Teague sees few people out, which is good, but lots of cars on Main parked at the curb which is bad because the plow's going to be coming through and the streets need to be cleared. Which means, of course, that he's going to have to make the rounds of all the gin mills and order a bunch of drunks to get their cars off the streets. And they're not going to like it. They'll give him a hard time and he knows it.

But that's part of the job.

The shovel has been passed and the shit needs to be scooped up.

He pulls to a stop outside the Broken Bottle and stands in the wind beneath its swaying Pabst Blue Ribbon sign for a moment or two, pumping himself up so he can get the job done.

But, he figures, if this is the worst he has to deal with tonight, then it won't be so bad. There are always much worse things.

He's right on that.

Because soon he'll meet them in the flesh.

It was all Tubb's fault and Gina had already decided that once he got out of jail, he was getting out of her house. Brother or no brother, she's finished supporting the eighteen-year-old lifestyle of a man nearly forty. There's only so much sisterly charity in her heart and the old well has run dry as a desert creek.

This is his second DUI in the last fifteen months, she thinks as she fights to keep the Toyota on the road against the howling onslaught of the blizzard. He'll be sitting ninety days this time at the very least and that sonofabitch deserves every hour of it.

God, what a storm.

It was bad enough on the way to Vermillion, but now the secondary roads are nearly impassable. She passed the plow not twenty minutes ago and already there is a fresh three inches of snow on the road. She won't make Craw Falls for another thirty minutes at this rate if she makes it at all.

Thanks, Tubb. Thanks a lot.

She can just about imagine the idiot curled up in a cozy jail cell sharing cigarettes with his incarcerated brothers while the storm screams and she fights for survival. Of course, she didn't have to drive all the way to Vermillion. Tubb and his stupid habit could have waited until Monday, but her ingrained martyr complex won out as it always did. Twelve years of Catholic school and a mother who made suffering an art form are to blame. Driving all the way to Vermillion in a blizzard is exactly what mom would have done for her baby boy, so Gina cannot possibly do less. It's unthinkable. After all, martyrdom is a competitive sport in the Keller family.

I love you, mom, and I miss you every day, but I'm getting real tired of out-suffering you—

The wind hits the car like a breaker heading ashore and Gina grips the wheel for dear life. The Toyota skids to the right, banks to the left, skating over the icy pavement. About the time it looks like she's heading into the ditch like a rocket, she gets it under control.

Jesus, but it was close.

The wind's whipping through the open fields, casting a curtain of white over the windshield. The wipers work frantically to clear it. The hi-beams look as if they're filled with pillow fluff.

Gina squints, trying to see where she is.

No other cars have passed in some time and the road is an unbroken sheet of white feathering out into the fields. She slows. She can't be sure if she's in her lane or edging onto the shoulder. The Toyota skids around a bend, the snow converging in an absolute whiteout. Visibility is down to less than thirty feet.

Then she sees headlights.

They're bearing down on her, closing fast.

Shit!

She's crossed the centerline and there is a semi coming right at her. The trucker blares his horn. White-hot fear floods her. There's no way in hell she can jerk the wheel to get out of its path; it has to be pulled to the right gradually or she will go into a skid. She eases it over and barely misses the truck, a logger loaded with pine. The Toyota comes within inches of it. If there had been an orange between them it would have gotten peeled. As it was, the truck threw a whipping mass of snow that nearly put her little car in the ditch.

The next twenty minutes are, thankfully, uneventful.

Finally, the Toyota tops a rise and Gina sees Craw Falls in the valley below, twinkling with lights like a kitschy Thomas Kinkade painting. It appears like a mirage in the desert and then disappears just as quickly in the blizzard.

Almost home, she thinks. Almost home.

When she's but five minutes from the outskirts, she cuts down a low sloping hill, pushing through four inches of drifting snow that covers the road.

And that's when the figure steps out into the headlights.

She lets out a cry and hits the brakes.

The Toyota careens to the left and right as it hydroplanes over the icy, snow-covered pavement. There's a grisly, boneless thump! as the figure glances off the bumper and is tossed into the storm.

The next thing Gina knows, the Toyota is buried in a snowbank right up to the windshield. She tries backing out, but the wheels just keep spinning. Trying to catch her breath, she hits the emergency flashers and forces her door open, stumbling out into the storm.

The wind rips into her instantly, making her face feel numb.

Her entire body is shaking, and it isn't from the cold. She hit someone and there is no damn way they're going to walk away from it. She has to call 911 and look for the body. The very idea makes her feel weak and terrified because she saw very clearly who she hit...or, more precisely, what she hit. There was no mistaking it.

She ran down a clown.

5

"Everybody just calm the hell down already!"

Sheriff Teague's voice is loud and booming over the karaoke mic. Even the bikers playing pool in the back room stop and take notice, leaning on their cues. The saloon goes silent. Nobody at the Broken Bottle utters a sound. Beers are forgotten, shots untouched, greasy slices of pizza cool on paper plates.

"Now," Teague says. "I didn't say I was closing the Broken Bottle down. I don't have the authority—"

"Damn right, you don't," a voice informs him, followed by drunken cheers and catcalls of support.

Teague shakes his head. "Thanks, Carpy. Next time I pull you over for weaving, I won't take your keys. I'll throw your ass in the slam."

Suddenly, George Carp's support drastically dwindles. He looks down into his mug of beer as if he might find courage in the suds.

Teague continues. "Now, as I said, nobody's shutting the Bottle down, I'm just apprising you of the situation. And that situation is serious. We got the blizzard of the century brewing out there. We're going to have a foot of snow by midnight and three more feet by first light. The State Police are closing the highway. The county isn't even going to try to keep secondary roads open. So, if any of you live out of town—like you, Carpy, for instance—you might want to make tracks while you can or find somebody to bunk in with."

Voices begin to argue and grumble across the barroom.

"Nice going, Sheriff," Brenda Prechek says. "You're killing my Friday night. I'm barely keeping the doors open as it is and you're taking the food right out of my mouth."

"Yeah," her husband Stew agrees.

In Teague's experience, Stew Prechek always agrees with whatever his wife says, whether that's the rising cost of pickled eggs and pizza sauce, or the heavy flow her monthly has visited upon her.

"I'm apprising every one of the facts," Teague says. "All of you can do whatever you want, but get your cars and trucks off the street. They're lined up out there at the curb and the city plow needs to get through. If they're not out of there in thirty minutes, they'll be towed and impounded."

People start pulling on coats and filing out the door, icy air and snow funneling in and casting paper plates about. The regulars and hardcore boozehounds stay put, grumbling under their breath about who has died and elected Will Teague God.

Brenda Prechek is fuming. "Yup, way to go, Sheriff. Looks like one more business bites the old hairy horn in this pissant town."

"Thirty minutes," Teague says, stepping off the karaoke stage which isn't much bigger than a postage stamp.

Brenda starts going on about the feds and cops sticking their oily fingers up everyone's asses and ruining the country. You can't have a gun and you can't even pray in schools anymore, she claims. "But that's what you get with all these liberals and their—"

"Shut the hell up, Brenda," Teague tells her.

"You gonna let him talk that way to me?" she says to her husband, who's so skinny he often gets mistaken for a pipe cleaner.

"Yeah, are you?" Teague says.

Stew looks from the boiling ire of Brenda to the sheriff...all six feet six of him in his leather squad jacket and squared-off shoulders.

He swallows. "Yes."

6

The blizzard coming down in whipping sheets of white, Gina stuffs her gloves in her pocket and pulls out her cell. She is going to call 911 and then go find the guy she has hit.

Between the cold and her own fear, her hands are shaking so badly that the cell seems to squirt from her fingers. It shoots through the air and disappears in a drift.

"Shit!"

Down on her hands and knees in the snow, she digs through the drift with freezing hands. It should be easy to find but it isn't. She digs and paws around until her hands are so cold she has to stop and put her gloves back on. Thin leather driving gloves. Useless against the cold, but great for fine manipulation. Still, she can't find the phone. It's too damn dark and the snow is too heavy. She struggles back to the car and grabs her little Maglite from the glove compartment. When she gets back to the area where she dropped her phone, she steps on something immediately.

Oh, this goddamn night is getting better all the time.

She searches through the snow and retrieves her cell. Nice. Her own weight has packed snow into the buttons. The display is cracked. She tries to work the snow free, but it does little good and particularly with her rubbery fingers. The buttons have no spring to them and the damaged screen is a blurry confusion of pixilation. On her knees, she feels like crying. The wind blows snow in her face. The chill works its way up the back of her coat. She can't imagine a more desolate and hopeless scenario. In ten minutes, she knows, she can be in town if she starts walking now.

If...

But she knows she cannot possibly leave the scene without checking on the person she has hit. The guilt would eat her alive.

You saw what it was.

And that's what really stops her. A clown? Out in a blizzard? The idea is absurd. Grim images of John Wayne Gacy parade through her head because, realistically, there is no sane explanation for a clown being out here. Nothing that doesn't chill her in ways the storm cannot possibly hope to.

The bottom line is that she is freezing.

Either she starts walking or she goes and looks.

The dreaded Keller martyrdom gets the best of her as always, reinforced by her long simmering Catholic guilt. Flashlight in hand, she pushes her way through the drifts. She doesn't have to go too far, no more than forty or fifty feet. The tracks of the Toyota are filling fast, but she can see the skid marks.

And she can see the blood.

It's nearly covered in snow, too, but in the beam of the flashlight she can see enough to know that something bled profusely.

That much blood... there's no way anyone survived it.

Yet, she sees no body.

But it's hard to be sure.

The snow is flying around her in sheets. Some of the drifts are well over three feet deep. A body could easily have been beneath any one of them. She prods a heap of snow near the blood spatter with her boot. Nothing. It's only a heap of snow. They're everywhere. For all she knows, there could have been a dozen dead clowns around her.

Don't be thinking shit like that.

No, there is nothing to do but march into Craw Falls and get the sheriff and his people out here. They'll know how to handle this. She starts walking and instantly stops. She hears something that just does not belong out here.

Listen.

The wind is moaning out across the empty fields, the snow whispering as it blows and piles up around her. It makes a sort of hissing sound. The world is a graveyard blown white.

That noise again.

A rattling sound...like a baby's rattle being shaken.

Fuck this, she thinks.

7

Gina starts back towards town, refusing to think, refusing to do anything but keep her legs moving as a shadow of terror envelops her.

She makes it maybe ten feet when her ankle is seized.

She lets out a manic, piercing scream into the storm as she sees what has her—a puffy, misshapen white hand. In the flashlight beam, it looks like a large glove. But it is no glove. Gloves don't have pink and purple vein networking and they certainly do not have long yellow claws.

Gina goes down into the snow, still crying out.

The hand has her in a crushing, viselike grip. It drags her through the snow and the next thing she knows, she's airborne, coming down hard and pile-driving head first into a snowbank. Frantic, she digs herself out, sliding back down to the road. Snow is jammed down her collar. She brushes it from her face. Her ankle throbs painfully.

She looks this way and that.

She sees no one.

The snow keeps coming down, brushing lightly against her parka. The wind howls through the trees. It's hard to imagine a more lonely, desperate, desolate situation. She keeps looking around, mainlining on fear. But she sees nothing and no one.

Yet, she knows she is not alone.

Terrified, her heart pounding painfully in her chest, she gets to her feet. Her bad ankle will barely support her. When she puts her full weight on it, white needles shoot right up to her knee. But what choice is there? If she stays out here, she'll freeze or that thing will get her. So she starts walking. If luck favors her—something she finds hard to believe—then maybe she'll be able to flag down a snowplow.

Move for chrissake!

She starts off, quick as she can. Her mind is locked down hard in survival mode now. All she can do is put one foot in front of the other. Her ankle feels like it's wrapped in bands of fire. She leans as much as she can on the other leg, hobbling but pushing forward.

She refuses to think about the danger she is in.

That will be for later.

She can just see the lights of town. In five minutes, she will reach the outskirts...if fate will only let her.

The rattling sound again.

Oh no, please please no more...

There is a blur of motion in front of her and she darts back, nearly falling. Snow gusts around her. Then something hits her. She falls down and immediately pulls herself up.

The clown is standing before her.

Huge and misshapen, its blue-and-white clown suit is filthy with dried blood. Its face is corpse-white, its nose red and bulbous, a pink vein networking like branching lightning spread over its cheeks and forehead. Green tufts of hair jut from its domed cranium like clock springs.

She has just enough time to take that in before yellow claws come streaking at her face, striking with enough force to drive her back four feet into a drift.

Screaming, she paws snow from her face.

She still can't see.

Her eyes are gone.

The clown's serrated claws have split her face open from scalp to chin, leaving four bleeding ruts. Her lower lip is nearly peeled off, her nose slit open, and her eyes nothing but ragged holes filling with blood.

About the time the pain and horror registers, so does the shock and trauma. Gina goes down and stays there.

So when the clown sinks its teeth into her throat, she is thankfully unconscious.

Twenty minutes later, Sheriff Teague figures he has a good handle on things. Just about every useless, pissed-up drunk at the Broken Bottle has read him the riot act and informed him—none too gently—how he will not be getting reelected for another term.

And that's just fine by him.

Goddamn town is full of nuts, misfits, and certified whackos. They don't need a sheriff, they need a fucking psychiatrist. There are less than 3000 people in Craw Falls and yet they have a disproportionate number of the state's head cases. It seems statistically impossible. There must be something in the water.

About half of the Bottle's clientele didn't come back after they went to move their vehicles. There is something about a cop on the premises that takes the fun out of things. Brenda Prechek busses tables, clearing bottles and mugs, glaring at the sheriff with no little ire. Teague isn't sure who she's more pissed at, him or her husband and he honestly does not give a shit. She's a black-hearted, foul-mouthed skank and he has no use for her.

He goes over to the window and studies the gales of the storm. It's turning into a real first-class piss-up, that's for sure. At least all those cars are off the street. That's a start.

He heads to the door, giving Brenda the same snarling, catty look she gives him.

Then the door flies open.

The wind and snow come blowing in, pushing Teague back a few feet.

Then the door closes, and he sees Beebe Chandliss coming at him. Her eyes are wild, choking cries coming from her mouth. She grabs hold of him, panting and gasping, dropping to her knees in her red Yamaha snowsuit.

"Jesus," Teague says, helping her into a booth. "What happened?"

It better not be Ritchie, he thinks. If he's been beating her again, I'll lock that sonofabitch up for six months.

But he doesn't think it is Ritchie.

She's frantic and winded, but he sees no blood or bruises. The only thing out of place, besides her mental state, are some rips in the back of her snowsuit.

She has her face in her hands and she's sobbing. When she finally starts talking, she makes little sense. She's blubbering and irrational, her nose running from the cold, eyes filled with tears. By then, a small crowd has gathered.

"Just take it easy," Teague tells her. He looks over at Brenda. "Get her a drink of something strong."

Brenda scowls at him. "That stuff ain't free, you know," she says with her usual sympathy.

"Get it," he snaps at her.

After Beebe gets about three fingers of Jim Beam in her and has a little coughing jag, she starts to speak a bit more calmly, picking up her story in mid-sentence: "... we saw the body... snow was just starting to cover it... it was all torn up." She finishes the rest of her drink in one swallow. "Oh my God... she was gutted, Sheriff. Gutted like a fucking deer." She stares at him, licking her lips again and again. "She was... we both saw it... she was hollow inside... she was hollow..."

A bad feeling stirring in his belly, Teague asks, "Who, Beebe? Who was?"

Stew Prechek says, "I think she's talking about a body."

"You think?" his wife says.

"We were scared," Beebe goes on. "We didn't have our cells, so we got back on the sleds and headed into town..."

It takes some time, but with patience and encouragement, they get the facts out of her. She and Ritchie were on their way back from Crow Lake on snowmobiles and they found the remains of a woman just outside town.

"The snow was flying," she tells them. "You couldn't see twenty feet. Ritchie was right behind me on his machine... then he was just gone."

She circled back and found his sled in the ditch, but he wasn't on it. The only thing that was, she discovered, was a lot of blood in the snow. Beebe claimed it looked like a bag of red ink had exploded.

"Then I saw him."

"Ritchie?" Carpy says.

She shakes her head. "No, it wasn't him." She looks out across the barroom as if she's still out in the storm. "It... it was standing on top of a snow bank staring down at me. It had big claws. It was a clown."

Teague stands there.

Everyone is staring at him. They're waiting for him to ask Beebe what she has been smoking. He sighs. It's going to be one of those nights and he knows it.

"A clown?" Brenda says as if she has never heard the word before. "A freaking...clown?"

Her husband is plain confused. "What...like the kind in circuses?"

"No, dumbass. The kind that fly jets," Brenda tells him. "How many kinds of fucking clowns are there?"

"I was just saying is all," Stew sighs.

Carpy giggles. "The kind that fly jets. I like that."

"Shut up," Teague and Brenda say at the same time.

Beebe seems oblivious. "It was a clown. It had claws. It got Ritchie."

She's in a bad way, but Teague knows exactly where she saw the body and Ritchie's snowmobile. He's going out there. "Take care of her," he says on his way out the door.

10

Teague has three deputies on that night, but two of them—Stills and Weg-ley—are on the other side of the county. Only Peanut, Olly Pease, is in Craw Falls patrolling the roads in an SUV.

He is taking his time, circling the edge of town, listening to WKBD, the alternative rock station out of Grand Forks, and playing some air guitar to Soundgarden's "Pretty Noose." He'd just gotten off the radio with the sheriff who'd said there had been some kind of accident outside of town. Details to follow. He told Peanut he didn't need any backup, to keep the roads clear of parked cars.

All of which is fine with Peanut.

Riding and listening to some good music is how he likes to spend his nights. He hates being a cop. The only reason he is one is because it's expected of him. His old man was county sheriff for like forty years and he expected his son to follow in his footsteps as fathers often did. All the Pease men were cops stretching right back to the 19th century and that isn't a tradition you fucked with lightly.

The thing is, Peanut is no cop. It isn't in him. He likes music. That's his thing. Since high school, he's played everything from country rock to thrash, funk to heavy blues. He likes metal best. It's the only real music there is in his opinion. And if you don't believe that, he's willing to bet he can convert you with a red-hot '82 Ibanez Destroyer and a Marshall stack that will blow your balls right off.

His old man passed from a heart attack six months ago and Peanut is now seriously considering hanging up the old badge and heading out to Seattle to see if he can grab some session work.

It would beat the shit out of this.

Oh hell, what's that now?

There's some weird-looking guy hanging out in the school playground. Shit. Peanut thinks momentarily of pretending he didn't see him (he often does this), but he knows he can't do that.

"Book 'em, Danno," he says under his breath. "Roll them black-and-whites."

11

Peanut pulls the SUV to a stop, telling dispatch his location and that he will be leaving the vehicle. The guy in the playground doesn't seem to be too concerned that one of Clay County's finest is bearing down on him. Peanut steps through the gate and into the playground where the snow is up past his knees.

"Excuse me, sir," he says, putting the beam of his light on the guy. It's thick with swirling snowflakes. "Can I ask what you're doing?"

The guy ignores him.

He's on his hands and knees scanning the snow with a small flashlight. After a moment, he stands up and what a sight he is. He's tall and bearded, his face craggy and his eyes narrow. He wears an ankle-length fur duster and a flat-brimmed Mormon hat. The duster is open, and Peanut can see a low-slung cartridge belt and a big, mean-looking handgun in a holster.

"Say what you got to say, officer," the guy says in a low, growling voice. "I'm kind of busy."

"Busy doing what exactly?"

"Hunting, looking for spoor."

Peanut swallows, letting his hand drop to his own weapon. "In a playground?"

"That's right. What I'm looking for likes little kids. It likes to sniff them out and eat them."

Peanut's throat feels like it's filled with sand. Here they are in the teeth of one evil mother of a blizzard and he has to happen upon this well-armed nutjob. The wind is blowing, and the snow is flying and try as he might, he simply can't pop the catch on his weapon.

Finally, he gets it out. "Can I ask your name, sir?"

"Clegg. Just Clegg."

"Now, Mr. Clegg, you have to admit that all this is a little peculiar. You're carrying a weapon and you tell me you're hunting something. In a blizzard. In the city limits."

"That's right."

"Would you like to tell me what?"

Clegg does not smile or frown; his face is unreadable. "Let's just say that I'm after a particular type of predator."

Peanut pulls his gun now. "I'm afraid that's not good enough."

Clegg sighs. "I'm no threat to you, son."

"That gun you're carrying says different."

Clegg laughs. "Son, that ain't for killing people. It's to defend myself against other things."

"You got a concealed permit?"

"No sir. There's no time for such things in my profession."

"And just what might your profession be?"

"I hunt things that kill people. That's what I do. That's my calling." He will elaborate no further. He keeps staring at Peanut suspiciously. "You ask an awful lot of questions."

"It's my job, sir."

Clegg shrugs. "Could be. Problem is, the kind of thing I'm hunting is very smart, very cunning. It uses camouflage to get in close to its prey. It can make itself look like a man or a woman...even a deputy sheriff."

Inside, Peanut feels like a stream that has run dry. His belly is filled with sticks and stones. Clegg is a lunatic. A first class wackadoodle. A bugfuck, as his old man would have said. "Mr. Clegg, I don't know what your story is, but I assure you that I'm a deputy sheriff. Now, I'm going to need to see your ID."

"It's over in my van."

Peanut has already seen it parked in the lot. Flat black, ugly, big tires. "Let's take a walk over there then. I'll need to see registration and proof-of-insurance. Please don't try anything, sir. I'd rather not have to shoot you."

"I won't if you won't, deputy."

"Before we do that, I'm going to ask you to drop that gun belt. And like they say in the movies, do it real slow."

"Can't do that."

Peanut tenses. "And why not?"

"Can't afford to be unarmed. I got too many enemies."

"Okay, sir. Now I'm not asking, I'm ordering you." Peanut's in a shooting stance. "Drop the belt."

"That's not a good idea in my profession," Clegg says.

"And what profession might that be?"

"I kill clowns."

Peanut nods. "Then I guess you better come with me."

12

When Teague gets to the location, the first thing he sees is a car buried in the snow bank. About half of it is sticking out into the road, three or four inches of fresh powder covering the trunk like a blanket. He shakes his head. It must have hit the bank like a missile to be buried that deep.

Of all things.

He stands there, the snow falling around him, the wind casting sheets of drift that play over the road. Other than the steady idle of his GMC and the occasional moan of the wind, it's silent out there and unbearably eerie. The headlights of his SUV fill with flying, agitated snowflakes. The red lights of his flashers turn the night into a storm of blood.

Narrowing his eyes against the blow, he can just make out some tread depressions. They're nearly filled in.

First things first.

According to Beebe, the body should be down the road a piece, lying right off the shoulder.

Teague makes his way down there. The tread marks are completely gone twenty feet down the road. With his flashlight, he scans the shoulder until he finds a place where the snow is oddly disturbed. He kicks around until he finds frozen blood, a lot of it.

"Shit," he says under his breath.

He searches around, poking in the snow, but he can't find a body. It doesn't make sense. Beebe said it was "hollowed out" and someone in that condition surely couldn't crawl off. There are no animals large enough to drag off a human carcass. A cougar or a bobcat might take a bite, but they wouldn't drag off the body of an adult.

Cursing, Teague climbs the snowbank and makes his way down the other side. He finds the snowmobile tracks. They top a rise flanking the woods. It's from this vantage point that Ritchie and Beebe must have initially seen the body. He follows the tracks as far as he can, but the storm has wiped them out. The blizzard seems to be getting worse and he can't see a thing. He finally gives up. He will need people out here. Lots of them. They will need to poke in every drift.

When he finally makes it back to the buried car, he digs his way in and checks the glove compartment.

Oh no, oh no.

According to the registration, the vehicle belongs to Gina Keller of 217 Long Acre Road. Teague has gotten to know her pretty well because of her brother Tubb, who is a shit-useless waste of flesh (as far as most are concerned). Tubb was bound and determined to drag her down to his level, but so far she'd kept her head proudly above the stink he created.

Now this.

It doesn't take a tree full of owls to figure why she'd been out in the storm. She must have been coming back from Vermillion where Tubb is in the slam on yet another DUI.

But there is no body.

Same for Ritchie Chandliss.

Teague climbs up into the cab of his GMC and thinks it over. The storm is worsening. He will need a State Police homicide and CSI unit up here. But until he has a body, they won't be interested. He will need to organize search parties, but that won't happen tonight. It will have to wait until morning when, hopefully, the storm will be over. There's just no way searchers can beat these woods in a blow like this.

He gets on the radio. "Dispatch, this is Three. Tell Rip I'm going to need a wrecker at this location."

"Ten-four. Request to see you at station, Three."

"Roger that."

Teague pulls back into the storm. At the very least, he will need to get that blood staked and roped off, but that will have to wait, too.

He wonders what's going on at the station.

He has a feeling that he will not like it.

13

Sometimes, late into the night, Carolyn Kewley will wake up in her empty bed and reach out for Tom, even though he left her two years before for a much younger woman. It's a funny sort of habit. One she practices when she's caught in that fuzzy never-neverland between sleep and waking when the little girl in her that believes in magic is in full bloom.

He's never there, of course.

She can wish it and hope for it all she wants, she knows, but that will not make it so.

Tom is gone, a dire voice in her head tells her night after night. He will not magically appear lying next to you this night or any other. Reach out all you want, but you'll never find anything.

This is the depressing, hopeless note she always falls back asleep on, suffering through nightmares in which she sees Tom in crowds but can never reach him and when she does, he invariably turns away.

During the daylight hours when adult anxieties and resentments rule her being, Carolyn hates Tom. He is the bastard who left her for a leggy little nymph after seventeen years of marriage in which she gave him all and everything. He used her, emptied her, sucked the sunshine from her soul and tossed her aside. She often fantasizes about terrible things happening to him.

But at night it is different.

At night, she is weak. Lonely. Brokenhearted. She still loves him and needs his strong arms around her, but they are never there. There is only the cool, empty part of the bed where he once slept.

So on this night of blowing snow and raging winds when she wakes to hear a rustling sound next to her, she is not frightened. She is, of course, still dreaming. Tom has come back because he loves her and there could never be anyone else for him. He is ashamed and dejected, begging silently for her forgiveness.

It is nice.

It is what Carolyn has been longing for.

"Darling," she says, reaching out and touching a form that is cold and ruffled. "Never leave me again."

"I won't," the voice says to her, "Never again."

There is something funny about the voice in that not only is it not Tom's voice, but it does not seem to be the voice of a man or a woman; it has elements of both and others that belong to neither grouping.

The form next to her sits up and she can see it silhouetted in the pale light coming through the window. It has a bulbous nose and bushy hair. It is a clown. Why it is here now on this terrible stormy night, Carolyn does not know. It watches her in the darkness of the bedroom and its eyes shine wetly.

Since it is only a dream and she has never had any fear of clowns, she holds her arms out to it.

The clown reciprocates.

It is heavy and large. It smells of musty trunks and rotting linen. Its breath is like raw meat as its presses its blubbery lips to her own.

This is all only a dream, Carolyn knows, yet it feels so real.

The clown's tongue is in her mouth, cold like that of a dog and she can feel what's between its legs pressing hard against her. Despite how very wrong it is and perhaps for that very reason, she is excited. She opens her legs and the clown slides into her. His shaft is icy and thick. It makes her cry out as he rides her. She bucks with orgasm after orgasm.

After a few minutes of this, certain she can take no more without exploding, the clown bites into her throat with sharp teeth that feel like cold iron. He tears out her jugular and sucks her life away as Dracula did to Lucy Westenra in Bram Stoker's novel (which Carolyn read three times in high school).

The clown fills her and drains her and only the pain tells her how very real it all is. She cries out in agony and passion, her entire being satisfied for the first time in her life.

As she falls into darkness, Carolyn discovers the secret of it all...that the most beautiful part of life is death.

14

When Teague gets back to the Sheriff's Department, he finds Peanut waiting for him. He looks excited, concerned, and confused. Not good signs in a cop. Not good signs at all. Teague likes Peanut—hell, everyone likes Peanut—but he knows he isn't much of a cop. Not like his old man, who'd been too much of a cop in many ways. Polar opposites.

"Will," Peanut says. "This is the craziest thing I've ever seen. You're not going to believe it. I'm not sure I believe it."

Teague sighs and walks straight over to his desk. He chews up a couple Rolaids, washes them down with a slug of coffee and chases this with three extra-strength Excedrin, the kind that are loaded with caffeine and will make your nerve endings hum like banjo strings for hours.

"Okay," he finally says, lowering himself into his chair. "I'm listening."

"Got a guy in lockup," Peanut announces.

"Good for you. Is there a reason for him being there?"

Peanut's shoulders slump. He doesn't claim to be a great cop but even he knows you don't just lock people up on a whim. His look says it all. "Guy's name is Clegg. He looks a little dangerous. I found him over at the school playground with this."

Peanut sets a big chromed-up .44 Magnum on the desk blotter. He sets a box of shells next to it. Teague raises an eyebrow. Hypervelocity hollow nose expanders. Christ.

"He have a concealed permit?"

"No."

"Any explanation?"

Peanut gives him a funny look. "He said he was hunting a type of predator."

"What type?"

"A clown."

Teague feels the contents of his stomach stir. "Clown?"

Peanut shrugs, looks embarrassed. In fact, he looks as if he wants to be many things at once. "Yeah, that's what he said. Not clowns at kids' parties or clowns in parades, but clowns that are predators. He said he was at the playground because they like to hunt little kids. They like to sniff 'em out and eat them. And... oh, God, this is bad..."

"Go ahead."

"He told me these kinds of clowns can make themselves look like other people. Like you or me or anyone to draw us in so they can feed on us."

Teague sighs. Clowns again. What the hell is going on in this town? Isn't the blizzard enough without this kind of nonsense? First Beebe Chandliss, now this Clegg guy. Goddamn. What did Beebe say? It was a clown. It had claws. It got Ritchie. Sure. Clowns with claws of all things. The scary part is that what Clegg said fits in a bit too seamlessly with that. And Ritchie Chandliss is missing and so, it would seem, is Gina Keller. And Beebe said the body she and Ritchie saw was female. Gutted like a fucking deer. The logical assumption is that the body is that of Gina Keller. All of it fit together too nicely. That's what Teague doesn't like about it. The skein of logic seems pretty solid...until you factor in that clown stuff. Then it skids to a halt.

Sure, on the surface 2+2=4, but he has been a cop long enough to know that in police work 2+2 often equaled zero or five or seventeen for that matter. When you added in the human factor, things got messy.

"Real messy," he says out loud.

"What's that, Will?"

"Nothing. Did you run him through the system?"

Peanut shakes his head. "Claims his name is Clegg, just Clegg. You have any idea how many Cleggs there are out there? We need a little something more. I went through his wallet. Nothing. Not even a Social Security card, a voter's ID card, or a library card. Nada. I sent prints out."

"Figures. What about his van?"

Peanut shakes his head again. "No registration or proof of insurance. Nothing. Lots of goodies in the back, though."

"Do tell."

"Well, he showed me his arsenal. Military grade stuff. Handguns, sniper rifles, full auto assault weapons, bear traps, antipersonnel mines, you name it. I saw grenades and what might be a flamethrower. He's got a dog, too. A big, evil-looking thing. Might have to get animal control involved with that."

Teague rubs his tired eyes. All of this has become a federal matter now. FBI maybe, but definitely ATF. They'll probably roast this particular nut as a homegrown terrorist which means the Attorney General's Office and Homeland Security. Shit, talk about clowns.

"All right. I better have a chat with the Clownhunter General."

15

Teague follows Peanut to the holding area. There are exactly five cells back there. When things get rowdy on Friday nights, sometimes it gets a little crowded. Teague steps into the cell and the prisoner, seated on the bunk, looks up at him. He appears neither scared nor concerned, more bored and annoyed than anything. He's a tall guy, wide at the shoulders, muscular and wiry. His beard is well-trimmed, his face weathered, his eyes gleaming like chips of flint. He looks as if he might be dangerous if you cornered him.

"Mr. Clegg," Teague says.

"If you want."

Whatever the hell that means. "My deputy says you've got a story to tell. And with all that hardware in your van, I really hope it's a good one."

"Probably nothing you'd want to hear."

"Try me."

Clegg chuckles, but his eyes are still dark, mean, snake-like in their intensity. He pulls out a cigarette and lights up. Peanut's about to tell him he isn't supposed to smoke in the cells, but Teague shakes his head. If the cigarette is going to get this guy talking, then let him smoke by all means.

"Sheriff," he says, blowing smoke from his nostrils, "there are things in this world that guys like you know nothing about. Things beyond belief. Nightmare things. Things that should not be."

"Like clowns," Peanut says.

Clegg ignores him. "Not clowns as you or I knew clowns when we were kids, but things that look like clowns but are monsters that drink human blood. Creatures that are pure evil who delight in human suffering. Don't ask me where they come from or how they can be, because I can't answer that.

I'm one of a small group of hunters that tries to keep this country free of the scourge."

Teague suppresses the need to tell him he's fucking nuts. "Why clowns? Why do they look like clowns?"

"Because it unnerves people, scares them," Clegg explains. "And little kids like clowns. They go right up to them. That's what these things want." He shrugs. "Sometimes they appear as other things, but this time it's clowns."

Teague sighs. "Okay. But who authorized you to hunt these dangerous clowns?"

"You wouldn't understand."

"I might."

Clegg has a look on his face that speaks volumes. He isn't being taken seriously and he knows it. But it doesn't seem to bother him. "Let's just say we're a secret brotherhood sworn to eradicate these things. And nothing, nothing will stand in our way. We canvass the country—and the world—hunting these things down."

"Well, I hate to be the one to tell you, Mr. Clegg, but that vanload of illegal weapons is definitely going to stand in your way just like this cell is. You're not going anywhere except maybe to prison."

Clegg is underwhelmed. Completely. "Well, you can believe what you want, Sheriff. I'm not going to waste my time trying to talk sense to your thick head. First off, your deputy here forgot to read me my Miranda rights."

Teague gives Peanut a withering look. If this goes to court, it will be thrown out and Clegg will walk.

"Secondly, sooner or later I'll get to make my one phone call. When I do that, I'll call a certain number and within a couple hours the state attorney general will be reaming your ass out."

"You telling me the attorney general sanctions what you're doing?"

"Of course not. He's as in the dark as you. But the people that pull his strings know and trust me. They won't be pulling them, they'll be yanking them. He'll hand you some shit cover story about how I work undercover for the ATF or the DEA or the Treasury Department. It'll sound good to you. I'll walk out of here and you'll be told to leave me alone."

Teague swallows. Surely, this guy is crazy... but why does he sound so damn sure of himself? "I guess I'll have to take that chance."

Clegg chuckles. "It's okay by me, Sheriff. This isn't my town or my county and these people didn't put me in office. By tomorrow morning, I'll walk, but you'll still be here having to answer questions. You're going to have a serious body count by first light and you'll be blamed for it."

"What the hell are you talking about?"

"I'm talking about what you have out there."

"And what do I have out there?"

Clegg finishes his cigarette. "You've got a colony here, Sheriff. A Class-A clown nest. The blizzard has this shithole locked up tight and the clowns have themselves a private hunting preserve. By morning, you'll have dozens dead. All those pretty little houses lined up out there and all of them nothing but meat lockers."

Teague is in a quandary and he knows it. Now he doesn't believe in clown monsters for one moment, yet things have been happening. Strange things. And Beebe Chandliss did say she saw a clown. Oh, it's too far out. He can't accept something like this.

"What the heck is that?" Peanut suddenly says.

For a moment, Teague hears nothing but the hum of the fluorescents, then there's something from outside, something rising above the moan of the wind. It sounds much like a scream. It's close by, maybe just down the block. He hears it again and this time it's louder—a wild shrieking sound that could have been an animal or a person or maybe a little of both. It dies away, then cycles up again into an unearthly wailing.

Clegg cocks his head, listening to it. He nods. "It's coming from that little park across the way. I laid some traps in the tot lot over near the swings and the merry-go-round. Looks like I got one of 'em."

"Traps?" Teague says, but then he remembers what Peanut said about the bear traps and panic grips him. Somebody got caught in one. Probably got their foot near ripped off. He looks over at Clegg. "If someone got hurt in your goddamn trap, you won't live long enough to make your fucking call."

He stomps away and Peanut closes the cell door, locking it.

"It's not a person," Clegg says. "You can take my word on that. I use handmade copies of 1880s vintage Oneida-Newhouse Number 15 bear traps. Cast iron with three-inch teeth. Whatever it caught, it ain't letting go."

Peanut looks at him and then runs after the sheriff. He isn't honestly sure who scares him more.

36

16

The park in question is down the block and across the street. It's called Little Willow Park because of the creek that runs through it. Teague, with Peanut behind him, grabs a riot gun from his GMC and makes his way over there, fighting through the wind and snow. The park is fairly large and in his mind, he can see it at high summer, rolling hills and green meadows, leafy thickets and duck ponds, concerts in the band shell on Tuesday nights, the baseball diamond and its gray splintered bleachers, the little bridge spanning the creek...and the tot lot.

The image of summer quickly fades.

It is not summer. Maybe it'll never be summer again. Maybe the cold white death of winter will last for a graveyard eternity.

Teague trudges across the street, leaning into the wind so it doesn't plant him on his ass. There is no one out. In the distance, he can hear one of the city plows scraping the road but that's about it.

Save for the moaning wind.

The rattling of icy tree branches.

And the cycling scream of whatever is caught in Clegg's trap. The last thing Teague wants is it to be some innocent citizen who stumbled by accident into it... God, he can just about imagine the agony they might be in and what it will look like when he finds them, ankle impaled by spikes... but he's really hoping it is a person because if it isn't that means it's time to rewrite the book of reality as he knows it.

Of course, it's a person, he tells himself as he follows the wrought-iron fence down towards the tot lot. You can't honestly believe it can be anything else.

No, no, of course not.

When they get to the gate, they find it open maybe five or six inches and frozen in place by walls of snow. He pulls on it, but it isn't going to move. There is no way either of them are going to get through. Down the way is a low stone wall that runs around the back of the park and Peanut leads the way down there. It's easy enough to get over it.

When they get into the thigh-deep snow on the other side and start fighting forward again into the wind, Peanut says, "We should have brought a pole or something to test the ground."

"Test it for what?"

"Well, we don't know how many traps Clegg might have out here."

Good point.

When they reach a point where the wind has eroded the snow down to the hardpack, Teague breaks a low-hanging limb off an oak tree and snaps the branches free. They have their pole. The tot lot isn't far. They push on through drifts that come well above their knees and sometimes up to their hips, carefully prodding the ground before them. The snow is flying in their faces, wind-driven and bitter cold. It engulfs them in sudden squalls, snow-devils twisting around them. The beams of their flashlights are filled with whirling flakes.

Whatever is in the trap is howling now like a wolf.

It's a shrieking, eerie sound in the blizzard. Teague keeps moving even though he wants very badly to hunker down and put his back to the blow. Out of the storm, he sees dark shapes emerging. Trees. Low shrubs. Then a slide, a jungle gym. He can hear the cleats on the flagpole dinging over at the veteran's memorial. The sound of the enraged beast is closer now. He sees the merry-go-round. In the wind, it's revolving slowly and not ten feet from it, he sees a shape, a shadow, a grotesque and aberrant something that is howling like a rabid dog, writhing and snaking back and forth.

Then a gust of wind throws snow in his face and he has to paw it away because he can't have seen what he thinks he has seen. Yet the image persists. It's like some great psychic fist that keeps punching his brain, working it like a bag.

He takes a moment and brackets the flashlight to the rail of the riot gun with shaking fingers.

Peanut is ahead of him, he skids forward, slips to one knee, and sees the thing in the trap, too. He gets to his feet, cries out, and staggers back, going promptly on his ass in a drift. Teague reaches out to pull him up and Peanut's face in the flashlight beam is blank with horror as if it has been scrubbed clean.

Then he is up and clinging to Teague like a frightened little boy, grabbing him and pressing himself to him, crying out nonsensically in a pained, shrilling voice as he stares at the clown in the trap. This is not Giggles or Bobo or some harmless limp-wristed kiddy party clown but a monstrous, malevolent wrath of pure evil wearing the skin of a clown.

It's not a clown, not really, a voice in Teague's head tells him. It's a demon. It's something from hell and if it gets loose, you've got a life expectancy of about thirty seconds.

It wears a shiny, silvery clown costume of green and yellow diamonds with fluffy white pompoms sewn down the front. The clown is a massive, huge sort of thing, much larger than even Teague himself who is a very big boy. Its face and balding head are skull-white, wrinkled and seamed, eyes like glittering rubies that cry trails of crimson tears. Tufts of bright blue hair grow from the sides of its head. Its mouth is puckered, lips split open in jagged cracks. Teague can see gums beyond that look red and raw like thawing, moist beef. Its teeth are yellow and viper-like. It breathes out clouds of fetid-smelling steam, a bubbling gray foam dripping down its chin.

"Oh Jesus, oh Christ," Peanut squeals. "Kill it, Will! Fucking shoot the goddamn thing before it's too late!"

Something he has already tried, the Glock 22 he carries sliding from his fingers and falling into the snow.

Teague shrugs Peanut aside and steps in closer, bringing up his Remington 870 pump and pointing it at the creature, a voice in his head wanting to shout, what the hell you doing out here, mister? And why are you dressed like a fucking clown? The idea of that is ludicrous, of course. In fact, it is downright insane under the circumstances. There is no reasoning with the thing before him. It keeps snarling and spitting, its white puffy fingers tearing at the secure jaws of the bear trap. It has claws and it tears at the metal, scraping them over the trap with a sound like knives on steel plating. Now and again, it seems to weaken and make a mewling sound, its ankle torn open, red-black blood sprayed up its pants leg like India Ink.

It turns towards Teague and roars with the sound of a dozen caged tigers. The heat and stench of its cry blows hot in his face, pushing him back a few inches. Its teeth gnash together like blades. If it gets free, it will gut the sheriff. It will split him open with its claws and yank out his bleeding entrails with its teeth. And that will only be the beginning.

Teague knows it.

The clown sees Peanut now and hisses at him. More of that inky black blood gushes from its mouth, flooding down its chin like poison sap and staining its white ruffled collar. It looks almost purple in the flashlight beams. Its tongue is like the stinger of a wasp, narrow and piercing and dripping with venom.

Peanut is digging frantically in the snow for his weapon and the creature seems to know it. As he comes up with the Glock, the clown spits a stream of sizzling goo at him that misses him by mere inches, hitting the snow and melting it into a boiling steam.

Teague hesitates no longer.

He sights in on the clown. The clown snarls. Teague fires. A hole the size of a dinner plate opens up in the clown's chest. It screams with agony, twisting and hopping, leaping right up into the air, the trap still holding it earthbound. Black juice splashes into the snow along with a great quantity of steaming tissue.

Teague works the pump and fires again, vaporizing the thing's shoulder. His next round goes right into its throat, nearly taking its head off. Blood and meat are carried off in a fine spray by the wind. The clown is badly injured, bleeding and shuddering and mewling. It's bent over backwards at the waist, its shoulders nearly touching the back of its legs.

Teague fires again and its torso erupts into a whirling hot meat storm... and things push up out of the smoking cavity. They look like squirming red worms that are easily two feet in length, steaming and slithering, they wriggle like tangled mating snakes.

Then Teague fires one last time, splashing the clown's face off its skull, and it drops into the snow, trembling, making snapping and popping sounds, a rubbery gurgling, then it goes still, its mighty jaws snapping shut one last time.

"Holy Jesus oh fucking Christ," Peanut says, dropping to both knees in the snow.

Teague stands there, the beam of his flashlight trained on the smoldering wreckage in the snow. Whatever in the hell it was, it's certainly no man in a clown suit. It's something far beyond that.

He reaches down and pulls Peanut to his feet once again and that's when they hear the deranged cry of a second clown.

17

Over at the Broken Bottle, the booze is flowing and the atmosphere is light now that the goddamn sheriff has gone on his way. Brenda Prechek has managed to simmer down being that most of her clientele has slowly trickled back in. The blizzard is still blowing out there but, as everyone knows, it'll take one hell of a storm to stop people from drinking in Craw Falls where alcoholism is as much of a natural rhythm as breathing or shitting.

Brenda holds court behind the bar, popping the caps off bottles of Pabst and Schlitz, filling mugs, and doling out shots. The pizza oven is cranking in the kitchen, turning out one thin crust pie after the other. In the backroom, members of the Dead Skulls motorcycle club are still playing pool, mowing down pizza after pizza, and swallowing immense quantities of beer. In the front, the juke is cranking out Travis Tritt and ZZ Top. The booths are full, the stools called for, and the tables filled. People are laughing. They are getting loud and drunk and that makes Brenda smile her greedy toothy grin. One of her most loyal customers, Leo Booth—AKA "Leo the Lush"—sees that look on her face and smiles himself. Being one of the biggest drunks in town, he is also a student of human nature.

"Did they get Beebe home all right?" he asks Bonnie Faust, the barmaid, when she brings him another bottle of Old Milwaukee.

"Yeah," Bonnie says above the din. "Her sister came for her."

"What do you think about that clown business?"

Bonnie shivers. "I don't want to think about it. Clowns scare the shit out of me. My mom hired one for my fifth birthday and I hid in the closet. He was creepy. His balloon animals looked like intestines." She shivers again.

Bonnie is very popular at the Broken Bottle. She's an attractive redhead with long legs, a pretty girl-next-door face, dazzling green eyes, and cleavage that just won't quit. She has a flirty demeanor the boys like and a take-no-shit attitude that the women find hilarious. A visiting businessman from Cleveland once offered her $500 if she would give him head out in his car. She turned him down. Six beers later, he offered her a cool thousand. Nobody really knew if she'd taken him up on it or not and Bonnie never said. She enjoyed the did-she-or-didn't-she mystique the episode created. The truth is, she didn't. Despite her looks and the fact that she is hit on dozens of times every night, she always goes home alone and shares her bed only with Herman, her monstrous battle-scarred tomcat. Herman is a real beast who bullies all the dogs in the neighborhood. Bonnie's not looking for any cheap thrills and she definitely doesn't want to get involved with anyone. She likes things uncomplicated. What she really wants is a ticket out of Craw Falls. The idea of spending her life working her ass off all week, then getting loaded and laid on Friday night as the grand prize just isn't enough.

Leo watches her sashay off with a platter of drinks, her swinging hindquarters igniting more than one dirty fantasy in his mind. He chuckles at the very idea and returns to his bottle of Old Milwaukee. It isn't even midnight yet; the real drinking is only starting.

By the time he finishes his beer, his bladder is begging to be emptied again. He staggers off towards the head, but there's a line waiting so he turns on his heel, nearly pitching right on his ass, and starts towards the door, nearly colliding with Stew Prechek who is bringing another pizza to the back room.

"Watch it, will ya, Leo?" Stew says.

Leo waves a hand at him, moves past a young couple that are making out in the doorway, and steps out into the storm.

18

Goddamn, what a blow! The wind is throwing snow around in a tempest. Leo starts wondering if he should have waited his turn inside.

He sneaks around the side of the building and out of the wind to do his business. He creeps through the snow towards the back of the Broken Bottle to his favorite pissing spot. He unzips and his willy doesn't care much for the cold. It looks like a snail that wants to creep back into its shell. He gets it working and sighs. Whenever the storm takes a breather, he can see the back parking lot of the Bottle that is shared with the apartment house next door. Beyond that, only the world engulfed in white. Now and again, he catches a glimpse of the old train bridge and the crumbling mill beyond which has been closed up since the 1970s.

The fields of new fallen snow are sparkling, the sky a pink vortex, the shadows of trees and light poles looking very dark and deadly like the blades of knives. He can see a hazy full moon above that blinks on and off like an old porch light. For a moment there, he thinks he hears a booming in the distance of the sort you hear during deer season, but the wailing of the wind muffles it so that he cannot be sure.

Besides, who'd be shooting off their guns on a night like this?

As he finishes up, his dick feeling like an icicle, he thinks about Bonnie Faust and her fear of clowns. A crazy, improbable, and utterly absurd fantasy parades through his drunken mind of him saving her from a demented clown and her being oh-so grateful. In his daydream, Bonnie's bed is equally as warm as her breasts when he pillows his face between them. That's a good one! A sixty-six-year-old stewpot and a twenty-four-year-old barmaid.

Sweet dreams are made of such things, he thinks.

As he zips himself up, he feels an icy darkness envelop him at the same time he hears footsteps crunching in the snow behind him. He wants to believe that it's only another guy from the bar, maybe one of those meat-eaters from the Dead Skulls, but he knows it's not. His heart trembles in his chest and blades of ice fill his stomach. He can see the shadow of what stands behind him and it's huge and distorted.

So turn around and see who it is.

That's the thing he doesn't want to do, the very thing that sinks him in a chilling pool of silver terror, but he knows he has to. Whatever is behind him gives off a hot stink of putrescence that makes him want to gag.

As he turns, he hears a low bestial growling that amplifies into the roaring of a savage beast. Seeing what makes it, he stumbles back, the roaring rising into a long, guttural crescendo of primeval wrath.

Leo trips and goes down in the snow, his heart threatening to pound its way right out of his chest. He can't be seeing this. The very idea is insane. Yet... there it is: a great hulking clown in big floppy shoes and a rustling, baggy suit of garish blue-and-black checks. Its face looks like a fleshy white skull, its lips black, its eyes gleaming pockets of yellow pus.

The clown advances and Leo feels a surge of pain in his chest. Oh, Christ oh please not me not me not me, a voice sobs in his head as the clown grins with a crooked smile of teeth that look serrated like steak knives. It reaches toward him with an oversized white clown hand that might have been comical in another situation but is not comical now because it isn't a glove. It's flesh. Bloated white flesh threaded by a black vein network. And the tips of the fingers end in claws. Thorny yellow claws.

With one last surge of survival instinct, Leo finds his feet and actually makes it two or three steps before the clown grabs him, spinning him around and disemboweling him. Leo falls to his knees, his lap full of blood and steaming viscera. Then the clown comes at him again and he gasps only once as it shears his face from the skull below.

As he slips into unconsciousness, he feels the clown's teeth sink into his throat and a barbed tongue jab into his carotid as the feeding begins.

19

"Shit!" Peanut says. "Shit! Shit! Shit!"

He watches Sheriff Teague bound away into the storm, tracking the shriek of the second clown to its source. He knows he has to follow. It's his job and his responsibility and there is no getting around that. Regardless, all he really wants to do is run in the other direction and get out of the park. Find a saloon and pour a stiff drink down his throat. But he knows Teague. The job is everything to him and he will not stop. So Peanut follows along, telling himself again and again that none of this can really be happening. The storm throws itself at him and pushing forward is like dragging a cinder block behind him.

He looks around frantically, but he can't see Teague.

Jesus, he has to be here.

Oh God, don't let me be alone out here.

His Glock in one hand and the flashlight in the other, he refuses to let himself panic. The tot lot isn't that big. Chances are that Teague is quite near him, maybe lost in the blizzard. Peanut calls out his name, but the storm has suddenly become not only violent but goddamned loud. He scans about with his light, but it seems to reflect off the moving shroud of snow.

"WILL!" he shouts. "WILL! WHERE THE FUCK ARE YOU?"

He charges forward, slipping and sliding, his face so numb he can't even feel his cheeks anymore. He pushes on, hearing the demonic baying of the clown from time to time, sometimes close and sometimes far away. He's cold from head to foot, but the sound of that horrible thing still has the power to chill him. The fence. Dammit! His light finds the chain-link fence that separates the tot lot from the rest of the park which means he's going completely in the wrong direction.

Swearing, he turns and collides with a huge form that seems to jump out of the storm. It hits him and he goes down on his ass, the flashlight spinning out of his hand. It's Teague and he doesn't look too damn happy. He hoists Peanut to his feet and says, "STAY WITH ME, DAMN YOU!"

Peanut grabs his flashlight and follows the snow-caked form of the sheriff deeper into the storm. Teague seems to know where he is going which is an absolutely amazing feat on a night like this. Now and again, he stops and listens. Every time he hears the clown howl into the blizzard, he moves closer to it, casting for sound the way a hound casts for scent. The clown's scream—because it does in fact sound like a scream, a screeching inhuman wail of pain and deranged fury—keeps coming and going, bouncing around in the storm, echoing with a shivery, baleful noise like a death-cry in an old comic book: "YAAAAAAAAAAHHHHHHGHHH…"

"THIS WAY!" Teague shouts, fighting his way forward. Peanut is right there behind him, the wind making him sway uneasily on his pumping legs. They are close now, very close, and he can feel it. If he needs verification of that, it comes with another bloodcurdling scream from the clown itself.

Then suddenly Teague is pitched on his ass and Peanut lets out a cry as a looming shadow is coming straight at him. He sees a massive, hobbling form and puffy white hands reaching in his direction. One of them paws out at him and he barely avoids its claws. More out of reflexive action than anything else, he puts two rounds into the shape and it roars and fades into the storm.

Teague is on his feet and Peanut sees the claw marks torn into the back of his leather squad jacket.

"WATCH IT!" he cries.

Peanut says, "WHAT?"

Then the clown is hobbling towards him again, its glittering eyes filled with an evil crimson light. It slashes at him and he backpedals, going down in the snow, catching a glimpse of its distorted, snarling face and the huge teeth that jut from its gums. There is an explosion as Teague fires on it. The clown takes the load of 12-gauge buckshot point blank, its shiny blue clown suit erupting into burning tatters that flame into the wind. It wheels away from them with a screech of pain that sounds doglike and is gone.

Again, Teague helps Peanut to his feet.

The clown leaves a spattering of dark blood in the snow. They follow it for maybe twenty feet before the storm erases it, then they stand there, feeling helpless, both of them white with fear.

Peanut scans about with his light.

Having survived several encounters with clowns now, he feels a badass confidence overtaking him. It is, he figures, the way soldiers in a war feel when they don't get wasted in their first few firefights. He keeps looking, searching for spoor of the beast. Over by the slides, he finds something.

"WILL!" he shouts. "OVER HERE!"

Teague comes at a gallop, kicking his way through drifts. He finds Peanut with his light trained on a great dark patch of blood—or something like it—that has stained the snow. A little further investigation and they locate the epicenter of it. They both see it. Peanut hears a demented laughter bounce around inside his skull. What they see in the blowing snow is a large, very large, floppy orange clown shoe caught in the teeth of one of Clegg's beartraps. A ragged stump juts from it. There is a knob of bone sticking out and trailing, ripped flesh frozen with clots of gore.

"The trap tore its foot right off!" Peanut says.

But Teague, down on his knees, studying the grisly object in the beam of his light just shakes his head. "No, this hasn't been torn... look at it... that fucking clown chewed its own foot off."

20

"Crazy shit, that's what I hear," Stan Barbacek says in the cabstand two blocks down from the Broken Bottle. He's sitting there with Flo Hemminger, the dispatcher, who waits patiently by the radio for calls that rarely if ever come in, painting her fingernails and *hmmming* to all he says.

"A clown of all things," he tells her, emphasizing it in case she isn't getting it. "That's the word. Beebe says a clown got Ritchie. Came out of the storm and pulled him right off his sled. Tore his throat out."

"Strange business," Flo admits, blowing on her nails to dry them.

Flo took over Taxi-A-Go-Go from her husband Mort after he pitched over six years before with a coronary. And six lean years they have been. She's barely keeping the doors open. If it wasn't for the Friday and Saturday night bar crowds she wouldn't even have been able to keep her head above water. There was a time, back when Mort ran the show, when Taxi-A-Go-Go had three cars out at night and four during the day. But that was back in the days before the veneer plant closed, sucking away 600 jobs and displacing a good portion of the population who either moved away or decided to stay in Craw Falls and wither on the vine.

"It's more than strange, you know," Stan points out. "If what they're saying is true, we've got more than some nut parading around out there in a clown suit but a psychopath parading around there in a clown suit. One that likes to tear out throats."

Flo listens, nodding. It's obvious that she thinks Stan is full of shit. This is no snap judgment on her part, but one established through many, many long years of listening to him exaggerate, twist, and reinvent every story he hears until it bears scant resemblance to the events that inspired it. Bullshit is

Stan's thing. It's like alcohol or drugs or porn to others; a secret, wonderful addiction, intoxicating and joyous. He can take the most minor of things and inflate them to conspiratorial levels and, interestingly enough, he can get people to believe him. A born politician, Flo can remember Mort saying. Stan has the gift of bullshit. He'd been driving for Taxi-A-Go-Go for over thirty years by that point and he seemed to have little ambition to do anything else, unlike most all the other drivers who came and went regularly. Flo supposes she feels sorry for him because Stan really is full of his own shit. He's one of those guys who always has some big deal cooking on the back burner, waiting to flare up red-hot. It never happens, of course, but he never stops believing it will or, at least, trying to get others to believe that under his skin there is a big, important sort of man just waiting to come out.

So Flo, being good-hearted, listens and nods as she has so many times.

"It's quite a situation, isn't it?" Stan goes on. "When you think about it? It's like something out of those old Hitchcock TV shows. A small town in the grip of a terrible blizzard and somewhere out there, a bloodthirsty lunatic stalks his prey."

Flo doesn't know about Hitchcock. To her it sounds more like the blurb off a paperback novel. She has a whole box of them in the office that she whiles away the time with on long, lonely nights. Her niece kept telling her to get a Kindle, but Flo can barely operate her DVD player.

"This can be national, you know. The big networks, the newspapers, you name it," Stan says, jabbing a finger at her. "Something like this can really make a town like Craw Falls. It can put it on the map. Get us lots of attention and make us some money. You wait, those newsies come in here and you'll be making it hand over fist, Flo."

She sighs, sounding much like the wind that plays around the windows. "C'mon, Stan. Is that what you really want? Craw Falls to be known as Psychoville?"

"You gotta play the hand that's dealt."

"I don't know. I can use the money... but if it means something like this, I'd rather be broke. It isn't decent to make a profit off the suffering of others."

"Shit," he says.

A call comes in and breaks up the festivities. It's Lyle Stubb and his wife, LuAnne. They're over at the Whistle Stop and they need a lift back home.

"They sound three sheets to the wind," Flo says. "Arguing like usual. You sure you can get through that storm?"

"My old Jeep'll go through anything, Flo."

He drops her a wink and heads out the door, a blast of wind and snow coming in that goes right up her spine. Even five minutes later after the oil heater in the corner disperses the chill, she still feels it crawling over her skin. She has worked the graveyard shift for many, many years, always enjoying the solitude and the quiet. But tonight, it's getting to her. In fact, she begins to peer around out of the corners of her eyes, watching the shadows and watching the storm through the window. The wind is howling, and she begins to feel very afraid.

21

Clown.

We're going to get a clown.

As Patti Wayland sits before the radio in the Sheriff's Department—which shares the same building as the county clerk-treasurer, the city health officer, and public works—she thinks about what Peanut said as he and the sheriff stormed out of the office.

"Clown," she says under her breath. "we're going to get a clown."

On one hand, of course, it's the most preposterous thing in the world, the sort of smart-assed remark she'd expect from one of the other deputies like Rich Wegley. God knows that little sonofabitch liked to run his mouth. And had it come from him, she would have shaken her head. But Peanut. Peanut's not the sort to make stupid, sarcastic little comments like that.

And as Patti sits there, thinking of that weird guy Clegg they've got in lock up and listening to the storm howling out there, she gets a chill up her spine.

That screaming, she thinks, sipping her coffee with a trembling hand. That awful shrieking that sent Peanut and Teague running out the door. What the hell was that about?

"Clown," Peanut said when she asked. "We're going to get a clown."

Only he didn't say it like it was something funny, but the most horrible thing he could imagine.

Now Patti sits and waits for them to come back so she can ask Peanut what the hell he was talking about. Clowns, of all things. She's been dispatching the graveyard shift for six years and she's seen (and heard) her share of crazy-ass shit, but this is one for the books.

There's not much traffic out on the police band and for reasons she's not entirely sure of, she finds this disturbing. The storm has pretty much shut the county down, yes, yet there's almost something unnatural about the silence that's getting on her nerves.

She sips her coffee and pages through her copy of Woman's World, which is a complete rag that she reads compulsively every week and she's not even sure why. She glances through articles about Kate Middleton's hairstyles, melting away belly flab with avocado shakes (probably works, Patti thinks, because they make you puke), and recipes for breaded chicken tenders and chocolate pie.

She tosses the magazine aside. "Junk," she whispers under her breath. "Weight loss secrets on the cover and fattening recipes inside."

This is a little joke between she and herself. It's meant to lighten the mood because the atmosphere of the station (and the whole goddamned town for that matter) is getting too heavy. Dear Christ, it's practically brooding. And that's the thing: regardless of how hard she tries to make light of things and ignore those dread instincts that are cutting into her belly, she cannot. They exist without her input.

Outside, the wind rises in pitch until it sounds very much like a scream circling the building. Snow is blown against the window across from her and she starts. She will not look over there because in the back of her mind she is afraid that something might be looking back in.

But exactly what, she does not know.

"Maybe a clown," she whispers.

It's meant to be another little joke, but it takes root in the dark soil of her mind and begins to grow, crowding her head with the white, grinning faces of circus clowns.

Shaking badly, she thinks, *I'm scared to death. Oh, God help me, but I'm scared to death.*

22

Jesus Christ, Teague can sure pick 'em.

This is what Rip Frazer thinks as he drives through the blizzard to pick up Gina Keller's car. A hell of a night to call him out of bed. The snow is flying thick and wild, the wind throwing sheets of it against the tow truck. The wipers are pumping back and forth, barely keeping up with it. He navigates down Central Avenue, following it out of town. The plow passed him five minutes before and already the street is drifting over. This will be one they'll be talking about for years, he knows.

Feeling pissy and very cantankerous, he pulls from his coffee and lights a cigarette, following the deep ruts down Central.

It's going to be a busy night and he knows it. He's already pulled out two cars and has no doubt that by morning, he'll have logged five or six more. Nights like this always bring 'em out. They always got to take a chance in a storm. They need milk or eggs or a loaf of bread, that last six-pack. It's always something.

Rip shrugs.

Of course, it doesn't matter much to him; he makes his bacon because of the poor judgment of drivers. That's what he's here for.

Still...what a night.

The wrecker actually shakes because of the gusting wind. The headlights are filled with thick, spinning flakes that have to be the size of quarters. They look like hundreds of winging cabbage moths. There's no one out. Rip is glad for this... yet, it unnerves him in ways he cannot truly fathom. Town seems too dead, a crypt covered in a white shroud. The wind creates jumping shadows and leaping shapes. Half a dozen times, Rip is sure he sees someone out there.

You're tired, that's all. Gonna be a long night.

Storms can do funny things to your eyes, he knows. Make you see things that aren't there and other things you wish were there. Human imagination, that's all. The mind is always searching for recognizable shapes and when it can't find them, sometimes it manufactures them.

Rip turns up the radio. Some talk show. He listens intently, moving the tow truck ever forward at a snail's pace. They're talking about ghosts, of all things. Some caller's saying how he saw the ghost of a woman in a white dress on the road out in the middle of nowhere. Rip doesn't care for this kind of stuff, not on a night like this. Another caller. This one claims that a ghost comes into his room and sits on the edge of his bed at night. A woman. But it doesn't bother him because he's used to it. The host finds that hard to believe. Now they're arguing about ghosts and whether you should be scared by them or not.

Rip giggles.

Now that's entertainment!

The radio goes in and out. Rip passes the Whistle Stop. Lights still on. A few cars out front. Even a blizzard can't stop people from drinking——

Did I just see that?

He could've swore there was someone standing on the corner, waving to him. Oh, that's crazy. Maybe it was a drunk from the Whistle Stop. He refuses to think about it or how they looked strange like they had some big, baggy costume on.

Five minutes later, still shaken, he arrives at the scene. A little silver Toyota is buried in the snow bank, grill first. This'll be an easy one. He turns on the emergency flashers and backs up to the Toyota. He drops the boom and slides the wheel lift in place.

Piece of cake.

He lifts the Toyota up and pulls it from the snow bank, just a few feet so he can check his rig. Pulling on his hat and coat, he climbs out. The wind punches into him, a tempest of spinning snow overwhelming him. He puts his back to it until it blows past. Even then, it's a crazy, wild night. He's wearing heated Carhartt overalls, still he can feel the frigid wind going right up his spine.

Down on his knees with a flashlight, he checks the rig and she looks fine.

Good. Get the hell out of here.

The wind hits him again and snow covers his face. Christ, he can barely stay on his feet. He makes his way back towards the cab of the truck and then stops. There's a sound out there. He's sure of it...something that does not belong. It reminds him of New Year's Eve for some ungodly reason. That's the association that pops into his brain.

It makes no sense.

Or maybe it does.

Standing there in the blow, he listens and, yes, there it is again. The screech of the wind blocks it for a moment, but only for a moment, then he hears it and it chills him in ways the storm cannot. It's a sort of rattling sound, a rat-a-tat-tat-tat noise. And then he knows what it is. It's utterly impossible, but there it is again. It's the ratcheting sound of one of those New Year's Eve noisemakers you spin on a stick. He seems to recall that they're also known as a gragger.

But here...in this storm?

It's crazy, it's fucking crazy. Who's going to be out here in this goddamn blizzard with one of those things?

Rip can't see much in the blowing snow and darkness, but that rattling comes and goes. He shines his flashlight this way, then that, seeing nothing but shadows that seem to dance and dart and sway, always moving back into the storm when his light gets near them.

"Someone out there?" he says.

The only answer he gets is that rattling noise. It's enough. Somebody's toying with him. Though part of him wants nothing better than to track them down and sort out their ever-loving hash, he decides he's getting out of there.

Then he hears another sound.

Not a rattling, but a thump-thump-thump sound. It's coming from the car. It can be coming from nowhere else. Rip is feeling scared now. His skin crawls in waves and he's not sure why. The thumping comes again, only this time it sounds louder and much more insistent.

Get in the truck, you idiot, he tells himself. *Get out of here.*

But what if someone's in the car? What if someone needs help?

It's ridiculous. If someone was in there, the sheriff would have found them. Rip begins to back slowly towards the wrecker. But when the thump-thump-thump comes again, he goes over to the car. There's snow heaped on it, yet he's certain that someone is pounding on the driver's side window as if they're trapped in there.

He approaches it carefully.

If there is someone in there, part of him does not want to know who it is. Rip is a big man who's worked hard all his life. He really fears nothing. But right then, everything inside him has shriveled. He's a little boy again hearing spooky noises in the night and he wants to run because he fears that he will find something in the car that will strip the gears of his mind smooth.

Yet, he now stands before the driver's side door. His hand reaches out and brushes snow free from the window. It seems to do this of its own volition.

There's someone in the car.

23

Rip can see a vague, shadowy shape slumped over the wheel. Whoever it is, he must help them. Swallowing down the dryness in his throat, a sharp prodding sensation in the pit of his belly that he recognizes as the release of fear-induced adrenaline, he grips the door handle. It's frozen. He has to work it back and forth. Finally, it gives. He opens the door and the dome light comes on.

He lets out a gasping cry.

What's behind the wheel is nothing alive, but a corpse. The corpse of a woman. She's dressed in a lavender parka that is splattered with old blood that has gone brown in the cold like chocolate syrup. Her head is thrown back, mouth frozen in an agonized scream. There's dried blood where her eyes should be, and a great trough gouged out of her throat. But as bad as all that is, what's worse is that she's open from chest to belly and there's nothing inside. All of her internals are missing. As the beam of his flashlight shines off the rungs of her ribs and the black hollowness of her body cavity, Rip turns away.

He only looked at the corpse for three seconds tops, but it's enough to haunt him a lifetime. He's woozy with the sight of it. But he can't fold up and he knows it. He must get back in the cab and call the sheriff... though how it was that the sheriff missed the body in the first place is beyond him.

Rip thinks: Maybe it wasn't there then. Maybe it was placed in there since.

Now that's the sort of thing he shouldn't be thinking about. Not here. Not on a night like this.

As he makes his way to the cab of the wrecker, he hears the rattling sound yet again. He shakes his head from side to side out of terror, yes, and frustration...and confusion. Something is not only wrong here, it is fucked up beyond comprehension. Those are the very words that play through his brain.

He has the most awful sense that when he stepped out of the wrecker cab initially, he stepped out of the world he had known and loved his entire life and into another where things were much darker and topsy-turvy in the worst possible way.

As he reaches the cab, trying to blot all the mad, careening thoughts from his head, he notices something that makes him want to break down in jagged laughter and scream his mind away at the same time——there's a balloon tied to the rearview mirror. A black, shiny balloon bouncing back and forth in the wind.

Now Rip is afraid to get into the cab.

The uncertainty freezes him there. He hears the rattling again and turns and... and there's a clown standing there. A goddamn clown. A clown dressed in a thin black silken jumpsuit with bright red pompoms running down the front.

Rip unconsciously blinks his eyes the way they do in movies when they see something that just can't be. For a moment, the image of the clown wavers like the heat coming off a flame. It shudders, gutters, then solidifies. The clown's face is as white as the belly of a fish, set with tiny black cracks like an antique vase. Its grinning mouth is vibrantly red and juicy as if it is bleeding, the eyes like glittering crimson scarabs in black ovals. Tufts of scarlet Bozo hair are bunched at the sides of its skull. They blow in the wind.

Rip breaks out in a sweat that is at first cold, then unbearably hot. It runs down his back. It steams from his face.

The clown steps forward and as it does so, its head spins round and round on its neck, making the rattling sound of the noisemaker he heard.

Rip feels a shriek building in his throat. It's getting larger and larger, inflating like a helium balloon and when it comes cycling out of him, it's going to be the big one: the scream of the deranged. It will take the wind out of him and drop him to his knees with horror. And it will take his mind. Oh yes. His mind will pop like a blood blister and all his sanity will come spilling out.

Run, a voice instructs him. *Run. Move. Hide. Scamper. Flee. Please, please, please do something! It's getting closer...*

And it is.

The clown is coming for him. It steps forward two or three steps, stops, and its head ratchets around and around on its neck. When the head comes to rest yet again, the face is blurred as is the flesh. Its red mouth and red eyes are running, mixing in with the garish bleached white of its face, becoming something quite like oozing, spitty pink bubblegum that is sagging and stretched out of shape.

Rip lets out a sound that is not exactly the scream he felt coming, but more of the pained yelping of an injured animal. He stumbles back and away, and the blizzard covers the clown, eradicates him from this world.

Snow is blowing from every direction now.

It whips and whirls in sheets, the wind driving into Rip with deadly force. It knocks him back and down and for a moment, he cannot see the wrecker. It is gone and he is cast adrift in some relentless, chaotic Antarctic storm.

When it clears, he sees that he is not alone.

A shape is coming out of the blowing drift, but it is not the clown. No, this is a lean female figure, a crooked, distorted walking cadaver. It is the woman from the car. The wind moans as it blows through her empty body cavity, her rib slats ringing out like tuning forks. She is gutted, broken, bones erupting from her skin like withered sticks. Her head is bent on her neck, her face gray and seamed from the cold, a shriveled leather bag, lips blackened and split open.

She has no eyes.

She reaches for Rip with scaly hands like the claws of graveyard rats.

He screams and stumbles away towards the wrecker and hears the rattling again. Then puffy clown hands cover his face. They are white and spongy like the flesh of a corpse.

24

As Stan moves his Jeep Cherokee slowly down the snow-covered roads, punching forward in four-wheel drive, he is thinking very deeply on what he said to Flo. She didn't seem interested but then she is never interested in anything that isn't green and folding. Typical business person. No matter. This is a goldmine, he decides, if you only work it properly. Now Stan doesn't want anyone else to get killed by some crazy-ass clown, but if it's going to happen anyway, then why not make a buck off it?

There has to be a way.

He just has to think of what it is.

Think, think, think.

If there is indeed a maniac out there haunting the storm then the guy who takes him down will be a hero. And that guy can use his hero status to elevate him into greener pastures. Stan starts getting excited as ideas roll through his head. His entire life he's wanted two things. The first is status and money, lots of both. He wants to be a big man, a mover and shaker. The second thing is he's always wanted to write a book. Something good. Something people would want to read. Maybe this is his chance. A sort of crime story penned by a cabbie who is on the spot of the clown murders, the Craw Falls Killer Clown. That's good. He likes that. He's always had a pretty fertile imagination, and this might be the opportunity to put it to good use.

The Whistle Stop is way across town.

In good weather, he would have been there in five minutes, but in this blow, it's a slow crawl at best and he knows it will take him an easy twenty minutes or more. The wind is screaming out there, dragging the snow in sheets across the roads, making trees and houses look like ice sculptures. Shadows sway and snow-devils spin through the streets. Stan has the wipers on full tilt and they can barely keep up with the onslaught. The headlight beams are filled with churning snowflakes. What a night. What a fucking night.

Clowns.

Clowns.

Stan has never really been afraid of clowns. To him, clowns are just clowns, but some people have a sort of phobia about them. How much of that is real clown phobia or acquired clown phobia is open to speculation. Ever since Stephen King wrote his book about Pennywise—Stan read it twice—and they made the movie about it, people who never gave clowns a second thought are suddenly afraid of them. It's pop culture programming. That's all it is. Marketing and hype. That's all it ever is. People don't know what they like/love/hate/fear, so you tell them. If you can build up enough hype, people will stand in line for whatever you sell. Whatever it is. They want the choices to be made for them. That's why McDonalds sells a lot of burgers and top forty songs sell millions and whatever TV show or movie Entertainment Weekly is pushing—probably because of money under the table—becomes a big hit. Anyone with half a brain knows it's all hype and marketing and selective programming. They know there are a lot better burgers than those at McDonalds, a lot better music than what is on the radio, a lot better movies than the latest crapfest Hollywood is shoving down their throats, and a lot better books than those that make the bestseller list. But most people don't have half a brain and those are the very people Stan wants to milk dry.

When they said there was a sucker born every minute, they really meant it. All you have to do is get people talking about it, posting it on social media, and sending it out on their Twitter feed. Bingo. You got big sales. Stan's old enough to know that the most famous actors/directors/writers or what have you are not the best in their field, but simply the loudest and the pushiest.

"There is no such thing as a good product; only good marketing," he says under his breath.

But back to the crazy clown.

Now, he invented that bit about Ritchie Chandliss getting his throat torn out, of course. But such exaggeration makes good marketing. Ever since he got the word about Ritchie, Stan has been selling it hard to everyone he met. He's already spread wild fabrications over half the town in only a few hours. He told Flo that Ritchie had his throat torn out. He told a couple old ladies from Grace Baptist church that Ritchie's body had been partially devoured. And he'd told more than one person that they hadn't been able to recover Ritchie's head.

He laughs out loud at the idea.

I've been marketing my book all night without even being conscious of the fact, he thinks and laughs again. *But how to keep the ball rolling? That is the question. There has to be a way. It is only a matter of thinking about it—*

Holy oh Jesus.

He hits the brakes and slides four feet through the snow. Some crazy sonofabitch stepped out in front of the Jeep and he nearly killed the dumb bastard. The snow flies in thick sheets and the wipers pump madly to clear it away.

That somebody is still standing there.

A clown.

Stan feels gooseflesh move in prickling waves from his scalp right down to the balls of his feet. The clown just stands there in the headlights, wearing a baggy suit of what looks like gray dingy sackcloth with bright green pompom buttons running down the front and stiff spoke-like yellow ruffles at the throat. The entire outfit looks like it's stained with dark splotches as if the clown has vomited blood. Its chin is glistening with it. Its face is long and narrow like a crescent moon with a stark, noxious yellow pallor, its lips a brilliant scarlet, the tip of its pointed hag nose the same color, exaggerated red eyebrows arching well up onto its seamed forehead. Forking black veins pulse just beneath the skin. It watches him with bright silver eyes glaring from scarified black sockets.

Then it grins at him, threadbare lips pulling away from pocked gums which recede to reveal long pink-stained teeth that are eager to sink into something soft and meaty.

It's not human, a voice in his head informs him. It ain't human. It's not a guy in a suit and makeup—it's a fucking monster.

Stan knows he has to do something.

He knows he is precious seconds from a dirty, ugly death... but his body will not move, his muscles will not react, and his limbs are numb as frostbite.

Do something, the voice warns him. *Do something right now.*

The clown takes two stiff steps forward. It holds out gray-white hands with long, skeletal fingers ending in the bright red claws of a night lamia. The flesh is badly worn at the knuckles and yellow knobs of bone have burst free. It comes closer, cocking its head on its ruffled throat, grinning sardonically with a cold appetite, eager to bury its talons in him. Its halo of red hair is moving, each strand alive and undulant like writhing blood worms.

Stan jams the accelerator down.

For a second or two, the wheels just spin, the Jeep swinging sideways, then they catch, finding a bare stretch of pavement and the Jeep rockets forward, striking the clown—which shrieks with rage—and rolling right over it.

Stan doesn't slow down until he slides to a halt in front of the Whistle Stop, popping the curb and smashing right into the snow bank.

Then he runs inside and before the regulars can ask him what the hell is going on, he starts pouring shot after shot of Wild Turkey down his throat.

25

Any moment now, they are going to bag that sonofabitch. Because even a fucking clown from hell is only going to get so far on one foot. At least, this is what Sheriff Teague keeps telling himself. The storm is coming on in a maelstrom and the clown's tracks are steadily being erased. That is bad. But what is good is that he, she, or it is bleeding a lot—if you want to call that black slime blood—and it stands out in stark contrast against the snow.

Teague moves carefully forward, not lagging because he doesn't have the time for that, but not rushing headlong into disaster either. He doesn't know what in the Christ any of this is about, but he does know that the clowns are monsters. They are predators. And he isn't naïve enough to believe that they aren't intelligent predators. There are lots of trees and bushes in the park, any of which can serve as a good ambush. And he knows from experience that he does not want to let this thing get in too close.

Find it and kill it, he tells himself. *Then get back to the jailhouse and demand some answers, some real answers, from Clegg.*

It sounds like a plan.

As he moves forward, frosted white with snow now, he keeps peering behind him to make sure Peanut is keeping up with him. So far, so good.

They are out of the tot lot now and into the park proper. The snow blows in weird and fantastic shapes that dance and leap around them, becoming leering phantoms and clawing wraiths, a cold dead white entity that wants to bury them forever in sepulchral white silence. The wind keeps blowing and howling, sometimes sounding like it is whispering and other times screaming in rage. It would have been bad enough just about any night, but tonight it's that much worse.

Teague is cold and his limbs are getting stiff. His face feels like slack rubber. He knows they can't keep this up for long. Hypothermia has a nasty way of sneaking up and overtaking you before you even know it's there. So he keeps the symptoms of it fresh in the back of his mind—clumsiness, disorientation, sleepiness, poor decision-making.

Shit. It feels like he already has it.

Keep going.

Which makes perfect sense, but he stops dead because suddenly he sees no more blood. It was there, sprinkled liberally over the white face of the snow... now it is gone. The drift blows, forming little whirlwinds and mad dervishes that play devilishly over the hardpack. Snowflakes whirl in his flashlight beam like hundreds of meat flies abandoning a corpse. He moves this way and that, beginning to feel confused and unsure of himself. It feels oddly as if something inside his mind has just rolled up like a carpet or drawn the shades. Indecisively, he watches the storm gather around them. It comes on heavy for a few minutes then lightens as if it's resting before pouring it on once again. The night goes black then white and finally a dull uniform gray like a tombstone. Whenever it momentarily clears, he can see the town beyond the park and it looks like a frozen crystal palace in a fairy tale.

"Will," Peanut says. "Will?"

Teague comes out of it, realizing he is being mesmerized by the storm and knowing it's imperative that he get out of it soon as possible.

"Here, Will. Over here."

Peanut finds some more blood and then they are hot on the trail again, the clown's trail haphazard as it cuts through the snow, moving to the left, then the right, side to side then straight on in a staggered circle. Yet, it keeps going. Regardless of the clown's injuries, the trail keeps going.

So do they.

Teague knows they could have been waltzing right into an ambush or trap, but something inside him tells him that this isn't the case. The clown doesn't have the energy for such things. It's weak. It's wounded. It needs a hole to crawl in, a place to hide so it can lick its wounds. And if they keep on its ass, it will never get the chance. Sooner or later, it will be forced to turn and fight.

The blood trail leads out of the park now.

It's on the sidewalk along with some half-buried, seesawing prints. It moves down the walk for maybe half a block and then out into the street, back and forth, back and forth... then it disappears out in the middle of the street as if the clown has caught a ride.

But that isn't the case.

The prints move across the street and up the snow-covered sidewalk. Except something has happened. They are no longer the loopy, drunken stride of someone injured but very uniform and they have been made by two feet.

"Can't be," Peanut says.

But it is, Teague thinks.

As incredible as it sounds and as biologically impossible as it might be, the clown has regenerated its foot. That's what they are seeing now. The print of a large floppy shoe and, next to it, the print of an equally large floppy foot. It's insane. They quickly backtrack across the street to make sure they have not lost the trail. They haven't.

"How can it do that?" Peanut asks.

Teague has no answers for him. How the hell is he supposed to know? He remembers one of those old Lon Chaney wolfman movies where the prints out on the moor go from the footprints of bare human feet to wolf tracks.

They follow them up the walk and then they disappear. There is no doubt where the clown has gone—right through the side door of the Broken Bottle. It has to be in there now, hiding.

"Let's go get that sonofabitch," Teague says.

26

Craw Falls, Craw Falls, Craw Falls.

It's a charming little picture postcard of a place, serene and quiet, green by summer and silver-white by winter. Clapboard church spires rise high into the blue sky, children laugh, and oldsters hold court on sagging porches. The rivers run pure and clean and the wind that whispers through the high pines smells of distant tomorrows and yellow yesterdays. All in all, it's a safe, friendly, wholly predictable sort of town. And it's also a dead-end shithole where you bury your hopes and dreams prematurely like children in autumn churchyards. It's a well-loved blanket, fuzzy and warm and familiar, its nap against your skin silken soft like the down of a baby owl. It's this and it's also a devastating blight that withers everything you are or can ever be into thorn-stemmed mortuary roses. It's a good life and a cruel death with nothing in between but misery and suffering that you cloak in things called love, friendship, and security. You tell yourself it's good, it's all good, that this is God's country you're living in, and that makes the hopelessness and stagnation of spirit go down that much easier when night calls your name and prepares a place for you.

This is how Flo Hemminger sees it on those long, lonely nights at Taxi-A-Go-Go as she waits for dawn with a broken heart and a jaded soul, waits for sunlight to play across the streets in golden fingers and bring the town back to life like Sleeping Beauty's long-awaited kiss. Then she can go home to her bed and stop thinking about Mort, about those last days they spent together before he died, of the things he said and how it felt inside when he held her hand or whispered in her ear. She can go home and pull the covers over her head and instead of thinking about him, he will come to her in her dreams and tell her, once again, about the little town in New Mexico they will retire to where the desert is a painted glory at your doorstep and the mountains rise high and wild like God's own steeples. How good it will be. How very good.

Thinking about it, her eyes mist because she is so very, very alone. She has friends, she has family, but deep down inside where it really counts, she is lonesome and lost, a deserted house standing in the middle of an empty desert. Day by day, there is more gray in her hair and more wrinkles etched into her face and down deep inside her there is pain that has no bottom.

Mort, she thinks. *Oh, Mort.*

Morning seems far distant now, a lifetime away. The darkness holds and Craw Falls is a bleak nightscape and the storm crawls over it like a voracious beast. She can hear it out there, moaning and howling. It throws snow against the windows and shakes the building, circling, ever circling, trying to find a way in to steal the warmth away. She tries to raise Stan on the radio to see how the pickup at the Whistle Stop is coming along, but all she gets is static. A bad night all the way around. And on a night like this, even the company of Stan is something.

Ever since he'd regaled her with tales of murders and clowns, she has felt a nameless anxiety growing inside her. She never really noticed before how the cabstand is a dark chest of shadows, that the only light comes from the lamp over the desk. How it casts a perfect circle of illumination like an island in a dark sea. Funny. It has never occurred to her. The cabstand—or station as her husband had once called it—is a narrow building that once housed a lunch counter many years before. Sometimes when it rains in the summer, Flo can swear she smells French fries even these many decades later. Where the counter and stools once stood, sits her desk and filing cabinets. The kitchen in the back is a storeroom now. There is still a grease stain on the ceiling roughly in the shape of Texas from the hooded range that once sat there. Upstairs is an apartment where Flo lives.

There is nothing else but an old ratty cellar that she refuses to visit, having a phobia of dark, cobwebby places.

All these nights she has worked here and never once noticed how the shadows bunch and gather in the corners, how the darkness seems to press in at every quarter.

Oh, would you quit. You're being ridiculous. You're letting what Stan said get under your skin.

Regardless, she gets up and steps lightly to the front door, locking it. Which makes her wonder if the back door is locked. She can't remember, but she knows she'll never relax if she doesn't check. She goes across the room and through a door which leads to a little corridor. The storeroom is on one side, the bathroom and a broom closet on the other. It is dim in there and she walks quickly down its length, around the bend to the back door. It's locked.

Thank goodness, she thinks, without really knowing why.

"Good God," she says under her breath, "what's wrong with you?"

27

Flo's nerves are on edge, ringing out like wind chimes, and her guts are flipping and flopping. She goes into the bathroom, throws the deadbolt, and helps herself to the stall on the end. It's a unisex place and Mort remodeled it himself, transforming the two small bathrooms of the lunch counter into one roomier version. There are two stalls, a couple sinks opposite them, and, farther down, two urinals.

Standing there, pulling her pants down, Flo is struck with the very real, inexplicable need to run. To get out of there as fast as she can before...before a fathomless darkness descends. It's insane and madly impractical, but she nearly does it. With her joggers down to her knees, she actually hesitates for a moment or two before sitting down and when she finally does, the worst feeling of expectation floods her.

You really have to stop this, she thinks, trying to be sensible.

Then she hears the door jiggle.

Dear God, it's come. It's come out of the night.

Maybe it's her imagination. Then it comes again. Somebody is jiggling the doorknob out there. Stan? Has he come back already? No, she doesn't believe that much as she wants to. Stan always knocks twice before coming in, saying something like, "Anybody home?"

This is not Stan.

This is darkness.

This is death.

She sits there, shivering now, fighting down an urge to call out, is that you, Stan? even though she knows it is not him. The door jiggles again. She shivers. Her heart plummets. Go away, please just go away. But they aren't going away.

The doorknob is not being jiggled now. Somebody is rattling it, twisting it back and forth and she hears a strange sort of groaning sound followed by a distinct popping noise and something metal falls to the floor.

The lock. They just broke the lock.

And, conceivably, how much strength would that have taken?

Flo knows how vulnerable she is, but she can't make herself move. She can't even make herself stand and pull her pants up. The door swings in violently and crashes against the wall and she nearly comes out of her skin.

Then for a moment or two that stretches out into three or four, there is nothing but the steady tom-tom beat of her heart and the sound of the breath in her lungs and the blood rushing through her head.

Silence.

It is unreal, surreal even—a seamless, silken sort of silence that is heavy and enclosing. It is the dread sound of neutrality you would know in the grave where the only noises are the chewing of coffin beetles and the corkscrewing of the conqueror worm. The bathroom—which smelled of lilac soap and pine cleaner moments before—now is positively rancid with a stench of leaf mold, rotting humus, and black wormy soil. It's a moist wet stench like something that might blow out vaporous and black from a flooded tomb.

Now there is movement and she gasps.

She hears the slip-slap¬ of wet shoes crossing the floor, shuffling in the direction of the urinals. The stench of crypts and open graves is stronger now, becoming a high, sweet putrescence that makes her want to vomit her stomach out. She hears a voice humming low and oddly obscene. She recognizes the singsong tone and thinks it is "Wee Willie Winkie." There is something horrifying and perverse about the idea, but she is almost sure of it.

There is a low, slow sighing like October wind playing about high gables, then the sound of water running. He's pissing. Whoever it is, he's pissing now. The stream goes on and on and as it does so, a pervasive hot stink of foulness fills the bathroom. It is the stench of urine from a cancerous bladder or maybe stagnant piss that has been sloshing around in the kidneys of a corpse for days and days and is now being squeezed out.

Flo has to bite down on her hand so she does not scream.

She shivers.

She sweats.

Bile kicks up the back of her throat.

She goes hot and cold, her brain reeling and threatening to turn out her lights at any moment. The piss keeps coming and coming and she's almost certain it has been going on for three or four minutes by that time. Its smell contaminates the air, making her nostrils sting and her eyes water and roll in their sockets. She counts off twenty terrible seconds, then thirty, forty, fifty... and the piss keeps striking the urinal. The flow is not diminishing in any way.

It's getting stronger... can't you hear it? a near-hysterical voice in her head informs her. *Can't you?*

And it is.

Now it's gushing out with the sort of pressure that is beyond ordinary human uresis. No bladder can do this. It sounds like it's coming out of a garden hose with a spray nozzle on the end. And whoever owns that equipment, they aren't just pissing into the urinal now but spraying the walls and floor. It sounds like a man washing his car, back and forth, back and forth.

Tears are running down Flo's face. Her entire body is shaking. She is biting down so hard on the back of her hand that she has drawn blood. The room seems to whirl and spin around her, black dots popping before her eyes as if she's being asphyxiated.

Whatever that individual is putting out, it isn't urine.

Not exactly.

There is a central floor drain before the stall door and she sees a river of black fluid reaching it, filling it and backing up, swirling in a great sluicing pool of corpse drainage. It's not just liquid. There are bits of tissue in it as well.

And still that horrendous pissing goes on and on.

Flo can't keep it together any longer. It's simply impossible. Her mouth frozen in a silent scream, she tries to pull herself up off the pot, the stink of urine up her nose and down her throat. As soon as she stands, the world spins like a top and she falls, banging her head against the back of the toilet.

Then darkness.

She isn't out long.

She's sure of that.

She comes out of it in a wild panic, shaking and confused, scrambling to her feet and pulling her pants up the rest of the way. Like a scurrying rodent fearing the talons of a hawk, she goes still, listening, feeling for danger. The pissing has stopped, and she is nearly certain she is alone in the bathroom. She can see the black stains on the floor. It looks like somebody has drained a dirty transmission in there.

Listen.

She does. There is nothing. Though this is a good thing, she is hardly relaxed or hopeful. She stands there until she feels secure and solid on her feet. She can't spend the rest of the night in the stall and she knows it. Steeling herself, she slides the catch on the stall door very slowly and very carefully. Still, when it breaks loose, it sounds loud in the stillness of the bathroom.

She opens it and steps out.

There is no one in there with her.

But there are footprints on the floor, huge, distorted footprints that lead away from the urinal and out into the cabstand. Whoever pissed that black ichor on the floor has left a trail of it leading out the door.

Those feet.

The shape of them.

The deadbolt is on the floor, along with some hardware and mounting screws.

Nobody could be that strong.

As she pushes open the bathroom door, she starts thinking about what Stan said about a clown. Those tracks certainly could have been made by large floppy shoes.

Oh, listen to yourself! That's insane! Clowns...big floppy shoes. You're not thinking straight.

But maybe she is. That's the most frightening part of it all. The footprints lead out into the cabstand. She has a choice to make. Either she follows them and faces what is out there or she slips out the back way.

And what? You run out into the storm with nothing but a hoodie and a pair of joggers on? You're sixty-three years old. You're not a kid.

That is reason talking. But she's not listening to reason; she is listening to instinct which tells her to get out of there and get out right now. So she moves quickly down to the end of the corridor to the back door. She throws the lock and tries to open it. The door will move only a few scant inches. It is iced in place, a wall of snow blown up against it. She puts everything she has into it, but it won't budge. It just won't budge.

The corridor fills with a hot smell of spoiled meat.

Oh God, oh dear God please...

She turns and a clown is standing there.

She feels the blood drain from her torso down into her legs. The clown stands there, watching her, its head cocked to one side as if it's confused about what she is doing. It's a man...or something like a man. He is tall, well over six feet, wearing a billowing black satin jumper with immense red polka dots on it. He even has red-and-black striped clown socks on. It might have been comical if it wasn't for the huge fish-white hands, the fingers clawed like a hawk and stained pink with blood. And that lopsided, bulbous head of pale blue-gray flesh, balding, with sprouts of shocking green hair. His nose is like a cherry tomato, his lips black, eyes white as the pale eggs of a spider, bulging and about to hatch. They are set in deep black ovals. They have no pupils, yet she knows they watch her.

She wants to scream but there is no scream in her.

The clown steps towards her, its black lips wrinkling back to reveal teeth...the yellow dagger teeth of a wolf or a monster from a comic book. They gleam and glisten with frothing white saliva that bubbles free and drips down the clown's pointy chin as if it's rabid.

And maybe on this dark cold killing night in this dark cold little town, it is.

The clown reaches for her. Its white puffy corpse fingers end in black seeking raptor talons that will split her wide open so it can swim in her blood. She can already smell its breath—marrowfat and cold raw meat.

Flo knows she is going to die.

There's no chance of surviving this.

Something in her begins to go dark like a candle fizzling as its wick burns out. The clown advances and slashes out at her with one white, clawed hand. The claws are very sharp, and they lay her open from forehead to mouth, slicing four very clean, very deep rents in her face. Blood explodes from them and sprays against the wall.

Then the clown leaps on her.

It moves fast before she falls right over. It takes hold of her in a powerful grip and her fingers tear at it, expecting the material of its suit to be satiny as it looks. But it's not satiny. It feels like flesh under her fingertips, living oily flesh. She is amazed by this and amazement is one of her final states of being as the clown tears her carotid open and buries its face in her throat, sucking and licking and guzzling the hot rich blood that flows free, satiating itself on it. Its grub-white eyes go pink, then a juicy red like Egyptian scarabs and finally the purple-red of blood clots as they swell to bursting, filling with stolen blood.

When Flo hits the floor, she has been drained like a cold can of beer on a hot day, crunched in a fist and discarded there, a shriveled thing, dead dry sticks in a puckered vellum bag of skin.

The clown stares down at her, smiling.

As it stumbles away, full to bursting, it grabs her by the ankle and drags her along with it like a little girl with a rag doll. It has sucked down so much blood in one feeding that red juice runs from its nostrils and trickles from the corners of its mouth. It finds the doorway that leads below and shambles away into the cool darkness of the cellar, Flo's head bumping on each step. It tosses her aside and stretches out on a nest of rags and bones. Belching loudly, it goes dormant, blood continuing to leak from its ears, its ass, even sweating from its pores from the overfeeding.

Like a man snoozing after a large Thanksgiving meal, it sleeps in gluttonous contentment.

28

At the Whistle Stop, Stan Barbacek stops at his third shot of Wild Turkey. Christ, he's got to drive and all. It's his duty. He's a freaking taxi driver. He can't afford to come undone; people count on him. That's how he sees it most nights, like he's on a mission or a magical quest—a guy with a tough job to do and if he doesn't get it done, others will suffer.

At least, that's how it is most nights.

Tonight, however, is not most nights. Tonight is about as unique as they get. Stan sits at the bar with Lyle and Luanne Stubbs, running it all through the reels of his brain. Not just the bit about what happened to Ritchie Chandliss, but what he himself saw out there in the blizzard.

Clown, he keeps thinking. *And not a psychopath clown, but a fucking monster clown, a clown from hell.*

That's the part he's having trouble wrapping his brain around. A clown from a horror book. He keeps telling himself that maybe it didn't happen the way he thought, but he's not buying it. He saw the teeth the thing had. He saw those eyes. The claws.

No, you saw it. It was there, all right. That was the monster that got Ritchie.

"You better slow down if you're driving," Brick Zutema says, polishing glasses and peering at an Australian rules football game on the tube.

"Just enough to warm me up, no more," Stan tells him. True, he's more than warm now. There's a glow inside him that seems to be spreading. But God knows, he needs it.

"Ah, let him get loaded," Winn McCoy says. "He ain't afraid of no pussy-ass drunk driving laws. Are you, Stan?"

Stan, knowing he's being baited, keeps his mouth shut.

"Hey, Stan?" Winn says, louder this time. "You ain't some faggot who's gonna let cops run your life, are you? Fuck no. Set him up again, Brick."

Brick sighs. "Just stay out of it, Winn."

"What? I'm a paying fucking customer, ain't I? Hell's your problem?"

Brick gives him a warning look and moves down the bar to serve another customer.

There's about ten people in the bar, mostly old soaks who've been hanging around the Whistle Stop for years and years. It's hard to find anyone in there younger than sixty. Even the music playing on the juke is that old——Jim Reeves just finished "He'll have to Go" and now Marty Robbins is "Singing the Blues." This is the sort of music Stan's mom used to listen to while working in the kitchen when he was a boy. The sound of it depresses him.

Down the bar, Jaylene Thone is singing off-key. Karen Baylen is with her. Everyone knows they're an item...except for Jaylene and Karen.

Winn is watching Stan. "See, buddy, you know why these laws are so fucked up? You know why an honest hardworking guy can't have a few and drive home?" He waits for an answer but doesn't get one. He adjusts the greasy brim of his Navy baseball cap. "Well, I'll tell you. Women. That's right. These sonofabitching Women Against Drunk Driving."

"WADD?" Jaylene Thone down the bar calls out. "Women and Dangling Dicks? I'm all for it."

There're a few peals of laughter over that. Some giggling.

"What are you pissing about?" Winn asks them.

"It's MADD," Brick enlightens him. "Mothers Against Drunk Driving. Not Women Against Drunk Driving."

Winn waves that off. "Fuck. Whatever. It's all the same. Them snatches got together and stripped our rights away. That's what happened."

"Oh, shut your hole," Jaylene tells him.

"Shut yer own!" Winn threatens. "It's only good for one thing!"

Jaylene slams her beer bottle down. "Yeah? What would you know? You ain't got nothing worth sucking!"

"Just ignore her, Stan," Winn says very loudly. "Never had a cock in her life. She's licked more slit than I have."

"Listen, you little—"

"All right, all right," Brick tells them as the volume goes up and up. "Everyone mind their own and drink their drinks. We're not having any goddamn fighting in here."

There's some grumbling, then Jimmy Rodgers starts singing "Kisses Sweeter Than Wine" and that soothes the savage beasts.

29

The silence is deafening.

This is what Margot Cheever thinks as she opens her eyes, blinking them slowly, bugged by something but unsure as to exactly what it might be. She hears the storm out there, endlessly moaning and groaning its displeasure. The wind makes the window rattle in its frame. Even in her bed, tucked warmly under the covers, she can feel the chill of it.

Not getting up, she thinks, *not quite awake. Nothing can make me.*

This gives a sense of comfort and her eyelids grow heavy and close as her head sinks deeply into the pillow. She knows, as she drifts off, that something woke her, but she ignores it. If it was the twins, well, they weren't known for their subtlety. If they needed something, they'd whine and cry until they got it.

Margot sleeps, dreaming that Jonathan is with her and not working the night shift over in Vermillion. It makes her feel calm and relaxed and her sleep is deeper. Twenty minutes later, she opens her eyes again.

This time, they do not flutter or threaten to close.

Something is wrong.

Though she cannot figure out what, she knows it to be a certainty. Like countless generations of mothers before her, she is psychically uplinked to her house and her children. They form a delicate ethereal web and like a spider, she knows very well when a single strand is plucked or broken.

Her throat dry, she reaches for the water bottle on the nightstand. She does not panic or leap out of bed. No, she listens and she feels, seeking out the disturbance with her mind, knowing she will find it if it's indeed there to begin with. Her intuition is disturbed. She knows something is not right, but she cannot place it.

She gets out of bed.

First things first. She'll merely tiptoe down the hallway and look in on the twins. That's the first thing. The second thing will be to make sure the furnace is still running. Everything else is pretty much pedestrian after that. Priorities. And life is all about priorities, she knows.

The hardwood floor is freezing beneath her bare feet. She pulls her socks on quickly. Like dressing, she has learned to do it entirely in the dark. The room is not completely murky. A sort of half-light from the storm comes in through the window and as she passes it, she can see that the streetlight on the corner is filled with whirling snowflakes. She worries momentarily that Jonathan—*God, how he hates being called that*! —won't be able to get home in the morning if it keeps up like this.

But on to more pressing matters.

The twins.

She steps lightly into the hallway, still listening, still feeling for something that she knows is there and does not belong, but unable to detect what it is. She turns on the hallway light. She sees no one, but is suddenly certain that someone is there, someone is in the house that does not belong. The very idea fills her with dread. A pervasive bone-deep chill moves through her in waves. She is scared now. Unsure. Threatened. Spooked. She is trembling with the fear of the unknown which is the worst possible fear imaginable.

"Jonathan?" she mouths silently, afraid to raise her voice and alert the stranger in the house that she is aware of them.

She is caught, held immobile by conflicting imperatives: the need to not move and the need to protect her children. The latter wins out. She moves down the hallway quietly in her stocking feet, certain she is overreacting (as Jonathan always accuses her of), but intent on vanquishing her fears. That's when things begin to get a little strange. She feels a curious weakness in her belly that is beyond apprehension. It becomes a nausea that overwhelms her, makes her double over and lean against the wall. But it does not stop there. Now she is dizzy, sweating, nearly feverish. The hallway blurs, becomes insubstantial, then solidifies.

And as it does, she sees a clown standing there some ten feet away. The idea of which, of course, is insane. A clown? In her house? In the middle of the night?

As she leans against the wall, physically and, possibly, psychologically ill, she has a desire to laugh at the absurdity of the situation because for one lean moment, she is certain that Jonathan came home early and is playing a terrible, sick joke on her.

But she does not laugh.

In fact, she chokes back a scream.

Because this clown is not cute nor funny, but blatantly horrible. It wears a checkered suit that looks as if it's stained with blood and not a little, but a fucking lot. Its hair is orange, its lips quite red, its eyes huge and filled with a glistening yellow drainage.

It grins at her.

It shows her its teeth.

The nausea and dizziness are nearly overwhelmed by a rising hot spike of pure adrenaline-infused terror. Margot feels as if she might pitch right over with it. She feels the need to hide in a closet or under a bed.

And what increases this very real terror is the fact that Mia and Michael, her twins, are with the clown. They stand sleepily to either side of it, holding its huge white puffy hands.

Margot lets out a strangled cry, trying to throw herself forward, and succeeds in going down on one knee. Her heart is hammering, her breath coming in dry gasps. She is shaking and delusional and overwrought with horror.

That clown...that clown, oh dear God, that clown will kill them...

These are the thoughts that drift aimlessly through her head like random clouds in a summer sky. She tries to rise and fails again and again. But she does not stop trying because Mia and Michael are with that goddamned clown and she knows it will kill them.

It grins like an evil monkey, a sardonic death rictus, all pink interlocked teeth. Its black pencil-thin eyebrows arch high on the shiny white dome of its forehead. It's evil by nature, she knows, and it will now do evil.

Margot cries out, screams for the twins to get away from that horror. But her voice, unfortunately, is an airless whisper. And the twins—who look up at the grinning clown with delight and wonder—probably wouldn't have heeded her warning anyway.

Now the clown's head makes a cracking sound and there is a visible seam running from its chin right up to its cranium, bisecting its face. Now the head opens like a clamshell and what is beneath is even more horrible to behold—a sagging, pulsating sack of pink flesh that is honeycombed like the skeleton of a bryozoan. It moves and shivers in peristaltic waves. Where its mouth had been, there is now a blunt collection of squirming tubes that expand and deflate.

The children giggle at the sight of this fresh horror.

Margot shrieks and flops about numbly on the floor.

The clown silently grabs Mia and hoists her into the air. She giggles happily as it bends her into a writhing, pretzel-like shape. Margot can clearly hear Mia's bones dislocating and tendons snapping as the clown twists and mangles her, working her like a balloon animal at a kiddie party. Her flesh even makes that rubbery balloon sound as it is reconfigured, legs knotted and pulled over the top of her head, arms corkscrewed behind her, head pulled down where her hips once were.

Now Mia is dropped, a freakish sculpture of gore that wriggles on the floor. Michael is seized and likewise mutilated and dropped before his mother.

The clown could have done many hideous, obscene things to Margot, but instead, it leaves her with two very appalling corpses as her mind vents itself in one final, devastating scream of pure horror that tears her sanity out by its black roots.

30

"Finish that one," Lyle Stubbs tells his wife. "Then we better go."

"Yeah, yeah," Luanne says.

This is what Stan is afraid of. When it's time for them to leave, that'll mean it's time for him to go back out into the storm…and what might be waiting there. He breathes in and out, trying to calm himself. If he wants to write that book, then he's going to have to deal with his fear.

Luanne swallows down the rest of her Seven-and-Seven, smacking her lips loudly. "Thinking of poor Ritchie getting his head torn off," she says, getting emotional as she often does when she's drinking (which is every night). A tear slides from her eyes, taking a trail of mascara with it. "Terrible thing. Killers out there and nobody to protect me."

Oh Christ, Stan thinks, *here we go.*

"Oh, you'll be fine, Luanne," Brick says. "You got Lyle to protect you."

She laughs. "Ha! Fat lot of good he'll do. He's no better with his fists than he is in the bedroom."

Lyle, who's practically comatose on Manhattans, comes to life. "Oh, shut your mouth, you old bag. And while you're at it, cross your legs—you're drawing flies."

"You see how he treats me!" Luanne starts sobbing for real now, tears and mascara rolling down her face. A single tear lodges between her lips which are painted a vibrant red. She whimpers and shakes, but her hair never moves. It's a massive helmet-shaped bouffant that has been carefully lacquered with hair spray. A hurricane couldn't dislodge a single hair.

Brick gives Stan the look which means, *get them the hell out of here, will ya?* Stan sighs inwardly. It's time then. Time to go out into the night and see what's out there.

"Okay, kids," he tells the Stubbs as they pick at one another as they have been doing since their nuptials, summer '63. "Let's get going before the storm gets any worse."

"And her mouth gets any bigger," Lyle says.

Luanne breaks into fresh tears.

Oh, God.

He escorts them to the door, waiting as they get their coats and boots on, which is quite an undertaking in of itself. Then it's time. Lyle holds the door open and the wind comes blowing in, bringing snow and frigid air. The regulars start bitching right away and Stan gives Luanne his arm.

"So afraid I'm going to fall," she says, "like my cousin Georgina. She broke her hip. Into the goddamn nursing home she went, and she never came out. God rest her soul."

Stan takes them out to the Jeep, the wind shrieking around them. Finally, he gets them in the back and gets the door closed. The snow is flying in dervishes and devils and he keeps seeing shapes moving in it, things with long claws and blood-red eyes. Then he's in the Jeep, too.

"You okay, Stan?" Lyle asks.

Shaking, breathing hard, Stan says, "Sure, just fine."

But as he backs out into the street, the hairs standing up on the back of his neck, he's anything but.

31

Oh, by Christ, would you look at that.

Mike Zutema, Brick's brother, moves his plow slowly towards the intersection of Plum Street and Central Avenue. He passed this way two hours before, but you wouldn't know it now—it's all drifted over. Looks as if he never plowed it at all. The blizzard is getting worse, if that's possible. The headlights of the plow truck are filled with whirling flakes the size of nickels.

"This is pointless," he says under his breath.

He decides that he'll make one more pass down Central, then he's calling it a night. All he's doing is wasting gas by this point. There's simply no way to keep the roads open.

Outside, the wind rises to a mournful howling. The truck shakes. A blanket of snow inundates the windshield. The wipers can barely keep up.

Mike pushes on relentlessly, thinking of other storms other years. This is among the worst he's seen, but he knows if he says that to any of the old timers down at the garage, they'll go on about horrendous blizzards back in the '70s and '80s. That's how they are. Don't even try to outdo their yarning; they'll just pile up the BS that much deeper.

Something hits the side of the truck and Mike barely even flinches. It gets noisy in a plow truck. You're always throwing chunks of ice around. No worries. But when it happens again, he slows the plow, wondering if something has broken loose on the truck. He waits but there is no repetition of the sound.

On he goes.

Another twenty minutes, then back to the city garage for a hot cup of coffee. The idea cheers him considerably. In fact, it makes him grin. Then something hits the truck again. More specifically, it hits the door. Not once, but three times—bang, bang, bang. Crazy. It's like somebody out there knocked. That's insane, of course, the very idea of someone running in the storm to keep pace with the truck. Yet, it wipes the smile from his face and breeds fear deep inside him. He's not sure why it scares him, but it gets into his blood and it won't let him go.

He speeds up, knowing it's dangerous, but he has the sudden inexplicable sense that there's something out there, something toying with him. And he's sure of it when there's a loud rapping at the door again. He nearly comes out of his skin. Out the driver's side window, he sees nothing but the storm and darkness.

Christ, you better slow down.

That's common sense talking, but common sense does not understand what he's feeling, the slow crawl of terror up his spinal column. He cannot shake it. When the rapping comes again, it's louder and more insistent and he knows he can no longer ignore it. Something has to happen. Either he tucks his tail between his legs and makes for the garage or he stops the truck right now and sorts this out.

Whatever it is.

Something hits the door again and he feels his dander rising. Maybe kids having a lark. Even though he doesn't believe this for a moment, he tells himself that he'll soon sort their shit out. He brings the truck to a stop, throws her in park and, gathering up every ounce of strength he ever had or ever will have, throws open the door.

The storm rushes in, papers blowing around in the cab, snow gusting right in his face. Even with the dome light, he can see nothing out there but the blowing drift sculpting itself into wind-driven shapes and leaping, lean shadows.

The wind screams and it sounds almost like a human voice driven mad with agony.

Mike leaps out with a tire iron from behind the seat. Having it in his hands makes him feel that much bigger, that much tougher, that much more of a match for whoever is toying with him. This is when he sees the bent, loose weather-stripping dangling from the bottom of the door.

He chuckles in his throat.

Sure, the wind took hold of it and knocked it against the door and that's all it was. All it ever could be. Goddamn idiot, he thinks. Boy, he'd never admit to this one; the boys would never let him live it down.

As he prepares to climb back up into the cab, he senses motion behind him. He spins around and sees nothing. But he was sure, he was so sure…more movement—to the left, the right, in front of him, behind him. Wherever his eyes aren't, that's where it is. Motion and a sort of swishing sound.

"Looking for me?" a voice says, and Mike nearly screams. If his throat hadn't gone dry with terror, he might have. The voice has a low, wicked hissing quality to it, reptilian.

A shape steps out of the storm and Mike sees it's a clown. A fucking clown of all things. In the blizzard of the decade, here's a clown. Despite the weather, he's dressed in a satiny white costume, one side set with black polka dots, the other with black stripes. A ruffled collar, also black, flutters in the wind. Mike doesn't know whether to laugh or to scream.

This is some kind of joke. Some kind of sick, fucked up joke. This guy is one of those freaks who dress like clowns and go around scaring people. Mike has already decided that he'll sort his shit out.

"Who the hell are you?" he asks, feeling the tire iron in his hand and wanting to use it.

The clown steps forward, a tall, gaunt, cadaverous fellow. His face is painted white as a corpse, his eyes pink, infected sores set in black stars, his lips pulled up in a black malefic grin. Even his nose is set in a black circle…except, closer now, Mike can see that he has no nose but the triangular cavity of a skull.

"I'm Mr. Skinsquab," says the clown in a rasping, awful voice. "And I'm going to eat you up."

Mike, nearly hysterical, swings the tire iron and it impacts with the clown's skull. There is a cracking noise and the crown of its head splits open, black blood running down its bald white scalp.

This is what Mike sees right before the clown's hand seizes his face, fingers sliding into his eye sockets like drill bits, blinding him.

32

Over at the Sheriff's Department, Patti Wayland's feeling not only frightened but lonesome and maybe even depressed. She's not sure what it's all about, but whatever it is, it's dug down deep inside her and she can't shake it.

Oh, you know what it's about, a voice says in her mind. *You know very well what it's about.*

And maybe she does, but she'd rather not admit it. This makes things easier to live with. Denial. It ain't just a river in Egypt. That makes her smile momentarily because it was one of her mother's favorite sayings. But the smile fades quickly enough. Everything inside her seems to drop down into a deep black hole.

She feels like she's on the edge of a panic attack.

She tries breathing in and out to calm herself, but it does no good. Her heart is hammering away in her chest, galloping like a runaway pony. This makes her even more nervous. But it's not just a case of bad nerves. She knows that. This is something bigger, something perhaps even immense.

Fear is inside her like cold sludge, moving, shifting, filling her veins. She's aware, very aware, that something is terribly wrong. She cannot put a name to it, but it's most definitely there. For the first time in her life, she's questioning the nature of reality as she's always understood it. She feels things that she has never felt before. In fact, she's almost afraid to look around because she might catch a glimpse of her world unzipping itself and see the eyes...the glistening blood orbs she always thought watched her from the depths of her dreams.

Stop this! she tells herself, nearly certain that she is not only losing her mind but that it has cracked right down the middle like an egg broken against the side of a pan. If you don't get your feet underneath you, you're going to fold up—

But wait... there is a sound.

Bang, bang, bang.

Her heart skips a beat and for a moment there, it seems like it might seize entirely. Then she realizes that what she is hearing is coming from the holding cells down the corridor behind her. Oh Christ. She unkinks slowly, breathes deeply and exhales. It's that nut they threw in the cell. That's all it is. God, what's wrong with her tonight?

Though she is not supposed to leave the radio, she figures it won't much matter tonight. It's a real cemetery out there. Immediately, she wishes she hadn't thought that, because it launches stark imagery in her head of rows of graves thrusting from the snow. A metaphor, surely, for Craw Falls this night.

Hesitantly, she goes down to the end of the corridor. She opens the door and there are the rows of holding cells. Only one is occupied. In the morning, she knows, when the roads are clear, its occupant will be transferred to the main lockup in Vermillion.

But for now, he sits there, staring at her. His eyes are heavy-lidded as if he does not close them much at night, and very dark. Intense, is the word, Patti supposes. He's sinewy, mean-looking, like some kind of vigilante from a spaghetti western.

"Why are you making that noise?" she asks him.

"I need to speak with the sheriff," he says.

His voice has a sort of accent to it, but she cannot place it. It's not exactly Midwestern or Southern or New England, but there's something there. He seems to form his words very carefully.

"The sheriff is out. He'll be back within the hour, though, and when he comes back, I'll give him the message."

"It might be too late by then."

"What are you talking about?"

He licks his lips slowly. "I'm talking, ma'am, about what's happening out there. The evil that has taken this town and will not release it until there's nothing but a lot of bones and corpses lying about."

Oh, he's mad, this one is. He's mentally challenged, unbalanced, disturbed. Goddamn crazier than a shoeshine in a shitstorm (another of Patti's mother's favorite sayings). Yet, down deep, she does not really think this guy is nuts. His face, though scarred and lined, is honest and calm.

"I need to get back to the radio," Patti tells him, feeling like his eyes are boring into her in a way that she finds oddly exciting and more than a little dangerous.

"There's no point," he tells her. "It won't work."

"It works."

"You sure?"

"Yes." But she's not sure at all. Last couple hours, the calls have been fewer and fewer. They've trickled down to nothing now.

He nods his head. "See? They've got this town wrapped up tight. No radios. No phones. No cells. No internet. They've got us right where they want us."

"I don't understand what you mean."

"I'm talking about the signal," he says. "The one they broadcast. See, they've knocked out communications with this town so we can't call in help and because signals from radio, TV, cells etc. might interfere with their own."

"You're not making sense."

"The only thing out there is the signal...their signal. That's the way they want it."

Patti shakes her head back and forth because this has to be raving, nothing but raving, but, again, she does not really believe it. Despite the chill coming in from outside, there is a light layer of sweat on her forehead and fear like ice just beneath her heart.

"What's your name?" he asks.

She tells him, not sure if that's a good idea or not.

"Listen to me, Patti," he says. "I've seen this before. They get a little town like this isolated by a storm and they go on a killing spree. By the time anybody figures what's going on, they're gone. That's how it works. That's how it always works. And don't look at me like I'm crazy because I might be the last sane head in this town. Unlike the others, I know what's going on. I'm not in denial."

"I don't know what you mean."

"Sure, you do. You're afraid only you're not sure what of. That's what they do. They poison the atmosphere of a place, weaken their prey with terror, then they attack. That's why you're afraid. I'm willing to bet this has been building for a few days inside you and you haven't been sure why."

She wants to disagree, but she cannot because it's true. This has been going on for days. A sense of unease, of expectation, of dread that she cannot put a name to. Her dreams have been invaded by the worst sort of nightmares. She has woken up again and again, shivering, sweating, unable to remember them but knowing they were terrible beyond belief.

"I... I need to get back to the radio," she mumbles.

"You do that, Patti. You try and call out to somebody, anybody, even 9-1-1 and you won't get anything. Trust me, nothing but dead air out there now. As they get closer to you, your fear will increase, and your anxiety will spike. Then... then you're going to come back here and let me out. Because you know you have to."

Patti nearly runs back to the office. She sits in front of the radio, waiting for calls that don't come. She's never been so terrified. She thinks of Clegg and knows he's right. That's the most terrible thing of all: he's right.

33

Over at the Broken Bottle, George Carp, pissed out of his gourd, makes a mad dash for the shitter because the pepperoni deluxe he chomped down not an hour before is beginning its march to the sea. Droplets of salty sweat the size of BBs roll down his face. It feels like there's a knife jabbing his lower intestine. He performs a merry, if not graceful, dance through the bar, making for the Men's room. It's like some oasis of relief in his mind. If he can only make it before he sprays mud down his leg.

Jesus, here's the door.

He makes it through and nearly flattens a guy washing his hands (who calls him a stupid fuck). The stalls are empty. Thank God. Carpy takes stall three because he needs to distance himself as much as possible from the heavy traffic at the urinals. This is going to be the mother lode and he knows it. Sweating profusely, squeezing his cheeks together, he barely gets his pants down and his ass over the toilet when his bowels explode.

It's real nasty business, loud and unpleasant. He's glad the bathroom is empty. It takes about five minutes for his bowels to thoroughly squeeze themselves out like a pastry bag.

When it's over, Carpy mops sweat from his face and sighs. He wipes himself and prepares to flush when the outer door bangs open and he smells something so terrible it overpowers what he has just produced. It's a stink of putrescence. The sort of thing you smell in the summer when there's a dead dog on the side of the road, its caved-in skull swarming with maggots.

Carpy sits back down and mainly because the strength has run out of him.

That stink. Jesus Christ, that stink. Nothing alive can smell like that.

He doesn't know what to think. Has a zombie come in to take a whiz? No, worse. Whoever it is, Carpy hears the clump-clump-clump of his shoes. They pause as if their owner cannot make up his mind which stall they want.

Shriveling inside, Carpy thinks, Not this one... oh dear God, not this one.

Five minutes before he was nicely drunk and feeling no pain, now he feels stone cold sober. He can hear the storm outside, ever-circling, as if it's hungry and wants to get in. But that's all he can hear save the buzzing of a fluorescent tube overhead. He might have thought he had imagined it all if it wasn't for that pervasive graveyard stench that makes him want to throw up.

Outside the stall: silence.

The silence of forgotten tombs.

Carpy is not just nervous and confused now, he's terrified. There's no sound out there at all and he dearly wishes somebody would come barging into the Men's room before he totally goes freaking bananas. But the silence is unbroken and he has the worst feeling that the rest of the world no longer exists, that it's just him and what stands outside the stalls, stinking the joint up.

So do something already!

Which is exactly what he wants to do, but that will mean opening the door and looking at what stands out there and he doesn't think he's up to it. But maybe even that would be better than sitting on the toilet, shaking, smelling his own shit, and wondering what sort of gruesome horror is waiting for him.

There's a footstep, then another.

He sighs. The smell is stronger, and he can feel it settling on his skin in a greasy, foul membrane.

The door to stall two opens and the visitor steps in, closes it, then settles onto the toilet. Carpy can hear him breathing with a terribly phlegmy sort of noise. He seems to be humming something under his breath, something strange but familiar that Carpy has not heard since he was a child, many moons ago.

Now's the time, now's the time.

Yes, time to get out. But before he does, Carpy—curious as he is disturbed—peeks under the stall. What he sees is a large, very large floppy shoe of the sort clowns wear and that makes him break out in a cold sweat. A clown got Ritchie Chandliss. You heard what Beebe said. And now, oh God, now

that same clown is sitting in the shitter next door. It's got to be the same one...
how many clowns could there possibly be out in the middle of a blizzard in
Cray goddamn Falls?

The stench is so terrible that Carpy can barely breathe. He feels woozy. His
head spins. He wants nothing more than to get off the pot, but he does not feel
physically able. Every time he moves, his head pounds. It's something...some-
thing with the smell coming off the clown. It's doing something to him, acting
like a paralytic. He doesn't have the strength to blow his nose, let alone run
from the stall.

As he tries to clear his head, he hears a steady drip-drip-drip from the stall
next door. On the floor, there is blood...and not just a little, but a great seeping
pool of it flowing around the clown's shoes and seeking Carpy's own. He has
never seen such bright red blood before. Movie blood. That's what it is, movie
blood like in some cheap vampire flick. Now it's gushing out of the clown,
raining to the floor, the pool enlarging until it's a great spinning whirlpool.

Carpy, sweating hot/cold bullets of perspiration, keeps his feet up because
he knows if he doesn't, he'll get sucked into that spiraling vortex of blood.
He'll drown in it. He'll get sucked into some bottomless ensanguined abyss.

His vision blurs, clears, blurs... dear God, he's having a stroke or a seizure
or something. Maybe an embolism is about to burst in his head like a bag
of blood, maybe...maybe... maybe it's already happened and I'm dreaming
this shit. This makes him feel hopeful for a moment until he sees that there
are objects in the blood pool on the floor. In fact, there are many objects in
it...swimming, wriggling things.

There seem to be hundreds in the pool, and he knows they are coming from
the bleeding clown in the other stall. Now they are inching up the toilet and
walls of the stall. They are seeking him out and he sees, really sees, what they
are—leeches. They can be nothing else. They are maybe three inches in length,
swollen fat like slugs, ribbed and very determined.

It's at this point, that Carpy screams.

He screams blue fucking murder, but he is not really sure if he's screaming
out loud or only in the confines of his mind. He still cannot move. The leeches
are crawling up his legs. They are on his shirt now. Dozens of them are seeking
his throat. He gets one of his hands moving and begins plucking them off like
blackberries from a bush. They twist and writhe in his fingers, trying to get

their oval suckering mouths on him. He squeezes them until they explode into a meaty slime.

Two of them have found his throat.

Their mouths feel hot on his flesh. There is a piercing as if a needle has gone in and then he can feel them sucking and sucking. They make moist, slurping sounds like infants feeding from their mother's breasts.

And this does it.

If nothing else, this really does it.

Carpy lets out a strangled cry and this time he can really hear it. It explodes from his mouth and then he jumps to his feet, slipping and sliding on the blood and the wriggling carpet of leeches. He throws the bolt on the door and bursts from the stall. His forward momentum carries him right into the sinks. He hits them, goes down, gets up. Still plucking leeches from his neck, he races for the door at the same time the clown flushes the toilet in the second stall.

Coming now, coming now to get you, a voice says in Carpy's head as he stumbles to the door. It's coming and when it gets you, it'll bury you alive in leeches and they'll drain every last drop of blood from you.

Then he throws the door open and is in the back room where the Dead Skulls are playing pool. They stop shooting and look at him as he races past, and they all begin laughing because his pants are down around his knees. By the time he reaches the barroom, he falls face-first and that really gets them going.

34

When Sheriff Teague comes through the side door of the Broken Bottle with a riot gun in his hands, people take notice. His face is pale and pinched from the cold, his eyes squinting and smoldering dark. He's after someone and he means business and they all know it. Peanut comes in right behind him and even though Peanut has always been (in the opinion of most) a fairly harmless and likeable fellow, tonight he looks much older, much more intense. The trademark goofy grin he wears is light years distant.

It doesn't even look as if he knows how to smile.

Everyone in the bar stops what they are doing. Brenda Prechek stops mixing drinks. Bonnie Faust stops serving them. Stew Prechek steps out of the kitchen in a flour-covered apron, a pizza in his hands. He freezes right there. As do the patrons at the bar and in the booths. If this had been a movie, the music would have stopped; too, but, of course, it doesn't. Molly Hatchet is still "Flirtin' with Disaster."

For some time, nobody moves, then Brenda takes the initiative. She comes wheeling from out behind the bar puffing steam and black smoke. "What in the name of Jesus H. fucking Christ are you doing, Will?" she wants to know.

"We're looking for someone," Teague says, his eyes sweeping the barroom. "And we aim to find him."

"What?" Brenda scowls and shakes her head. "KILL THAT FUCKING JUKE!"

Bonnie Faust does, getting some dirty looks from the Dead Skulls on account that "Flirtin' with Disaster" is kind of like the club theme song along with "Dirty Deeds Done Dirt Cheap by AC/DC and "I'm the Only Hell

(Mama Ever Raised)" by Johnny Paycheck, as well as a half-dozen other hard rocking and outlaw country songs.

Now the barroom of the Broken Bottle is quiet.

"We tracked somebody in here," Teague explains. "He came in the side door."

"Well, who?" asks Brenda.

"Yeah, who?" echoes Stew.

"A clown," Peanut says. It comes right out of his mouth unbidden. Sometimes that's just the way it is with him—things come out of his mouth that shouldn't.

Now the silence is not only thick but heavy. For maybe five seconds it hangs there like something ready to fall.

Then Brenda says, "A clown? Oh Christ, not that shit again."

But nobody else says a thing because they're all remembering what Beebe Chandliss said about what got Ritchie, her husband. It was a clown. It had claws. It got Ritchie. They begin to bunch in a little closer as if they're in the need of warm human contact at that moment, the idea of demonic clowns wandering out in the storm leaving them cold, colder than maybe they've ever been in their lives.

"This is no shit," Teague tells them. "We saw it. We chased it. It came in here and my guess is it's still here somewhere."

Everyone looks around fearfully, except for Brenda. "C'mon, Will. Ain't no damn clown in here. Don't you think we'd have noticed if fucking Binky the Clown walked in here? I'm behind the bar for godsake, I'd have seen him. How stupid do you think I am?"

Teague decides he won't answer that one. The fact remains that the clown came in and if no one saw him—something he finds very hard to believe—then this business has just gotten weirder than it already was.

About this time, there's a scream and Carpy comes running into the barroom and falls flat on his face to the laughter of the Dead Skulls. Everyone can see that his pants are down around his knees. People try not to chuckle, but many are not successful.

Teague shakes his head and brushes snow from his jacket. "Carpy... what are you doing?" he asks.

Carpy stares up at him from the floor, looking sort of stunned like a deer caught in headlights. He shakes his head back and forth, scrambles to his feet and then starts wailing. "Was on me...all over me...crawling on me...leeches sucking the blood out of me... blood was everywhere... it was everywhere! And that clown! It was in the stall! It was the one that killed Ritchie and it's in the shitter! IT'S WAITING IN THERE RIGHT NOW!"

Carpy is shaking and spitting and drooling. He hitches up his pants with trembling hands, his eyes rolling madly in their sockets. He keeps trying to talk but all that comes out is a sort of hysterical gibberish that no one can make sense of. It has all the cohesion of a snipped string.

By this point, the Dead Skulls have pushed their way into the barroom led by the club president, Clyde Taggert. Clyde is a real beast and not one of Will Teague's favorite people. He's been in state prison for assault and federal prison for narcotics trafficking. He's about 6'5, 350 pounds, and has a swastika tattooed on his forehead like Charlie Manson. With him is Nathan Free, his sergeant-at-arms, a walking pile of bricks, and another Skull named Skunk, who did time for armed robbery years ago.

"Hell's going on, Will?" Clyde asks.

But Teague just shakes his head. He wishes to God he knew, he really wishes he did. Everything is warped and out-of-perspective. Reality has torn the seat out of its pants and he doesn't know what to think.

Brenda gets Carpy a drink: Jack Daniels, straight-up in a beer glass. Carpy downs it, sputters and gasps, then says, "Right in there...goddamn clown is in the shitter. I saw it. It's right in there waiting."

Teague licks his weathered lips. "Okay, you're coming with me," he says, motioning towards the bathroom.

"No, I ain't!"

"Yes, you goddamn are."

They start towards the bathroom. Clyde and Nathan Free join them, both carrying their pool cues like baseball bats, ready to do some swinging.

"Peanut," Teague says. "Get on the radio, tell Patti where we are. And nobody leaves, you get me? Nobody."

"Yes, sir."

35

As they move off into the back room, one of the toughs at the bar says. "You think you can stop me if I wanna go, Peanut?"

Peanut swings the business end of the riot gun in his direction. "Yeah, pretty sure I can."

After that, nobody jokes with Peanut. This isn't the laid back, easygoing Peanut they all know and love. This isn't the guy who played guitar in high school and smoked dope behind the bleachers. This Peanut is dead serious. He gets on the radio and calls Patti Wayland at the station, but all he gets is static.

"Must be the storm," he says, but it's obvious from the tone of his voice that he does not believe this for a moment.

The silence is unbroken after that.

Something which drives Brenda Prechek crazy because people are tense and they're not ordering beers and pizza, and this is the second time tonight that Will Teague has kicked her business in the nuts and she's not at all happy about it.

"Clowns," she says. "Goddamn clowns. I think the only clown in this town is our fucking sheriff. Far as I'm concerned, he's violating my civil rights to run a business and make a profit. Somebody ought to bring a lawyer in on this and slap a class-action suit on his ass, then we'll see how self-important that sonofabitch is."

"Brenda," Stew says. "How about you just shut up for once?"

Which to those at the bar is equally as shocking as a killer clown out in the blizzard because Stew never says boo to his wife. Brenda runs him down and runs him ragged, tells him when to shit and how much to produce, but he never talks back to her. As Carpy himself has said more than once, Stew wears the pants in the family, but they zip on the side.

Brenda glares at her husband. Her look says it all. *Mmm-hmm. Okay. You wait. You just wait, you little bitch. I'll sort you out.* And no one doubts that, given time, she will do just that.

But for now, everyone waits silently.

And more than a few of them look around suspiciously, wondering where the clown from hell might be hiding or who might be hiding him.

36

Teague has to drag Carpy along with him like a precocious little boy on his way to the school principal to get what's coming to him. Clyde and Nathan are right behind them. Teague is not fooling himself, not by a long shot. He knows what he saw in Little Willow Park. He knows that, despite his common sense, these clowns are not human. They're not some idiots dressing up to scare people. They're something else. They're monsters. They're deranged fucking monsters from a horror show. How that can be he does not know and right now he has better things to do than try to make sense of something that is essentially senseless.

Outside the door, he stops.

He looks at Carpy who is trembling, beads of sweat rolling down his face. Then he looks back at the two Dead Skulls who look excited as if they've been waiting for something like this their entire lives.

The riot gun held in two white-knuckled fists, Teague says, "Push the door open, Carpy."

Carpy, who's very close to pissing himself, breathes in and out, nods uneasily, then moves quick, kicking the door open like a cop in a movie.

Teague rushes in, scanning about with his weapon and seeing nothing. That's his first impression. His second is that there is no blood on the floor. The way Carpy described it, you would have thought it was awash with the red stuff wall to wall, flooded like the decks of a tall ship in a violent storm.

But there's no blood.

But that doesn't mean there's no clown.

He moves farther into the Men's room, swallowing down pure apprehension that seems to fill his throat. Carpy has entered the bathroom now, probably forced in there by Clyde Taggert. Teague goes to the first stall. The door is ajar. He kicks it open. Nothing there but a toilet and the toilet paper dispenser. At the second stall, he hesitates a moment longer because this is the clown's stall—if what Carpy said can be taken at face value, that is—and in his mind, he can see himself kicking it open and some demonic form with blood-red eyes and gnashing yellow teeth leaping out at him, tearing out his throat before he can even squeeze the trigger. Under ordinary circumstances he would have rejected this as pure fantasy, imagination creeping in on him and trying to steal his nerve... but after what he saw in the park, well, he knows there are horrors that exist in the dark corners of the world that gnaw on human bones.

Just do it, he finally tells himself. *Don't you dare look weak in front of Clyde fucking Taggert.* He sharpens his teeth on weak, indecisive men.

Teague breathes in deep. The door of stall two is ajar like stall one. With a burst of bravado, he kicks it open and sees not a thing. There's nothing in there.

"Where's your fucking clown, Carpy?" Clyde asks. "If you're making this shit up, you and me are gonna have words."

"Quiet," Teague tells him.

Okay, maybe he hasn't found a clown, but there is a smell in the air, an after-odor that is out of place. It reminds him of yellow, fusty hay rotting in a barn. It's there and then it's gone.

He approaches stall three. The door is halfway open. He kicks it in the rest of the way and all he sees, again, is a toilet. There's a smell in the stall, but it has nothing to do with clowns.

"Jesus H. Christ, Carpy," he says. "Couldn't you have at least flushed?"

Carpy goes over there sheepishly. The Skulls are laughing at him again. He steps past Teague and flushes the toilet. "I was kind of in a hurry you know," is his only defense.

Clyde stands there with Nathan Free looking pissed. "Clowns. Blood on the floor. My ass."

"And don't forget the leeches," Nathan points out, barely able to keep the contempt out of his voice.

"I saw 'em!" Carpy says, pushed beyond acceptable limits by it all. "There was blood! There was leeches! There was a fucking clown!"

"Okay, simmer down," Teague says.

The thing is, he believes Carpy. He believes every word he says because he knows him. Carpy might be a lot of things, but he's not a good liar. In fact, he's terrible at it. He's not the brightest guy in the world and he has all the imagination of a steamed clam. What happened in there, Teague does not know. Much of it might have been subjective, but something happened and that something must have been pretty damn bad to get Carpy this worked up.

37

Back in the barroom, everyone waits pensively.

"Not a damn thing," Clyde says, and you can almost hear a great communal sigh come rushing out. Everyone was strung tight as wires and now, thankfully, they can relax because it was some kind of fucked up joke. That's all it was: a joke.

"Clowns," someone says. "Carpy, you fucking moron."

People laugh nervously now.

This is a good one. This has all the makings of a fucking legend. Ten years from now...hell, twenty...they're still going to be razzing Carpy about this, telling with great exaggeration how he saw clowns in the shitter and stumbled out, ranting and raving, with his pants down around his knees. This is the sort of tale that will get bigger with every telling.

Brenda Prechek could care less about Carpy or what he said. She polishes a couple of glasses, then sets them down loudly on the bar top. "So let me get this straight," she says and everyone there knows she's winding up like a batter getting ready to knock one out of the park. This is going to be ugly. "You, Sheriff, come barging into my place of business with Deputy Fife, waving fucking guns around and scaring the shit out of everybody because you're hunting clowns. Clowns for chrissake. And this because Beebe Chandliss who's half out of her skull said Ritchie fell off his sled or some damn thing and she claimed she saw a clown. Am I correct on this shit?"

"Brenda, c'mon," her husband Stew says.

"And, worse, you're listening to this bullshit Carpy is saying about clowns in the fucking bathroom when we all know that Carpy is a fucking dipshit and you can't believe a word he says. I already told you no clowns came in. I've been behind this goddamn bar since three this afternoon and if Pennywise or Dumpling the Dancing Pedophile came in, I would have carded them. This is the kind of police work you do? This is what my fucking taxes are paying for?" She casts an acid leer from Teague to Peanut. "I guess I only got one more question—which one of you is the Skipper and which one is fucking Gilligan?"

There's some uncomfortable laughter, but it doesn't last long. The tension between Will Teague and Brenda is strung tight, so tight people are afraid to trip over it.

Teague, to his credit, does not completely lose it. He chooses his words carefully. "Brenda, now I've put up with a lot of shit from you through the years, but right now I've had it with you and your mouth. There's things going on in this town that you don't know about. Ritchie Chandliss is missing. So is Gina Keller. I have reason to believe that the body Beebe Chandliss and her husband saw was that of Gina. And that's just the tip of the iceberg. So, if you want to keep your liquor license and yourself out of jail, I suggest you shut the hell up before you dig yourself a hole and bury yourself alive."

Brenda, sneering, opens her mouth, then shuts it again. If she's looking for backup from her clientele, she's shit out of luck. Not a one of them will meet her eyes.

"Let's just all calm down," Stew says then. "That's what we need to do. Just calm down and take it easy."

Peanut makes a grunting sound. "If you'd seen what we saw over in Little Willow Park, you wouldn't be talking like that. There's clowns out there and they're monsters."

"Peanut," Teague warns him.

But too late because everybody heard what he said. Monsters. They look around now, real fear beginning to creep into them. The Dead Skulls merely look curious, but it's beginning to edge into them, too. Everyone stands there silently. Outside, they can hear the wind moaning as it circles the Broken Bottle. It sounds evil, angry, and somehow voracious. At that moment, that precise moment, they believe in many things thought long forgotten in the closet of childhood. Particularly, they believe in the boogeyman and that it wears the face of a clown.

Bonnie Faust is the first one to break the silence. She stands there, her arms wrapped around herself as if there's a chill on her she can't shake. "That's not true. Tell us that's not true, Sheriff."

Teague gives Peanut a withering look. "We saw some things," is all he'll say. "Some...bad things."

"But monsters?" Stew asks.

There's some grumbling from the regulars. Nobody knows quite how to take this. They don't believe in monsters for a minute, yet they are not so sure. Not tonight with the things going on. And not with that hungry mother of a blizzard howling out there like a starving pack of wolves.

"What sort of bad things did you see?" Clyde Taggert wants to know because he can see how uneasy the subject makes Teague.

Before Teague can answer that one—or manufacture a reply that won't send people running for the doors—they all hear a drink being set down loudly on the bar. They turn and there sits Leo Booth. In the excitement, everyone forgot about old Leo. But that's understandable. Leo the Lush is forgettable. He spends so much time in the Broken Bottle that he's often mistaken for a piece of furniture.

Brenda stares at him suspiciously because she honestly cannot remember him being there a few minutes before. But he must have been.

"Chances are," he says in a ragged whiskey voice, "what you have out there is some sort of psychopath that likes to dress as a clown. I'm too old to believe in monsters and fairy tales and I'm pretty sure the rest of you are, too. No, it's a psychopath all right. Who knows what set him off? The storm? The night? Maybe something inside his head. He's probably been living among us for years, but we didn't spot it. You'd be surprised what can be right in front of you sometimes."

"It ain't no psycho," Peanut says, prepared to launch into the particulars of what was seen in Little Willow Park less than an hour before, but another look from Teague makes him shut his mouth and keep it shut.

Leo takes down the rest of his drink in one swallow. "Oh, but you see, son, it must be for it cannot be anything else...now can it?"

Leo keeps talking and Teague listens intently even though he knows that Leo is a veteran bullshit artist. Only Stan Barbacek over at the cabstand is better at slinging shit. There's something strange about the caliber of Leo's voice. Teague feels kind of sleepy at the sound of it. It's as if that voice is spinning a cocoon of dreams around him and all he wants to do is shut his eyes. What Leo is saying is patently untrue; this is not a psychopath they're dealing with but something more along the lines of what that head case Clegg over at the jail was saying—a nest, a colony of monsters. So even though he knows this to be true, Leo's voice is weaving itself around him and he's not so sure anymore what he saw in Little Willow Park.

At that moment, one of the Dead Skulls drops his beer bottle and the noise seems to snap Teague out of it. He blinks his eyes a few times and shakes the cobwebs from his head. By the look of the others, they were falling into dream, too.

Leo casts a sort of ugly look at the Skull who dropped the bottle. He licks his yellow teeth. "Point being," he says, "is that you got a guy who dresses as a clown. Not a monster, you idiots, but a man in a mask or what not."

"You don't know what you're talking about," Peanut tells him.

Leo laughs with a grating sound that is uncharacteristic. "Son, I know things you wouldn't believe."

Brenda shakes her head. "Leo, I known you my whole life. You used to hang around this bar when I was girl in pigtails and my daddy owned it. You didn't know squat then and you don't know squat now."

"Wait a minute," Nathan Free says. "Leo was in Vietnam. He's a veteran."

"That don't mean he's got a lick of common sense or a working brain cell in that stewed brain of his," Brenda is quick to point out. She jabs a thumb at Stew. "Lookit my husband there. Four years in the Navy and you see how he is."

"Huh?" Stew says.

Leo utters that perfectly awful laugh again that reminds Teague of a rusty hinge on a gate. "Well, what would you have us believe then, my dear? That there are monsters in the storm? Monsters that look like clowns? What sort of monsters are they? Vampires? Werewolves? Green-blooded creatures from another world? Hmm? That's strictly kids' stuff."

There's something striking Teague very wrong about Leo tonight. Something off. Something strange. But he can't quite put a finger on it. It's been a long day. Things aren't making a lot of sense anymore.

"All right, enough jawing," he tells everyone. "First off, no one's leaving. Not until I say so. Peanut, you go out there and check the snow. Nobody but us has come in since the clown. You check for tracks before the wind erases them. You see other tracks leaving then our clown has gotten away."

"Out there?" Peanut says.

"Yes, out there. Clyde? Nathan? You go with him. Make it quick. I want you back here in ten minutes. The rest of us'll wait."

Clyde and Nathan pull on their coats and hats. Teague doesn't like sending his deputy out with those two, but under the circumstances, he figures it'll be all right. Besides, he just doesn't trust Peanut to control this bunch.

Wind sweeps through the barroom as Peanut and the others head outside. Clyde has to fight with the door to get it closed.

Teague waits, watching everyone.

The clock is ticking.

38

Jesus, it's like the freaking North Pole out there as Peanut turns his back to the blow. The snow is flying, and the wind is screaming. It's a hell of a night. Already snow is piling up in the street. He looks down Central Avenue and it's desolate and somehow menacing with the storm. The streetlights look like ghostly moons fading into the distance.

"Don't see anything," Nathan Free says, pushing long black hair out of his face.

"Nada," says Clyde, nearly shouting.

Peanut scans about with his flashlight. The drifts before the front door to the Broken Bottle look undisturbed. He wonders how long it would take the wind and snow to cover prints and he's not sure in a blizzard like this.

"Nobody went in or came out," he says regardless.

"Snow could have covered them," Nathan suggests.

Clyde shakes his head. "No, not this quick. If somebody came in or left in the last half hour or so, we'd see something. There'd have to be something. Some depressions maybe."

Peanut swallows down his anxiety. He's hoping, really hoping that the clown went on its merry killing way in the night. After what happened at the park, he doesn't honestly think he's up to anymore of it. He doesn't care what anyone thinks; he saw what he saw. And it was no fucking guy in a mask. There were two of them and they were monsters, real monsters.

"Let's go," Clyde says.

Clyde has always made Peanut nervous the way he makes a lot of people nervous, but tonight he's glad to have him. He might be a criminal and a felon and a real meat-eater by nature, but the guy has balls. Real balls and the talents to back them up. Clyde leads them around the side of the building and it turns out he's right about footprints in a snowstorm—Peanut can see the prints that Teague and he left, along with the larger, nearly buried prints of the clown. They're still there, all right.

But no others.

"Well, he didn't come out then," he tells the others, nearly shouting into the wind.

"At least not this way," Nathan says. "But there's a door in back. The delivery door."

Peanut nods. He'd forgotten about that. The delivery door in back faces on the parking lot that the Broken Bottle shares with the apartment building next door. When he was a kid it had some fancy name like the Armiston Arms or some such shit, now it's nameless.

They have to head into the blow now. It really comes screaming across the parking lot, throwing sheets of snow in their faces and it's a struggle to stay on their feet. Twice, Peanut slipped and went down and twice he felt Clyde's strong hands hoist him back up.

After much to-do and swearing, they reach the back of the Broken Bottle. Right away, Peanut shines his light around, but doesn't see much. Outside the delivery door, the drifts appear untouched. At least, as far as they can tell. But the wind is stronger back here and the snow is flying with great force, obscuring everything and filling the air with churning flakes.

"Looks like somebody came by here," Nathan says.

He's closer to the rear of the apartment house. There's a stairway leading up to the second floor. Its underside is set with icicles that look like the teeth of saurians.

Peanut and Clyde go over there.

Sure, somebody did pass this way, but not recently. The depressions in the snow are telltale. They're barely there. Could have been someone leaving the apartment house. Could have been lots of things.

"All right, enough," Peanut says. "We did what we had to do. If that clown left, it didn't leave by the door."

"Wait," Clyde says. "Put your light under the stairs."

Peanut does not ask why. He swallows down his unease and does as he's asked. Under the stairs, in the shadows, there is something under the snow, something irregular that does not seem to belong. Could be bags of garbage or something else equally innocent, but he does not believe it. His heart begins to slowly sink into his belly.

Nathan, down on his hands and knees, paws away some of the snow. What is uncovered is a hand, a human hand frosted with ice.

"Oh shit," Peanut says.

Clyde helps Nathan brush away the snow from what lies beneath. The cadaver is that of a man in a parka. It looks like he was twisted in half. His body cavity is cleaved open, his throat torn out. His head is attached by a few ligaments and threads of flesh. The blue-gray face is locked in a scream and they all recognize it.

"It's Leo," Nathan says, his voice dry and cracking.

"Can't be," Peanut says even though he recognizes the parka and the remains of the man who wears it.

Clyde digs in the cadaver's back pocket and finds a wallet. He is fearless, that man. "Leo Booth," he says.

There's silence for a moment as the three of them look at each other, fully aware of what this ominous discovery means. The wind blows and the snow begins to cover Leo again. The shadows are hostile forms creeping around them.

Peanut, just out of his head, shaking, close to tears, says, "It can't be fucking Leo. Leo's in the bar. We saw him. We all saw him."

Nathan says nothing.

Clyde looks from the corpse to Peanut. For the first time, there is fear in his voice. "I don't know what's in the bar, but it ain't Leo Booth."

Back in the bar, the sense of unreality has gotten worse. Carpy waits there with the others. He has not spoken in some time and maybe that's because he is afraid of what he might say. He sits on a stool watching Will Teague because everyone is watching Will Teague—the regulars, the three remaining members of the Dead Skulls, Bonnie Faust, Stew Prechek, and particularly, his wife Brenda. She's like a pot that has come to full boil on the back burner and now her lid is beginning to rattle.

"I'm expecting an apology after this witch hunt is over," she tells the sheriff. "This is the second time tonight you've caused trouble in my place of business. There's other bars in town; you don't have to pick on this one just because you have a grudge against me."

"I don't have a grudge against you," the sheriff reassures her.

Which, of course, does not reassure her at all. She stands behind the bar with that black, evil scowl on her face, eyes narrowed and dark as the hair on her head. She reminds Carpy of one of those figureheads they used to carve on the bows of ships. That's how she looks at that moment—like something carved from teak weathering a storm.

"I wonder how legal it is to hold people against their will like this," she says pointedly. "Especially at gunpoint. Seems like there would be a law against it, don't you think?"

"Yeah," Stew says.

He doesn't really care for his wife's tact, but he's so used to agreeing with her that his mouth opens automatically in support. His face is blank, but his eyes are haunted.

"I believe we fiddle while Rome burns," Leo the Lush says as he fills his glass with Jim Beam.

"Hey!" Brenda says. "How'd you get that bottle?"

"Magic, just magic," he tells her.

"Well, you better have the magic to pay for it."

"Certainly, certainly," says Leo.

Of all the people in the bar, it occurs to Carpy, Leo is the most relaxed. It's a day at the beach to him. Everyone else is tense or agitated, but not Leo. He must have a pretty good shine on to act that way. Carpy has been drinking and drinking, but he's in such a high state of anxiety the liquor doesn't seem to touch him. Nothing can stop his hands from shaking and his heart from pounding.

"This is certainly an interesting situation," Leo says to the others with an expansive wave of his hand. "Here we all wait, wondering, worrying, thinking. Our lives are in the sheriff's hands. What will he do, I wonder, if his deputy and the others don't come back?"

"Shut up, Leo," Teague says.

Leo chuckles and is it Carpy's imagination or is that laughter just plain cold and mocking? It's the laughter a doll or puppet would make if you pulled its string. It's not lost on the others: some of the regulars pull away from him.

"You feel all right, Leo?" Bonnie asks, picking up on it, too.

"Fine, my dear, fine." To prove this, he offers her a wide and toothy grin. His teeth look very long and very yellow.

Carpy feels a chill run down his back. This ain't right, he thinks. None of this is right. He's drank with Leo for years and his teeth never looked like that before. He never saw him grin like...like a stuffed crocodile. But it's more than that. The atmosphere of the barroom feels strange as if there's something in the air——too much of something or not enough. The hairs at the back of his neck are standing on end.

He tries to swallow but his throat is dry.

"How long is this going to take?" a woman named Madelyn Kenner asks. She's there with two friends of hers, both of whom look not just unhappy but frightened.

"Not long," Sheriff Teague tells her, but it's clear from the tone of his voice that he's not sure. At that moment, he's not sure of anything.

"Still can't get any damn reception on my phone," she says. "Can a storm do that? Can it knock out cell reception?"

"Storms can do all sorts of things," Leo tells her. "They can knock out cell phones and create weird electrical activity in the atmosphere. Sometimes they call people into the night, never to be seen again."

"Leo, I'm warning you," Teague says.

Leo's standing not five feet from Madelyn now and Carpy, who's been watching him, cannot seem to remember him getting up. He grins at the others, licking his lips with a wet, slurping sound. But worse, Carpy notices, he's drooling. Droplets of saliva roll down his chin and his eyes seem to have gotten very large and very glassy. They shine like oily vellum.

"Sit down, Leo," Teague says and it's clear from his voice that he knows something is happening here and something worse is on the way.

Leo titters with a perfectly awful sound and Carpy is reminded of a film he saw in school many, many years before about not talking to strangers. A cautionary tale. In the film, there was a man who drove a long black car and enticed children to take rides with him by offering them candy or letting them play with a puppy he kept on the front seat. When he got a kid in the car——and he got several in the film——he laughed like that, with a tittering/snickering sound like a witch in a fairy story.

The wind outside rises to a shriek and Leo steps towards Teague. "I don't think they're coming back, Sheriff," he says with a sort of nasal drone (and is it Carpy's imagination or does he sound exactly like the pervo in that film?). "The question is: what will you do now? How will you safeguard us against what's out there when it comes to tear out our throats and yank out our intestines? What will you do? Will you have the courage to do the right thing?"

Before Teague can answer, one of the Dead Skulls, a real bad boy named Charles Penley, but known in the club as Mongol, says, "He told you to sit down, so sit the fuck down, you goddamn maggot!"

Leo cocks his head, as if he's listening to things the others cannot hear. "He told you to sit down, so sit the fuck down, you goddamn maggot."

Mongol bristles. "Are you mocking me, you little shit?"

Leo cocks his head again. "Are you mocking me, you little shit? Are you mocking me, you little shit? Are you mocking me, you little shit?" he repeats in a high falsetto that rises in volume to a shrill squeal. "Are you mocking me? Are you mocking me? *Mockingmemockingmemockingmemockingmem-ockingmemockingme—"*

"You little motherfucker," Mongol says, advancing.

Leo should be intimidated because Mongol is a crazy sonofabitch, and everyone knows it. He once stabbed a guy seven times in a bar fight and, on another occasion, ripped off another man's nose...with his teeth. He's been in prison and in the state hospital more than once.

But Leo does not sit back down, he keeps talking nonstop and the perfectly insane thing is that it's all gibberish and coming so fast nobody can really be sure what it is that he's saying:

"...andishalldotheterriblethingsbecauseichoosetogutyousuckyourbloodrapey-ourdaughtersandfeeduponyoursonsstrangleyourinfantsintheircribsheehahahow-canyoustopmebecausenoneofyouwilleverleavethisplacealive———"

A couple people scream, and a few are sobbing and Teague shouts, "SHUT UP, LEO! YOU GODDAMN WELL SHUT UP RIGHT FUCKING NOW!"

But Leo isn't shutting up and at that moment something inexplicable happens—everyone's cell phone begin to ring. Carpy doesn't have one (he thinks the government tracks you with them), but he hears the ringtones and they're all the same. He starts to laugh with a demented sound because he recognizes the tune. It's the same one the clown was humming in the shitter, the one he could not remember: "Little Bunny Foo Foo."

"Hell is going on here?" Brenda cries out.

And that's a good question because, suddenly, things have changed; nothing is as it was before. Reality, as such, has completely broken down.

Carpy watches it all with his mouth hanging open, dazed and confused, the sound of Leo's voice and the constant jangling of the "Little Bunny Foo Foo" ringtones putting him into some kind of fugue and isn't it interesting how he never even noticed before that Leo was perfectly bald save for those spiky green tufts of hair sticking out of the side of his scabrous skull? Or that his face was the dead-white of a corpse pulled from a river? Or that his eyes were yellow as piss in a snow bank, bleary and liquid, the pupils like bright red beads?

Isn't that just fucking amazing?

But he's trapped in a sort of stupor, oblivious to what is going on around him. People are screaming and falling out of Leo's way because Leo, of course, isn't Leo at all. At the moment "Little Bunny Foo Foo" rang out on everyone's cell phones, Leo began to move with a serpentine side-to-side motion like some grotesque hand puppet that was worked from inside. Then, without further ado, he simply split open like an egg and a clown was born.

"GET AWAY FROM IT!" Teague shouts. "GET THE FUCK AWAY FROM IT!"

He wants nothing more than to get a shot at it, but nobody is doing anything but falling into one another. They're Weebles that wobble but don't fall down. And the clown is right in there with them, dancing and swaying and spinning around and around in a blur.

Then it stops spinning and looks right at Teague, daring him to shoot with all the innocent bystanders in the way. It has big orange shoes and a shiny blue costume set with garish yellow polka dots. Teague knows it's the clown that escaped him in Little Willow Park.

It snarls and bays at him.

Its face is a dripping, ulcerous ruin. It has a red clown nose that looks cancerous and rotten, a crooked mouth that is a black smear and gnashing yellow teeth.

It sticks its tongue out at him which is black and bifurcated like that of an adder.

Mongol suddenly snaps out of it, pulls a knife because he's long been a stabber. He rushes the clown and buries his knife in it...four times. With the last plunge, he opens it up from belly to chest and the clown roars with volume and animal ferocity. Before Mongol can even think of withdrawing the blade, black blood, clumps of waxy yellow meat, and red tendrils explode from the open body cavity of the clown.

Mongol screams once before the tendrils—which are like pulsating ropes of blood—seem to ensnare him, pull him in, twist him completely out of shape.

Everyone hears his bones snapping and tendons breaking. They are all sprayed with his blood as the clown opens his throat, severing his carotid. It does not gently sip from the artery like a pretty boy vampire in a paranormal romance, it gulps from it, it slurps and licks and splashes gore in every direction. Then it raises Mongol above its head like a bottle, upends him, and lets what blood is left rain down over it.

Then it tosses his drained corpse over the bar where it collides with all the bottles of liquor Brenda has so carefully arranged for her serving convenience.

Most people are clear of it by then, but not Brenda. She keeps a baseball bat behind the bar for rowdy nights and she comes out swinging, cracking the clown in the head twice before it takes hold of her with blood-spattered white hands and bites into her shoulder.

Just a nip.

Just enough to show her pain, then it drops her and advances on Teague.

40

The barroom becomes a hive of chaos as people scatter in every direction, tripping and falling over one another as they try to escape the clown which is clawing and slashing at them, blood-drenched and deranged in its ravenous fury.

Teague's had all he can take.

He charges forward, knocks a woman out of his way, and fires on the clown. The riot gun puts a fist-sized hole through the creature, spraying white stringy meat and inky blood over the bar top...meat which squirms and then begins to crawl slug-like in the direction of Brenda Prechek who is slumped over from her shoulder wound.

The red tendrils that erupt from the clown are profuse and animate, whipping and coiling like dozens of angry vipers from a common nest. The tips of them are barbed and punch into several regulars who scream their minds away as they are yanked within striking range of the clown's puffy white hands which have sprouted hooked gray talons like those of an owl.

Teague tries to get off another shot, but Bonnie Faust, absolutely hysterical with terror, slams into him and her legs tangle with his own and down they both go.

Another of the Dead Skulls (a large and violent man called Pebbles for some obscure reason) is one of those who have been impaled by the slick red tendrils, which jerk and yank him like a marionette. One of them has pierced his left eye socket and a yolky mass of ocular tissue has splashed down his cheek. Another is in his rather large round belly and it can be seen corkscrewing beneath the skin like some perfectly hideous parasite. Yet another has drilled into his groin and it appears as if Pebbles, a mighty, bearded gorilla of a man, has pissed himself—with blood.

He fights and moves with amazing agility for such a large man. Though he is nearly struck senseless with agony, he grips the tendrils with burly fists, pulling at them. But they are greasy and undulant, secreting a pale pink slime that burns his hands like battery acid.

By the time Teague disengages himself from Bonnie Faust, the clown has reeled in Pebbles like a thrashing catfish on a hook.

Then the most horrific thing happens.

The clown's blood-smeared mouth opens incredibly wide like that of an egg-eating snake. The fangs slide back and a gushing, vomitous torrent of milky-yellow bile engulfs Pebbles, whose cries become a high-pitched chok-ing/gobbling sound.

Then he begins to dissolve.

Like a wax figure beneath a high-intensity heat lamp, his flesh goes liquid and bubbling, hanging from his face in sluicing, steaming ribbons. His re-maining eye sizzles and pops in its socket. The cartilage of his nose becomes warm, pliable putty. He slaps manically at his face as if it's on fire. But his hands are useless things—the skin dangles like confetti, the flesh beneath a mucid emulsion that goes to simmering, slopping jelly like the rest of his body.

This happens very, very quickly.

Out of the clown's mouth comes a sort of tube-like proboscis with a puckering, blubbery flange of lips at its end which immediately begins sucking the biker's liquescent flesh from the clattering framework of his skeleton.

By this point, Carpy and several of the others are down on their knees, minds overloaded with horror and green with rolling waves of nausea.

Peanut is back by then and he nearly goes out cold at what he is seeing.

But not Clyde Taggert.

He sees Pebbles, his club brother, dying in a perfectly gruesome way. Such an insult to the Dead Skulls must be answered. Such a wrong must be avenged. It's the code of the outlaw biker.

Shrieking with rage, he charges in with absolutely no conception of what he's going to do. He's mainlining on pure adrenaline-charged instinct. As the clown reaches out for him, he throws himself athletically over the bar, grabs two fifths of Don Q 151 by the necks, then climbs back up atop the bar.

What he does then is as suicidal as it is amazing.

He leaps off the bar, ducks behind the clown, and smashes both fifths down on his white, bony, and blood-beaded skull. The clown is drenched in alcohol.

Clyde leaps back then, shouting, "LIGHT THAT FUCKER UP!"

Nathan Free, long used to fighting at the side of the club prez, flicks his Zippo and a long yellow flame licks from it. Without hesitation, he tosses the lighter at the clown. The Don Q ignites and the clown is swallowed in flames. It spins around and around, letting out an agonal, yelping cry as it burns.

This was something it had not considered.

Now it is hurt. Now it is being tortured beyond endurance. Its tethered victims fall away as it stumbles off. Flaming bits of it fall to the floor as it races away. It strikes one of the pool tables in the back, leaving a burning streak on the felt where its hand brushes. It bashes into the jukebox, then tosses itself at the side door, taking it right off its hinges in an eruption of flame. It escapes into the night, blazing like a human torch.

It can be heard screaming in the storm with a positively unearthly, strident wailing.

Peanut who watched it all, drops to his knees. "Jesus," he says.

When Stan Barbacek finally, finally gets Lyle and Luanne Stubbs home, he has to help both of them through the storm and up the steps. By that point, they're both out of fight and insults. The last ten minutes of the ride, they were both blubbering and holding one another in the backseat, professing their undying love for another the way they must have fifty odd years before during the heady days of the JFK administration.

It might have been touching if Stan had not seen it a hundred times by then.

Now it's simply pathetic.

After he finally gets them inside and gets the door shut and locked behind them, he thinks, thank God, they got each other. I suppose it's all they really need. Besides, as tired as he is of their melodramatics, he knows they're both in their seventies and time is running out. One of them won't wake up one of these days and the other will last about two weeks alone.

Stan knew he'd miss them when the time came, but as he leans into the blizzard, making for the Jeep, his mind is occupied by one thing and one thing only: clowns.

As he backs out into the storm, he keeps telling himself that this is his time, and this is his chance. But he needs an angle. The right sort of angle. He's already seen the clown tonight—hell, you hit it and drove over it—and he needs to see it again. If it's dead, it's dead, but either way he needs to find it and this time he needs to get it on video. That's how this has to happen.

As he drives, moving very slowly because of the deep snow, he thinks back on the clown. Something he's not real comfortable with because the memory is more than a little unnerving. Still, he goes through it in his mind. Every last detail. It's all still very fresh. One thing is for sure, the clown is not human. It's a monster. What sort of monster, he cannot say. A zombie, a vampire, a werewolf, a demon from hell... and maybe, just maybe, the sort of thing that inspires such tales.

Instead of heading back to Taxi-A-Go-Go as had been his original plan, he goes over to 9th Street where his place is. He has a camcorder there. He makes it there without mishap.

Leaving the Jeep running, he climbs the stairs to his humble bachelor's quarters. Sure, it's not much—bedroom, bathroom, kitchenette, tiny living room—but it serves. Standing there, taking it in, Stan wishes this was an ordinary night. Clock out at three, drink a couple beers, eat a frozen pizza and watch the tube, climb into the rack about the time other people ("normal" people as they like to refer to themselves) were leaving for work.

But tonight is not going to be that kind of night.

It will be unique in his experience. In his bedroom, he retrieves a camera bag that contains his nephew's Apeman action camera that he borrowed to video a bachelor party at the Amvet's hall two weeks before. He'd been meaning to return it, but now he's glad he hasn't. In the bag is everything he'll need for clown hunting: extra battery, SD card, clip-on LED.

Now it's time to capture a clown on film.

Back in the Jeep, he gives Taxi-A-Go-Go a call. First on his cell—no dice, no bars at all—then on the radio. "This is Two calling in. Pick up, Flo," he says, but there's no reply. "Car Two... you there, Flo?"

Nothing.

Maybe she's in the can. Hell, maybe she fell asleep. Stan thinks nothing of it. He's sure they'll meet up again later. And on this point, he's absolutely correct.

42

Over at the Broken Bottle, it's pandemonium.

Teague figures it's bad enough that they've got a body count, but they've got wounded, too. Mongol and Pebbles of the Skulls are both dead. Brenda Prechek has been bitten. Two other people were impaled by the clown's tendrils and several others were slashed by its claws. It is, without a doubt, a Class-A clusterfuck. They need the coroner in here, State Police CSI, and as much backup as they can get. An ambulance is priority. People are bleeding. They're in pain. Several are in shock.

It's definitely a worse-case scenario.

They need help and Teague has the awful feeling that they're not going to get it. Not tonight. Not in this fucking storm.

Then what? he asks himself. These people are counting on you to make something happen. You can't let them down.

The highway was shut down now. But if things are bad enough—and, oh boy, they sure as hell are—then the county would open it with a grader or plow to get emergency services through.

Peanut comes back in with Nathan Free. Wind and snow cycle into the barroom. "Will," he says, pulling the sheriff away from the injured, trauma-tized, and distraught. "I can't raise anybody on the radio. Even the emergency channels are nothing but static."

"I tried 9-1-1 three times," Nathan says. There's a funny, scared look in his eyes. "I can see the cells being out, I guess. Maybe even the radio... but it's everything, Sheriff. Internet. Cable. CB. Even the landlines are down. What kind of fucking storm can do all that?"

"We're buttoned up," Peanut adds.

Teague sighs. "Shit."

It means they're on their own. They're trapped in Craw Falls. The only possibility is to load the injured into some 4 X 4s and get Public Works to plow them a path to Vermillion. The State Police post is there as well as the county hospital. But to do that will mean abandoning the town to the fucking clowns.

He wished his other two deputies, Stills and Wegly, were here. They were out there somewhere, no doubt locked in by the storm. This was a real mess.

"Will, this is too much," Peanut says. "You know it. I know it. It's like we've been isolated on purpose."

Teague keeps remembering what Clegg, the clown hunter said. You've got a colony here, Sheriff. A Class-A clown nest. The blizzard has this shithole locked up tight and the clowns have themselves a private hunting preserve. By morning, you'll have dozens dead. All those pretty little houses lined up out there and all of them nothing but meat lockers.

He doesn't know what to think. This is insane. It's all perfectly insane.

"What's going on here?" Peanut wants to know.

Teague shrugs. He has no idea and he's not about to start speculating.

"What we need to do," Clyde Taggert says. "Is arm ourselves and kill these fucking clowns."

Two of his Skulls are dead and he's crazy with anger. His psychotic temper is legendary. He'll do something dangerous before the night is through.

"We need to get these people taken care of before we do anything else," Teague tells him. He turns to Peanut. "Here's what I want you to do. You and Nathan go over to the office and get our medical gear. After that, stop over at Tony Russo's place. He was a combat medic in the first Gulf War. Tell him we need him. Arrest him if you have to but get his ass over here ASAP."

I can't believe I'm sending him out with Nathan Free for chrissake, he thinks.

But the way things are going, he would be deputizing the other Dead Skulls before long.

"And watch yourselves," he warns them as they go out the door. "Keep trying that radio, too."

Clyde waits there with the other surviving Skull, a dude named Skunk who is bad news like the rest of them. He is well-named judging by the odor wafting off him. He watches the sheriff through thick-lensed glasses. Teague sees him as sort of an automaton awaiting an order. And the only one that can cut that order is Clyde.

Teague turns to him now. "How many boys you got in your club?"

"Eighteen."

"How many in town?"

Clyde shakes his head. "There was just the five of us. Most of 'em live outside town, probably holed up in the storm. A few are over in Vermillion at a wedding."

Teague sighs. So Clyde, Nathan, and Skunk are all he has. With Peanut and him that gives them five plus anybody else they can scare up. Not enough to get the injured to Vermillion and police this town, sort out what's hunting it.

"What do you got in mind?" Clyde asks.

Teague thinks about it a moment but knows there's no alternative. "When Peanut and Nathan get back, I want to introduce you to a guy named Clegg."

"You mean Red? Guy that owns the Shell station?"

"No, this is another Clegg," Teague says. "He hunts clowns for a living."

43

If we're going to do this, Stan Barbacek thinks, *then let's do it right.*

He cuts back slowly from 9th Street towards Central Avenue. The snow seems to be getting worse, piling up in drifts and frozen white waves in the street. So far the Jeep is handling it. It had better handle it; the idea of being out on foot in the storm is unthinkable. With a combination of four-wheel drive and wily driving tricks picked up from decades of ugly Midwestern winters, he's near sure he'll get through. The last thing he wants to do is to pack it in, particularly when his gut sense is telling him there's a fortune to be made if he can get some real clown footage.

Without losing his life, that is.

That's the last thing he's worrying about though because you have to gamble to win. It's one of life's little rules.

As he drives, watching the falling snow filling the headlight beams, he thinks about his mom for some odd reason. His dad died shortly before Stan's fifth birthday, so his memories of him are a little vague. But Mom, well now, she was quite a lady. She worked two jobs to keep food on the table and raised Stan and his kid sister up right. Maybe they never had a lot, but there were clothes on their backs and a roof over their heads. Mom was great.

One of her cardinal rules was that you had to believe in yourself. Come hell or high water, Stanny, she used to say, you'll learn that there's only one thing you can count on in a pinch and that's yourself. That was one of her favorites, along with, if you want something bad enough and you're willing to work for it, you'll get it. Nothing can stop you. Which, in a way, has always made Stan feel uncomfortable and more than a little useless because there's always been many things he's wanted, but he's never been willing to work for any of them.

That's always been his problem.

He's spent his life as a talker and not a doer. Lots of big plans but few, very few, concrete results. It makes him kind of glad Mom didn't live to see the failure he'd become. He's certain she would be disappointed. He can hear her voice in his head. Stanny, you got to grow up. You've got skills but no ambition. Get a move on! Time's running out! That's why, starting tonight, things are going to change. Whatever is happening in Craw Falls, it's like nothing anyone has seen before and he's going to be right on top of it.

Feeling by turns empowered and more terrified than he's ever been in his life, he turns onto Central Avenue.

He picks up speed slightly so he can punch the Jeep through a few high drifts. He has the road to himself. About a block or so up from the Whistle Stop, he sees lights blinking. It can't be the caution light; that's two blocks away. Must be a stalled car with its hazards on. It's hard to tell with sheets of snow obscuring everything.

Wait... that's not a car, it's a city truck.

As he gets up close to it, he can see it's a plow truck. It's just sitting there with its lights blinking and the driver's side door open. Odd. It's as if someone stepped out in a hurry, but never came back.

Stan pulls the Jeep over and waits.

He's got a feeling about this.

He gets on the radio and tries Flo again. Still nothing. There's no traffic out there at all. The static is like nothing he's ever heard before. Sounds like a cold hissing sibilance. The sort of thing that might issue from a subterranean snake pit. Probably just some weird atmospheric thing, but he's not convinced.

He tries his cell. Still dead, not a bar to be had.

He starts thinking how peculiar it all is. That demon zombie clown (he didn't think that was an exaggeration), radio down, cell service toes up. When he was at his apartment and tried to get the weather on TV, the cable wasn't working either. Like...like Craw Falls fell off the edge of the world or got sucked away into another galaxy or something, he thinks. He remembers an old Outer Limits or Twilight Zone or something where that happened. Of course, that was just a show and he never took it seriously... now, well, he's beginning to think differently about a lot of things. In his many years of bachelorhood and working the late shift, he'd spent a lot of time eating TV dinners and watching old movies, everything from film noir to sci-fi, westerns to horror to screwball comedies. But if ever there was one about a killer clown in a snowstorm, he must have missed it.

He watches the plow truck.

No one has returned.

There's only two guys who could have been conceivably driving it, Chip Vandermay or Mike Zutema. There's no one else. Public Works in Cray Falls these days consists of four full time guys and two part-timers. Plowing at night is overtime. There's no way Chip or Mike would let any of the guys with less seniority get a piece of that.

"Well?" Stan asks himself under his breath.

He's been waiting ten minutes now. Neither Chip or Mike has re-turned. Truck is still running. Door still open. And even if they had stepped out——where would they have gone? Nothing was open. There were a few stores, a carpet warehouse, a True Value hardware, a video store, and a senior center where the old fogies got together three times a week to play Rummy and Crazy Eights. But nothing that stayed open past eleven.

So where are they then?

Stan doesn't know, but he figures it's time to start shooting his killer clown doc. He digs the Apeman camera out of its bag.

Action...

44

For the first time since he's worn the uniform, Peanut really feels like a cop. He spent the last six years pretty much wasting his time with speeding tickets, parking violations, and petty domestic disturbances. Things that in the grand scheme are pretty much Mickey Mouse... but now, well, all that's changed. Now there's something going on that requires real police work. Now the town is really in danger. Finally, Peanut is doing something that matters, and he feels like the uniform not only fits but that he's filling it out.

As he drives the GMC over to Tony Russo's on Long Acre Road, he talks nearly nonstop. Nerves, got to be nerves. "All these years," he says. "All these years. Christ."

"What're you yabbing on about now?" Nathan Free asks him.

"Monsters."

"Monsters?"

"Monsters," Peanut says. "All these years I thought they were bullshit. You grow up and your mom and dad tell you werewolves and witches and space monsters and all that are make-believe. No such thing as ghosts or boogeymen. No monsters in lakes or Abominable Snowmen up in the Himalayas. It's all fantasy. Imagination. And now I know better. It's like the whole world has been turned upside down, ain't it?"

Nathan shrugs. "Oh, I knew there were monsters."

"You did not."

"Sure, I did." Nathan pauses, staring out into the storm-tossed night. "When I was twelve, my old man took me and my kid brother fishing up in the high country above Wolf River, out past Black Heart Creek. We got our fill, all right. Last day up there, right before sunset, we smell something real bad. Like a hundred skunks let go at the same time. We hike up above this waterfall and we see something down below us at the water's edge. Kind of thing you might call a sasquatch. It was bigger than a man, hair-covered, real fierce-looking. It saw us, let out a whooping sort of cry and disappeared into the woods. We never saw it again."

"You're shitting me."

"No, I'm not. All kinds of things in the world, bro, both good and evil, that people never see. But it don't mean they don't exist."

Peanut moves the GMC slower now as the snow gusts, shaking the truck. It covers the windshield. The wipers keep pumping, trying to clear it.

Nathan Free is a full-blooded Blackfoot Sioux from the Standing Rock rez. Maybe what he says is true. Maybe he knew about monsters all along. A week ago, that might have been bullshit... but now Peanut is willing to believe just about anything.

"Maybe it's different for you people."

"What people?"

"Native Americans, I mean. Maybe you guys are more in touch with that weird stuff than whites are. Maybe you know things we don't. I don't know. I was always told monsters weren't real."

Nathan utters a cynical chuckle. "You know why you were told that?"

"Why?"

"Because the adults that told you that were scared," Nathan explains, as if it's the most obvious thing in the world. "See, if they admit there's monsters and spooks, they'll never sleep at night. Denial is easier. If they admit that there's holes in their version of reality and that if you look through 'em, you'll see shape-shifters and devils and the walking dead, it will be acknowledging that their belief system is faulty and what scares them most is real. They'll never have peace of mind again. That's why they laugh at scary stories and roll their eyes at monsters, because it all cuts too close to home, it exposes their secret fears, and makes them doubt their own sanity. It's just like guys in a war, man. They laugh and joke even though they're riding the edge of the knife the whole time. It covers up the truth, which is that they're scared shitless. Makes it easier to live with."

Peanut never heard it put that way before. It makes perfect sense. "You know what, Nathan? You're fucking wise. You really are wise."

"I try."

Peanut drives for another five minutes, then pulls into the snow-covered driveway of a little brick ranch house.

"You better let me handle this," he says, "since it's official business."

Nathan looks away and rolls his eyes, but he nods.

45

Peanut hops out of the cruiser and struggles through snow to the porch. In the headlights, he is lost amongst millions of glittering snowflakes. It's like entering the static of a TV screen. The wind tries to peel him off the steps, but he hangs on. He pounds and pounds on the door. That's how you do it when you're on official police business.

Finally, the porch light comes on. The door opens. Tony Russo is there looking ornery, even more ornery than usual.

"Peanut? What the fuck do you want?"

"There's been a…a sort of an accident. We need a medic."

Tony, a gruff and solid little man with the personality of a nutcracker, sneers at him. "So call an ambulance, fuckhead."

"We can't get one in the storm."

"Too fucking bad."

"Tony, goddammit, Will wants you right now!"

"Tell him to kiss my fucking ass," Tony growls. "Now I'm shutting the door, so piss off."

Peanut, still feeling like a real cop, walking the walk and talking the talk, sticks his boot tip in the door so it cannot be closed. It's what tough cops do in the movies.

Tony's eyes go dark as his mustache. "Get your fucking foot out of my fucking door, you asshole!"

"You're coming with me!" Peanut insists.

"Fuck I am!" Tony says.

He opens the door wider, stiff-arms Peanut in the chest and then slams it shut. Peanut stumbles back, slips on a patch of ice and rides down the steps on his ass.

The porch light goes out.

"You okay?" a voice asks.

Nathan Free is standing there, big and bristling. He offers Peanut a hand and pulls him to his feet.

Peanut brushes snow from himself. "That sonofabitch! He won't get away with this!"

"No, he won't," Nathan promises him. "You made it official business, now I'm making it Skull business. In other words, we do it my way."

Peanut stands there in the snow and wind, bending to it like a sapling. He watches Nathan go up the steps to the door. Unlike him, Nathan does not knock. He kicks the screen door until the aluminum face is dented in and the sheet of safety glass falls out. He means business.

The porch light comes back on.

Oh boy, Peanut thinks. *Here we go.*

46

Stan moves up on the plow truck like he's approaching a sleeping grizzly bear. He's tense head to foot, shivering and sweating at the same time. Amazed that such a thing is even possible. The plow truck is just a plow truck, but for reasons he cannot fathom (or refuses to), it scares the shit out of him. It's a beast. A monster waiting in the storm. At any moment, it will wake up and bite him in half. It will snap his bones with blunt yellow teeth and lap up his blood with a tongue like a rubberized canvas belt.

Shit, you better shut down your imagination for the duration or you just ain't gonna make it, son.

Okay.

He can do this.

There's also the possibility that what he may find will have nothing to do with clowns at all. He'll discover Chip or Mike laying over the seat, dead of something perfectly prosaic and earthy as a heart attack. It happens in weather like this. People push themselves too hard and pay the price. Every year, it seems, Stan hears about someone who had a heart attack while shoveling snow.

But Chip and Mike wouldn't have been shoveling snow, he reminds himself. They would have been pushing it.

Enough gymnastics for his overworked imagination. He turns on the camera and the spot illuminates the truck.

"Why would a city plow truck be abandoned in the middle of a blizzard?" he asks out loud, providing narration for his images. "That's the question I'm asking myself. Abandoned, door open. It's more than a little troubling. But this is a night for trouble. My name is Stan Barbacek. I'm a cab driver in the little town of Craw Falls, South Dakota. A place our own mayor once described as being little more than a 'smudge on the state map.' Tonight this smudge is in the grip of a terrible blizzard. But there's more than snow and cold and wind out here. Something much more dangerous."

Good. Don't overdo it.

He moves closer to the truck now, his heart thumping in his chest. He pans the camera along the box on the back that is filled with road salt. As he gets near the door, the wind takes it, making it creak back and forth on its hinges.

"Let's have a look inside," he says.

The light of the camera is thick with flying snow. He can feel the cold right into his marrow. He nears the door and it swings open completely in the wind. He jumps back, startled. He can hear his blood coursing in his ears. His hand is trembling on the camera. He puts both hands on it to steady it.

He steps next to the door, the snow coming up to his calves.

Inside the truck, there's nothing.

He doesn't believe it, eyes darting from the viewfinder and back again. Nope, there's nothing. This was a buildup that led nowhere. But that's fine. It's great atmosphere for his doc.

"No driver," he says, "no anything. What does it mean? Where did the driver go and, better yet, what might have called him away into the storm?"

He continues to pan from the empty cab and back to the encroaching storm where shadows move and prowl, fantastic shapes sliding through blowing sheets of snow.

"The world is white and deadly tonight," he says, "pregnant with menace."

Hey, that's good.

Though he is scared shitless, he continues to film. He circles around the truck and comes around the back.

He points the camera towards the ground. "There's no footprints anywhere that I can see. But they wouldn't last long in weather like this."

His nerves are like pins pricking him from the inside. His flesh beneath layers of clothing is tingling. Part of it's from the cold, yes, but not all of it. He can feel that he is not alone out here. Something is near. Something jumping away every time he turns. It feels as if it's close enough to reach out and touch him at times.

Breathing hard, he retreats back to the Jeep. He shuts the camera off. In one smooth motion, he gets inside and locks the doors.

There's nothing. Nothing at all.

This is what his common sense is telling him, but it seems hardly convincing under the circumstances. No, something was out there. He's positive of it.

As he pulls away and around the plow, the four-wheel drive finally biting in, he tries the radio again. He still can't raise Flo. It's getting to the point that he's starting to get more than a little concerned.

He drives down past the Whistle Stop. The lights are still on and the party continues. The need to go in there and be with people is nearly overwhelming.

He keeps going until he reaches the place where he hit the clown. The storm has erased nearly all the evidence, but he hops out anyway, filming the scene.

"This is where it happened. This is where I encountered the clown not long ago," he narrates, filming the drifting street, snow-devils spinning away into the night. "As incredible as it sounds, I hit the clown here. And... I think I rolled over him. He should still be here, shouldn't he? And he would be, if he was human."

Leave it there. Let the viewer's imagination fill in the blanks.

The storm picks up its fury, the wind moaning and tossing snow around. Curtains of it whip around Stan, sounding like granules of sand as they glance off the windshield. This doc is important to him, but not so important that he's going to ignore the signs of hypothermia. He needs to keep his wits about him, regardless of what else happens. Weather like this can kill you just as easily as a maniacal clown.

A sound.

He freezes there, listening. His core temperature was low before, but now it seems to have dropped into the subzero range. He's shaking, feeling disoriented. Maybe hypothermia is really setting in and maybe, just maybe it's something much darker.

It's there again, he thinks. I can feel it.

Still, he stands there, the storm marching in at him from all directions. What's happening here? He's only fifteen feet from the Jeep, but he can no longer hear it running with the constant mournful wailing of the blizzard. And he can't see it. The snow swirls around him in a maddened, insane vortex, blocking out everything. The cold is like silver needles piercing him. This must be hypothermia. He feels groggy and confused, yet terror that is bright and hot is exploding in his chest.

He moves.

Dear God, he finally moves.

He stumbles this way and that, going five feet, stopping, retreating, striking out in a different direction again and again. And in his mind, he can see himself with a bird's eye view, turning circles within circles within circles.

Stop it! Stop it! a voice in his head cries out frantically. *You're not out on the Arctic tundra! You're in the middle of the street in goddamn Craw Falls! You can't get lost! If you walk in any direction for any length of time you're going to run into the Jeep or a storefront or a telephone pole!*

But where are the streetlights?

Shouldn't he be able to see them? Maybe not with any true clarity, but a hazy glowing indication of them? They're gone. The entire world feels as if it's gone and Stan has been transported into some impossible glacial realm of biting cold and reaching shadows, a polar chaos of snow and wind. Using the camera, he aims the spot in every direction but there is only that enclosing wall of whiteness like some great blowing shroud that wants to suffocate him and bury him deep in the drift, put him asleep until he's nothing more than a frozen steak.

"I don't know what's happening here," he says in a shrill, agitated voice. "It makes no sense... but I'm not sure where I am or what's going on..."

Then he senses movement.

He's sure of it. It's behind him, to the left, to the right. He hears footsteps in the snow, fey steps like ghosts treading around him, baiting him, torment-ing him, making his head reel and his mind fragment like the snowflakes gusting around him in a cyclonic whirlwind.

Whatever haunts the storm, it's here with him now, dancing around him, filling his mind with clawing shadows. He sees the grotesque, leering faces of clowns now. They circle around him, blurred and flapping like sheets on a line. Scarlet eyes in black triangles. Narrow faces of shining white greasepaint flut-tering from the skulls beneath. Grinning red-smeared mouths and tusk-like fangs. Bloated white hands reaching for him.

Please go away.

Oh, dear God, leave me alone—

He panics and vaults away into the night, driven by sheer animal fright. He can feel the clowns moving with him, hollow eyes watching him and swollen lips eager to press against his throat.

Bam!

He runs right into the Jeep and goes down, the wind knocked from him. Scrambling to his feet, he grabs the camera out of the snow, hobbling towards the door, bent over and gasping.

Then he's inside and he can feel the heat unlocking the frost in his bones like skeleton keys unlocking vault doors.

Whimpering in his throat, he looks out through the windshield and the storm appears as it always has. He can see the hazy globes of the streetlights. The storefronts to either side. Something happened out there, and his greatest fear is that it will happen again if he does not get moving.

He puts the Jeep in drive, heading for Taxi-A-Go-Go. That's where he'll be safe.

Peanut does not know what might possibly happen next, he only knows he's standing there in the cold and snow, watching Nathan Free literally kick in the door of the Russo household. He cannot even think of all the laws he's breaking allowing something like this to go on. Yet, he's pissed and, God help him, he's enjoying it.

Nathan pretty much rips the screen door from its hinges and as he does so, the inside door opens and there's Midge Russo, Tony's wife. She's in her bathrobe, looking like she's ready for bed.

"GET OFF MY PORCH!" she shrieks. "GET THE FUCK AWAY FROM MY HOUSE!"

She's a wildcat, ready to scratch out eyes, spit and claw. Peanut knows her well. She's every bit as ornery and evil-tempered as her husband, maybe more so. He took her in once for disturbing the peace at the Whistle Stop and she nearly bit his throat out. She was full of acid and molten lead that burned anything that got in her path. Once they got her into a holding cell, she—drunk and mainlining on a pure white seam of hate—threw herself continually at the bars, screeching and squealing and telling anyone that got in range how their mothers sucked dick and their fathers licked ass.

She's a real handful.

And right then she looks more pissed than usual.

Not that Nathan cares.

He grabs the door and throws it open, almost pitching Midge on her sizeable ass. She charges at him and he shoves her down, warning her to stay out of his way.

"Tony!" he calls out. "Get your ass down here now! If I gotta come get you, I'm going to give you a beat down!"

By then, Peanut is entering the house. He has to diffuse this situation before it gets really ugly, something it is scarce inches from now.

"YOU DIRTY FUCKING INDIAN COCKSUCKER!" Midge screams. "YOU MOTHERFUCKING WOOD NIGGER! GET THE FUCK OUT OF MY HOUSE OR I'LL TEAR YOUR EVER-LOVING FUCKING BALLS OFF!"

She's going to launch herself right at Nathan again and he will not put up with shit like that, Peanut knows. Oh, Christ, this whole thing is going from bad to worse. Peanut then makes his biggest mistake: he gets in between Midge and Nathan who is waiting for Tony to show.

Midge goes right at him.

Peanut tries to keep her away from him, but she's an electric, hissing mass of muscle and piss and attitude. "YOU USELESS DIRTY FUCKING CUNT! YOU COCKSUCKING PIG-ASSED FUCKING COP!" These are the words that spray from her lips like venom from the mouth of a spitting cobra as she goes after Peanut. Her nails come streaking at him, slashing his cheeks and forehead and scraping over his eyelids which he wisely shut. He tries to fight back, but she's hysterical and savage like some tribesman jacked up on peyote. She slaps him. Punches him. Then knees him in the balls and drops him to the floor just as quick.

Then she turns and fires herself at Nathan like a bullet. He sees it coming and before she can get her nails into him, which are now broken and bloody, he punches her in the face. Her head snaps back and her eyes roll back white. She hits the wall and bounces off it, face-planting to the floor.

48

Holding his nuts, Peanut is sweating and hurting, curled up in a fetal ball. He should have seen that coming. Midge is a wicked woman. She's a fighter with a string of assaults. Now she's lying three feet away from him, whimpering.

Then Tony comes sheepishly down the stairs. He looks from Nathan to Midge, shrugs, says, "What's this all about?"

Just like that. That calm. That unconcerned. Which Peanut, knows, should not surprise him because he's been called over here more than once by the neighbors when Tony and Midge were really going at it. One time, Midge showed at the Broken Bottle, the left side of her face a livid purple bruise. She claimed she fell down the steps even though everyone knew Tony had given her a beating. Not long after, Tony ended up in the hospital in Vermillion, a barbeque fork stuck in his belly. He claimed he tripped with a platter of burgers and impaled himself. Everyone knew it was payback from Midge.

"We need you over at the Bottle," Nathan says. "Some people have been attacked. We can't get an ambulance in here with the storm. In fact, we can't even get word out. Highway's closed. Phone lines are down. Cell and internet are out."

"You're fucking kidding me," Tony says, lighting a cigarette. He steps over the form of his wife and goes in the living room. He tries the phone. Then his cell. Then his laptop. Nada, nada, nada. "Hell is going on?"

"Clowns," Peanut groans from the floor.

"What about 'em?"

"They're killing people," Nathan tells him. "It's like nothing you've seen before. We got injured people. Sheriff wants you at the Bottle right now."

Swearing under his breath, Tony suits up in polar fleece, snow pants, and parka. It's obvious from the look on his face that he's not buying this business about clowns, but on the other hand, he's not about to risk pissing Nathan off.

Nathan pulls Peanut to his feet.

"Oh Jesus, oh mother, I think she broke 'em," Peanut whimpers.

"What's your problem?" Tony asks as he pulls on his hat.

"Your wife kneed him in the rocks," Nathan says.

Tony grunts, looking from his wife to Peanut. "What? It's your first time? Don't be such a pussy. She stuck an olive fork in my left ball once. You'll live."

"Cocksucker, cocksucker, I'll get you for this," Midge moans on the floor.

The three of them pile out the door, Nathan having to help Peanut who's bent over like an old man. The wind and snow hit them right away, pushing them together. Unlikely compatriots—a bent-over cop, a biker, and a small bulldog of a man.

"No radio you're saying?" Tony says as they go down the steps.

"Nothing."

"That don't make sense. C'mon," he says.

"Where we going?" Peanut asks.

"Next door. Old man Peel. He's got a ham radio setup. He talks with people in Belgium and Antarctica and goddamn Vietnam. If anybody can get word out, he can."

Peanut's not sure if he likes the idea, but Nathan seems okay with it so he goes along. It'll just take a few minutes and what's the worst that could happen? Feeling his aching, swollen balls, he decides he doesn't want an answer to that one.

Off into the storm they go.

Back at the Broken Bottle, Bonnie Faust waits with the others for Peanut and Nathan to get back. The two dead Skulls have been covered with plastic dropcloths, so no one has to stare at their damaged forms. The injured are gathered in the booths, covered in blankets. Their wounds have been tended to best as possible under the circumstances.

Outside, Bonnie can hear the storm bearing down on them. In her mind, it's like no storm Craw Falls has ever seen before or will ever see again. It never stops. Most storms blow themselves out given time, but not this one. In her mind, it's not a storm at all, but something else, some frozen malevolent entity of pure chaos that has sucked in cold winds and heavy snowfall from every other blizzard ever known and brought them here, exhaling that wrath against the town for the sheer purpose of trapping everyone within its confines like mice in a killing box.

Carpy sits to one side of her, scared and brooding. To the other is Madelyn Kenner and her two friends, Lynn and Elaine. All three work over at Farm Bureau insurance. They decided to go out for Madelyn's birthday.

And they sure picked the wrong dang night, Bonnie thinks.

"I'm going to get Brenda upstairs," Stew says.

Bonnie figures that's a good idea. The bite is bad, but hardly life-threatening, yet Brenda is acting funny. Silent, for one thing, and that's a pretty good gauge that she's not doing well because she never shuts up. Stew helps her up and leads her to the doorway in the back that connects with the stairs up to their digs above the bar. Brenda is trembling. Sweat is running down her.

But her eyes, look at her eyes.

They are glassy and staring. They do not blink. She watches Bonnie, a crooked half-smile on her face. Her gaze is startling in its intensity.

Bonnie is glad when she's gone.

"She looks like she's crazy," Madelyn says and the sound of her voice startles everyone, save maybe Clyde Taggert and Will Teague.

"She's been through a lot," Bonnie says, thinking it is the right thing to say at the right time.

"Who hasn't?" Elaine snips.

The thing is, Brenda does look crazy. She doesn't look like somebody who is hurt or frightened, a victim; she looks like someone who is preparing to hurt or frighten, a perpetrator. This makes no sense and maybe it makes all the sense in the world if you think about it. Which is something Bonnie is not about to do. That's a dark road she does not wish to walk, one that will lead into an equally dark wood where inhuman things gibber and grin.

Keep your head. That's the most important thing. If you do nothing else, keep calm and reasonable.

She figures this is important because Madelyn and her friends are on the verge of a panic attack, Carpy can barely keep his lower jaw off the floor, and Clyde and the sheriff appear to be locked into a battle of wills.

"How long we gonna wait before we do something?" Clyde asks.

"As long as it takes."

"I'm not gonna wait here all night. Not while those things are out there killing people."

"We'll wait as long as I say we'll wait," Teague says, raising his voice. "At least until Peanut and Nathan get back."

"You can't hold us," Skunk says. "It ain't legal."

Teague smiles thinly. "In a situation like this, as county sheriff, I can declare martial law if the situation warrants it."

Bonnie knows that's not true, but she's not about to say so. For the time being, Teague's authority has defused the situation. Clyde goes back to the bar. Skunk follows obediently behind him.

Bonnie knows Clyde as everyone in Craw Falls does. He can be a pretty good guy, pretty levelheaded and decent, but he has a hair trigger. When he loses it, look out, there's going to be a body count. He's one thing and Skunk is quite another. Skunk is a smelly, filthy man with long greasy hair, an oily smile, and bad teeth. He wears Coke bottle glasses and is, in her opinion, dangerous. He's been watching her all night and he's still watching her, leering at her through his thick lenses like a child molester watching a schoolyard.

If we were alone, Bonnie thinks, he'd rape me. At least, he'd try. Then he'd probably kill me.

Sighing, feeling soiled from Skunk's eyes, she waits for the others to get back. Particularly Nathan Free. Nathan is not a savage like Clyde or a predator like Skunk. He seems intelligent. He's generally reasonable in all things. The other Skulls, with the exception of Clyde, seem to fear him. He'll keep Skunk in line.

Hurry, Nathan, hurry.

50

When they get over to Old Man Peel's house, Tony pounds on the door as if it's two in the afternoon and not well after midnight.

"He's got to be home," Tony says. "He never goes anywhere."

He pounds again for a few more minutes in which Nathan and Peanut grow increasingly impatient.

"Listen, we don't have all night," Peanut says.

Tony ignores him, pounds again, then reaches down and tries the knob. It's open. "This ain't right," he says. "He always locks his doors. He's OCD about it. He used to have a cat. He'd let it out and lock the door while it went to do its business for godsake."

"Well, that's not our problem," Nathan says.

Before he can say anything else, Tony has let himself in. Peanut gives Nathan a look and they follow him inside. It's warm in there anyway. That's a plus. About the only plus they've gotten this night.

Peanut wants to tell Tony that they just can't barge into peoples' houses anytime they choose... but after what he allowed Nathan to do at Tony's house, what's the point? He keeps his mouth shut.

Tony goes in like he owns the place and it's obvious he spends a lot of time there. He turns on lights and looks around. "Hey, Jimbo! Where the hell are you?" he calls, tracking snow across the carpet and into the kitchen. "Jimbo? JIIIIIIIIMMMMMMBO! Wake the hell up already!" He looks in the pantry as if old man Peel might be squatting in there amongst the Campbell's Chicken Noodle Soup and Kraft Macaroni and Cheese. He opens the refrigerator and looks around.

"Pretty sure he won't be in there," Nathan says.

Tony laughs at the very idea. "Ah, I come here a lot. I always help myself. Trust me, you're married to someone like Midge, you need a hideout to lay low."

Peanut, his balls still hurting, understands perfectly. But he also knows there's injured at the Broken Bottle and Teague is going to fucking scalp him if he doesn't get Tony back there and soon.

Tony pulls off a beer from the fridge. "Want one?"

"That's it," Nathan tells him, grabbing the beer from his hand and throwing it in the sink where it shatters. Then he grabs Tony and slams him against the wall. "You think this is some kind of fucking joke? You think we're playing around here? We got two fucking dead men at the Bottle and like five injured. You think that's funny?"

Tony, a veteran hardass in most respects, knows when he's met his match and when he's in the presence of a real meat-eater. He squirms and looks like he needs to piss real bad. "No, no, Nathan... c'mon, it's cool, man. It's cool."

Peanut has to suppress a giggle. Boy, what a cop Nathan would have made! A real friggin' Dirty Harry. The sort of badass take-names-and-kick-ass late show flatfoot that Peanut always dreamed of being.

"Show us this radio now, shit-fer-brains," Nathan tells Tony and it's no polite request.

Tony moves quickly then. No time for another beer or a cold chicken leg. He leads them to the back of the house and only stops when the temperature drops noticeably.

"Oh, shit," he says, turning away.

Peanut nearly loses his lunch. There's a body hanging from a door, an old guy, maybe in his seventies. Somebody has driven a butcher's knife through his neck and into the wood behind him. He dangles four inches off the floor. His face has been peeled like a grapefruit. There's blood on him, on the door, splattered on the walls. A trail of it leads into a room.

Lookit those prints, Peanut thinks. *Just lookit those prints.*

"This Jimbo?" Nathan says.

"Yeah," Tony tells him, leaning against the wall. "That's him."

Nathan pushes the door (and what's hanging from it) in. The bloody prints lead to the window that's been shattered. The glass is all over the floor so Peanut figures the clown came in through it, then departed the same way.

"This was his station?" Nathan asks.

"Yeah," Tony calls from the hallway.

The HF radio is shattered on the floor along with what might have been a tuner. There's a mic on the desk, a few books, a pad of paper with a large bloody thumbprint on it, but that's about it. Everything else is on the floor, tangled in wires and coaxial cables.

"It's been destroyed on purpose," Peanut says, thinking out loud. "This was no accident. It's all part of shutting us down."

"What the hell are you talking about?" Tony calls from the hallway.

Nathan steps from the room with Peanut in tow. "He's talking about what's going on. What's taken this town. And what's planning on killing each and every one of us."

Tony stands there, staring at them. Maybe he was thinking it was all some sort of gag, but he's not thinking that anymore. In fact, he looks about as scared as anyone Peanut has ever seen.

51

Stan Barbacek, still in something of a daze from what he just experienced, pulls the Jeep to a stop before Taxi-A-Go-Go. He's not entirely sure what happened out in the storm, how much was real and how much was hallucination. He sits there, gripping the wheel, his forehead touching his hands. He's scared and nauseous and unsure.

I don't know what I'm doing, he thinks. *I really don't know what I'm doing. I'm messing with shit way above my pay grade and way beyond anything I can understand.*

What he needs at that moment and needs very badly is someone to talk to. That's the thing. He grabs his camera bag and goes out into the storm to the cabstand. The first thing he discovers is that the door is locked. C'mon, Flo, tonight of all nights? He knocks a few times, then fishes out his key and unlocks it. The wind is blowing so hard he can barely get the door open and when he does, it's nearly yanked from his hand.

Finally, he gets it closed and stands there in the warmth, just breathing. "Flo?" he says. "Flo, you around? God, that storm out there. It's like nothing I've ever seen before. It just keeps going and...going and..."

Whatever else he was going to say is gone. The words dry up long before they reach his tongue. He's suddenly overwhelmed by a sense of dread that's completely nonspecific. The atmosphere of the cabstand seems black and rotten. Trembling, telling himself it's just the cold coming out of him, he steps farther into the stand. There's a terrible smell in the room that's gaseous and foul.

He steps over to the radio.

On the desk is one of those paperback novels that Flo is always reading, a stack of magazines, a call log, a cup of coffee. There's only static coming over the radio.

"Flo?" he tries again, this time more quietly. The sound of his own voice breaking the stillness unnerves him.

She's not here, a voice tells him. *She's not here at all.*

Though there's no way he can know, he's nearly certain that it's true—Flo is not here. She's not in the stand and she's not upstairs in her apartment. She's gone. Erased. Eradicated.

The room is L-shaped. He steps around the desk and sees the rest of it. There's the couch. A coffee maker. A fridge.

And huge black footprints on the floor.

He stands there, staring at them, knowing what must have left them but pretending he's wrong, that he's making false assumptions.

Whoever they belonged to, it looks as if they walked through a puddle of dirty ink. And what possible sense does that make? Stan does not know. The only thing he's certain about is the shape of those prints. Nothing could have left them but large, floppy clown shoes.

Without really thinking, he pulls out the camera and starts filming. He provides no narration. The sound of a voice in this unbroken, ominous stillness would be too much. The prints lead through a doorway into the corridor. Here, they're everywhere. Leading from the bathroom at the end, going down the length of the corridor. There's a flurry of them.

His heart thudding in his chest, he stands there. He doesn't know what to do. Common sense tells him to call the sheriff. But before he does that, common sense also tells him that he had better search the place first. Otherwise, what can he say? She's gone, I know she's gone. Something terrible has happened to her. What's that? No, I didn't really look around. I just panicked and called you. Yeah, it wouldn't sound too good.

But the idea of searching the place...well, it's almost more than he can take, especially after what he's seen tonight.

He thinks: You could always get back in the Jeep and call the sheriff, claim you're stuck or something and that Flo isn't answering. That you're worried.

Stan sighs.

He likes the idea, what he doesn't like is the idea of having to live with his own cowardice. Besides, Flo is one of his oldest friends. He cannot walk away from this (whatever this is). He owes it to her to find out what's going on.

"Okay," he says under his breath. "Okay."

He walks down the corridor to the bathroom. Whatever happened, this seems to be the source of it or the center of activity. Drawing in a deep breath that rattles in his chest, he opens the bathroom door and steps in there... oh Christ.

This is definitely the source of that reeking black fluid. God, it's everywhere. There's an immense sticky puddle of it on the floor. One of the urinals is painted black. It's sprayed all over the floors.

And the smell...like a backed-up sewer.

Could that be what happened here? he wonders. A backed-up sewer? Maybe. But that still does not explain those prints. The idea of walking in that stuff to check the stalls is unthinkable. He squats down. No, he can see no feet in them. They're empty. The only thing he sees other than that black goo, is the door lock on the floor.

It's been forced.

He pans the bathroom one last time with the camera. It's important, he decides, to have some sort of record of this. Okay. He leaves the bathroom. He follows the floppy clown prints down the corridor. He notices with a combination of interest and dismay, that there is another set of prints, smaller ones, mixed in with the others.

Flo's?

Got to be.

Stan hesitates a moment, his heart thudding in his chest. Fear is crawling over his skin like spiders. He can barely draw a breath. The atmosphere of the cabstand is thick with menace, palpable with evil. It's as if he's standing in a rising pool of it. At that moment, his mouth so dry he cannot swallow, he remembers every ghost story he ever heard as a kid. They come back to him, filling his skull with drifting, phantasmal images, haunting his very bones.

Well? he asks himself.

WELL?

He has to consciously will himself to move forward now. Anxiety unlike anything he has ever known before threads through his nervous system. A nameless fear inches up his spine on caterpillar legs. He knows that if he does not steel himself and do this now, he never will. His frayed nerves will win, and he will run for the door.

And you won't stop either, a voice tells him. You'll run until you're back home, cowering under the bed.

Fighting against his own pragmatism, he moves around the bend at the end of the corridor. He expects to see nothing. Just the cellar door and the back door leading out to the alley.

He does see these things, but he also sees a whole lot more.

There's blood on the floor.

Enough to make his stomach heave with a sickly roll. It stands out in stark contrast against the smudged black footprints. There's more blood on the walls, a spattering of it as if someone tossed a bloody rag against the stucco. There's even some on the ceiling.

Whatever happened here, it was devastating and lethal. The blood can only be Flo's. The stale, metallic odor of it—like rust and dirty pennies—makes waves of revulsion roll through his guts. He knows if he keeps pushing this search, he's going to find her remains (by this point, he no longer believes she is alive).

There's a blood smear on the floor leading directly to the cellar door. There's also a glaring red handprint on the door itself. As shocking as it is, Stan finds it hard to believe it's accidental. It's too...planned somehow, as if it was left there to incite his imagination and disgust him.

He gets a good shot of it with the Apeman cam. His hand is surprisingly calm, even if the rest of him is not.

The handprint is huge. It's not from an ordinary human being.

A clown hand, Stan tells himself. Big and soft and horrible.

Now it's really a matter of the cellar: does he go down there, possibly further muddling a crime scene or does he go for help? The latter is the logical choice. But human beings are not logical creatures—they are intuitive and instinctive.

He nudges the door open with his boot.

Big mistake, he tells himself.

52

Upstairs of the Broken Bottle, Brenda Prechek lays in bed, burning up with fever. She's in a bad way and she knows it. She tosses and turns, makes groaning sounds deep in her throat. Hot sweat beads her face. When she throws off the covers, she shivers; when she covers up, she sweats. It feels like she has the flu.

Her eyes open and she looks around the dim room. The only illumination is the orange glow of a nightlight in the corner. For a moment there, she does not recognize her surroundings.

Why am I here? she asks herself. *Where did they take me?*

Then she realizes with some agitation that she's in her own bed. Stew was there, now he's gone. That's the only blessing. He's such a nervous, indecisive little man. His mothering annoys her.

"Stew? Are you here?"

No answer. He probably went back downstairs to the bar. Probably to study Bonnie Faust's tits in more detail. Although they have a good working relationship and Brenda even considers her to be a friend, at that moment she hates her. The image of Bonnie in her mind makes Brenda gnash her teeth.

The anger subsides and Bonnie falls asleep again. It's not a pleasant transition. Not like cozying up in bed and slowly drifting off. No, this is more abrupt. It's like somebody pulls the plug on her like an appliance and she falls into darkness.

Right away, she dreams of the snow and the wind that batter the Broken Bottle and what moves through it, whirling and dancing, jumping and singing. Fantastic clown-faced forms in scarlet and black uniforms, ghastly apparitions that twirl and beckon. She sees herself moving with them, rushing with them into the polar depths of the storm like a terrible river, a maelstrom that draws them all down, deeper and deeper, into a sucking black pit of cold laughter and grinning white faces.

She wakes a few minutes later, convulsions rolling through her.

There's a voice in her head, a wise old voice.

They're down there, all of them, living it up. You're out of the way and that's the how they want it. Now they can look at Bonnie's tits. Now they can touch them, suck them, bite them.

Without realizing what she's even doing, Brenda finds herself on her feet. Her logic and reasoning are skewed, febrile. She knows and she does not know. But the voice tells her what has to be, and she listens to it. Her eyes shining like smoky glass, her mouth set in a scowl of hate, she finds the stairs and starts down them, one at a time.

Listen! Can you hear them? Can you hear the perverted games they get up to when you're not there to watch over them and set them straight?

Yes, yes! She can hear them. They are laughing and drinking and singing. Bonnie is probably naked and they're taking their turns with that fucking wench, that dirty slut. Though Brenda's head spins, her thoughts flying apart in her skull like dandelion fluff, she knows they conspire against her and it's all she really needs to know.

Stew is one of the first to see her.

"Brenda," he says in that soft, mucky voice of his that she despises. "Honey, you should be in bed. You should—"

Brenda screams at him with a terrible animal squeal, her hands going for his face, her nails laying open his cheeks. He is everything that is wrong in her life. Everything she hates. Trying to protect himself he falls away. Others move towards her and one of them is Bonnie Faust. Brenda goes after her, too, with manic rage, knocking her down and then Will Teague is coming after her and other people, faces, faces everywhere.

Brenda screams again and runs past them, making for the back room and the door the clown took off its hinges. It is loosely wedged in its frame. She pushes it aside and runs out into the storm. It finds her and covers her immediately, drawing her deeper and deeper into its depths. There are voices calling out her name and she runs from them.

There is another out here.

The one that waits for her.

The one that will protect her from the others who want to put her in a cage. Stumbling, running, crawling, but moving ever forward, she hears the voice calling out to her, summoning her to a place where the others will never, ever find her, a secret and special place.

By then, the blizzard has her. It has turned her forward and backward, upside down and inside out. She is lost in a secret wonderland of snow and icicles and silver cutting wind. She finally falls to her knees. She's dressed only in a hoodie, jeans, and socks. Her hands are numb as are her feet, her face pinched blue by the cold.

"I'm so glad you came," a voice says.

Brenda looks up and there's a clown standing there. She blinks, but its image does not fade. No, in fact, it becomes more solid. A moment before it fluttered like a mirage, but now it's real. She stares up at it, not with fear, but with wonder and awe and astonishment. In her mind's eye, it's every clown she has ever known—Bozo and Cooky, Buttons and Coco and Ronald McDonald.

"Who…" she manages. "Who are you?"

The clown looks down at her and explodes with laughter that is not remotely merry or delightful. In fact, it's a terrible sound like the braying of a wounded animal. Its breath blows in her face and smells of raw meat.

She notices that while her breath blows out in white clouds, the clown's does not.

Still laughing, he stares at her, boundlessly amused. He wears a billowing checkered suit that flaps in the wind. There are thick tufts of orange hair to either side of his head. They are shaggy and tangled like the mane of a beast. His face is white, his nose immense and bulbous like a ripe tomato. His soupy yellow eyes are set in painted red bands, his mouth a smiling, exaggerated black grin. His eyebrows are painted high up on his forehead.

"Why, my dear, my pet, my little one," he says, "I'm your friend. I want to play with you tonight and I want you to play with me."

He strokes her face with one pudgy white finger. Brenda's mind seems to go in and out of focus like a camera lens. She understands with childlike glee and trembles with adult terror.

"But for now," says her new friend, "there's only me! And I like to jump!" He hops into the storm, disappearing momentarily, then reappearing right behind her. Then his mouth is at her left ear, hot and blubbery. "And I like to sing!" He screams into her head until she doubles over with the pain of it. "But mostly, mostly I like to dance!" He tells her, grasping her by the shoulders now, his pulpous face pressed close to her own, his hot meat-breath in her face. "And tonight, my precious one, I'm going to dance! I'm going to dance in your skin..."

Brenda lets out a perfectly girlish cry. But it's too late by then, far too late, because her new bestest friend unzips himself like a garment bag and shows her exactly what he keeps inside.

53

The passage leading to the cellar seems darker than anything Stan has ever known before. Every shadow in the world has congregated here. In the light from the corridor, he can see the steps (three or four of them anyway) descending into that awful darkness. The hairs on the back of his neck stand on end. The fear he knows at that moment is perfectly instinctual as if he's staring into the cave of a carnivorous beast.

And maybe he is at that.

The basement. He has not been down there in three or four years. There's been no reason to. He keeps nothing down there and neither does Flo. She virtually has an atavistic dread of cellars. No one knows why.

At that moment, Stan shares her phobia—it's as if everything that has ever scared him is down there, waiting. Every crawling, bug-eyed, yellow-toothed nightmare he imagined as a boy or dreamed of as an adult.

Though he knows all that is hyperactive imagination, what is not is the smell that rushes up from below, a cloying subterranean dankness of things long buried and those that should be buried.

He watches the darkness through the viewfinder of the camera. His hands are now shaking so badly that the image is probably jumping all over the place.

"I don't know what I'll find down here, but I expect the worst," he narrates. "This may indeed be my epitaph."

He fully expects something shaggy and slavering to charge up at him. But that's not going to happen, and he knows it. What is below is not a horror that will come to you; you must come to it.

This, then, is the acid test.

Does he have the nerve to go down there and face what waits on its own turf... or does he get out now?

He reaches for the light switch. He has made his choice. Maybe there never really was a choice. Swallowing dust in his throat, he fully expects the light below to be burned out or broken. The logic of countless horror movies assures him that it must be.

But it is neither.

It flickers to life, but provides uneven illumination, casting a mutiny of shadows in all directions. It continues to flicker. The light is like that of a guttering candle.

Unarmed, shivering with irrational fear, he goes down there, step by heavy step. At the bottom, he pans the camera from side to side. The camera spot shows him what he knows is already down there: the cracked stone floor, the water-stained fieldstone walls, the cobwebbed beams overhead. He sees the furnace and hot water heater, some ancient mold-stained sandwich boards from when the cabstand was a lunch counter.

There's nothing else and he knows it.

The only ones whoever come down here are the meter reader and the furnace guy.

Stan moves towards the back.

There is a brick partition and beyond, sort of an ell where coal was once probably stored. There are no lights in this section, only that of the camera. In the back of his mind, he figures the video he captures will be his last testament.

The idea frightens him, but it does not stop him.

As scared as he is, he knows he must see what's down here. It's important and not just for his doc.

But a weapon.

He needs a weapon.

But there's nothing and even if he had one, could he really fight against one of the clowns?

He approaches the partition, sweating profusely, expecting his life to end at any moment. Then he moves around it. What he sees makes him freeze in place.

A clown.

It's not moving, not doing anything but laying atop a heap of rubbish like a hibernating bear—sticks and straw, bones and rags. A nest. That's what it is, a nest. He wonders if he rolls the clown off it if he'll find an egg. Regardless, something like this was not built tonight, but over many days or weeks.

How long has this been going on? a voice in his head asks. How long have they been preparing for this night?

It's a question without an answer. He keeps the camera on the clown. He tightens the focus. He's still anchored to the spot, knowing he needs to get out of there. But he doesn't. Something tells him there is no immediate danger.

The clown is inactive. Dormant. Something.

He or it is a swollen, foul thing. Bloated like a spider that has just sucked the blood from dozens of flies. The stench of corruption coming from it is sickening. It wears a black, satiny suit with red polka dots which is crusted with whorls of dried blood and foul drainage. Its face is dead-white, lips smeared red, eyes like blanched olives floating in oily brine. A purple-blue vein networking can be seen just beneath the skin.

Blood has leaked from its mouth, nostrils, and eye sockets, staining the nest of scraps beneath it. One of its white blood-spattered hands is thrown over its midsection. The other dangles over the side of the nest, palm upward. The flesh of the wrist has shriveled back like a poorly fitting glove, exposing a gray fibrous tissue.

No more. You need to get out of here right now.

Stan backs away, not daring to take the light off the clown. It reveals something like a cast-aside pile of rags pushed into the corner.

It's Flo.

The realization of this comes with a sharp, bright pain in his chest. She's a puckered, drained carcass like the carapace of a fly on a window ledge dropped from a web high above. The clown has fed upon her. If there was a weapon handy, Stan would have used it on that fucking leech.

This more than anything breaks his paralysis. He turns and runs, tripping up the stairs and making it into the corridor before going on his face. As he pulls himself frantically to his feet, he sees something has changed in the worst possible way.

There is writing on the wall, a crude and perverse finger-painting of words. On one wall, it reads:

HOPTOAD
Waz
HeRe

And on the other:

hoptoAd sez
SeE Ya soOn,
LittlE BuNnY FooFoo

It's enough. It's more than enough. None of it makes sense—Hoptoad and Little Bunny Foo Foo—but all of it fills him with a shriveling white terror. Some part of his mind that is still functioning by that point tells him he is not seeing it. That it's a hallucination of the most dreadful variety. But he does not care. He runs through the cabstand and out the door, slipping and sliding in the snow.

It's only when he's behind the wheel of the Jeep and the doors are locked, that he begins to scream hysterically.

54

At the Broken Bottle, it's Stew who moves first after Brenda disappears out the door. He is not, by nature, a man of action. He likes to take things slowly, step by step, with plenty of time to consider the ramifications. But after Brenda goes out the door, he goes after her.

Will Teague is amazed at how fast he moves. Before he can even hope to stop him, Stew is out the door. No jacket. No gloves. No hat. He does not even stop to think; he merely acts.

Teague knows he has to go get him. There's no time to waste. He wishes Peanut and Nathan were back.

Clyde Taggert pulls on his heavy coat and hat. "C'mon!" he says. "That fuckwit will die out there!"

Teague is right behind him. "Carpy, Bonnie... keep an eye on things!"

He has complete faith in the latter, but the former...oh Christ. Still, there's no time to think about it. Teague races out the door in close pursuit of Clyde. Here's the crazy thing: twenty-four hours ago, Clyde and the Dead Skulls were a nuisance to him. A group of hard-riders and troublemakers that gave him no end of grief through the years. Now, they are a necessary evil. In fact, tonight Teague has come to count on them.

That's what it's come to, he thinks as the cold finds him and makes him recoil.

Clyde is fast. He's spent years running from and/or evading the law and he's lost none of his spunk.

"CLYDE!" Teague calls out. "SLOW DOWN FOR CHRISSAKE!"

Clyde skids to a halt and Teague catches up with him.

"Let's use our heads or we'll all get lost out here," Teague tells him.

Clyde looks like he's about to disagree, thinks better of it, and nods his head. "Okay," he breathes.

Using his flashlight, Teague scans about and finds the prints of both Stew and Brenda pretty easily. "Let's go before they're gone but stay with me."

55

The storm has not lessened in its ferocity. The wind is still howling, throwing drift around, and the snow is still falling. The town is socked in bad now. It'll take days to clean up the mess. These are the thoughts that go through Teague's head as they follow Stew's prints that have pretty much fouled and obscured Brenda's. At least he was smart enough to follow them and not go off in the opposite direction. That was something.

And right now, I'll take anything.

Clyde is a born tracker. He stays on Stew's prints unerringly. He stops now and again to point out things. "Looks like he tripped here" or "fell down in this drift." Things like that.

"Wait," Teague says.

"What?"

"I heard something."

Now they both cock their heads to the storm, ears perked. They hear the wind, the snow falling against their coats. There seems to be nothing else out there but the near-steady drone of the blizzard itself. It sounds like some gargantuan, impossible beast breathing.

Then...a sound.

The wind distorts it, but they're almost sure that it's Stew calling out for Brenda. It does not sound far away. They move off, keeping on his trail. They'll have him any minute now. As for Brenda, who knows? Teague does not even speculate on this in the back of his mind. It's going to be hard enough to get Stew back to the bar let alone his wife.

"STEW!" Clyde calls out, the storm making his voice reverberate oddly. "STEW! TELL US WHERE YOU ARE! WE'LL HELP YOU!"

He must hear them, because he screams out his wife's name again. His voice sounds not just frantic but insane.

Teague and Clyde try to push forward but the storm intensifies. It batters them with wind. Sheets of snow like waves hit them one after the other. Teague has never seen anything like it. It pounds him with such force that he is put to his knees in a drift.

Clyde helps him up and nearly gets knocked over himself. His face blasted white with snow, he says, "I never...never seen anything like this."

Teague nods. If he didn't know better, he would think that the things that hunt the storm are in control of it, using it to further their own ends, trap people so that they are easy prey. It's silly perhaps, but he is not convinced it's sheer fantasy.

The punch of the storm downgrades and they are able to move again. Now they hold onto each other. The snowfall is so heavy, great rumbling walls of it pushing at them from conflicting directions, that Teague's light does not penetrate it. It's reflected off of it. Between the snow and the darkness, it's like being in a storm in Antarctica at dead winter—if you stray, you might be swallowed by the weather and never be seen again.

They hear Stew again.

This time he's closer.

A single struggling finger of hope worms inside of Teague. They've got a chance, by God. They might just get to him. As it turns out, they don't get to him, he gets to them.

Teague senses movement, turns, and there comes Stew, stumbling forward, blown white with snow from head to foot. He bashes into the sheriff and goes down.

"Brenda," he says. "Oh God..."

"We better get back or we won't make it," Clyde says, pulling Stew to his feet.

But that means abandoning Brenda and Teague does not like the idea. Though he rarely admits it out loud, he believes completely in what he does for a living. Being a cop is all he's wanted since he was in fourth grade. The way he sees it, the job of a county sheriff is less law enforcement and more helping people in any way he can. People fuck up and break laws and he tries not to get too heavy-handed with that, but as far as helping others in time of need, he's nearly fanatical as any good cop should be.

"Sheriff!" Clyde shouts. "Will..."

Teague nods and follows behind him. He catches up with him and helps him with Stew who is both physically and mentally wasted by that point. They need to get him somewhere warm before he dies. He's already frostbitten and hypothermic. Time is of the essence.

56

Bonnie does not like Clyde and Sheriff Teague being away. It leaves her with the injured, the dead, and...Skunk. He's still watching her as he has been all night. Not looking her in the face, of course, but gazing intently at her breasts and ass.

"This is all kind of crazy, isn't it?" Madelyn Kenner's friend Lynn says. "I mean, why are we waiting here? We already told the sheriff what we saw. He's got our names and numbers. Why should we stay?"

"Sheriff don't want no one leaving," Carpy tells her. "That means no one."

Madelyn's other friend, Elaine, nods in agreement. "Well, I'm glad I'm not the one to say it, but this is crazy. If we don't leave soon, we'll never get through that storm."

"You're right," Madelyn says.

"You can't," Bonnie warns her.

"Sorry, but this is still a free country and you can't stop us."

She's right and Bonnie knows it. Though the idea of whittling away at their little group bothers her, she knows there's nothing she can do to keep them. Funny how they waited until the sheriff was gone to assert their independence.

"I wouldn't do it," Carpy says.

Skunk, of course, picks up on the conversation and slithers on over. "Don't listen to him," he says. "Teague can't hold you here. He don't have the authority. You wanna go, then go."

As he says this, his eyes climb up Bonnie, from her crotch to her breasts. Bonnie fears him. He's a monster. A sexual predator. Without Clyde or Nathan around, there is nothing to restrain him from indulging in his sick fantasies. And she's pretty sure that one of them involves raping her.

He continues to stare salaciously at her. Magnified by the glasses, his eyes bulge like those of a frog, huge and glistening and repellent. She can see the grease in his hair, his crooked smile and bad teeth, the oily and pocked complexion of his face.

He sickens her because not only is he repulsive to look at, but what's inside him does not even seem human. He's an unappealing shell with a reptile inside that's waiting to be born.

"Why don't you take a picture," Madelyn says. "It'll last longer."

Skunk is not in the least bit offended by this. He grins and it's a perfectly vile sight. "I'd like to have a picture," he tells Bonnie. "I'd like that a lot."

"What a fucking creep," Madelyn says.

Skunk bristles. He might be a creep, but he doesn't like people calling him one. Even he, apparently, has his standards.

"Why don't you mind your own business, bitch?"

"Why don't you crawl back in the sewer you came from, you fucking worm," Madelyn tells him.

"Slimy little piece of shit," Lynn says.

"Don't be too hard on him," Elaine tells them. "He hasn't had a good piece of ass since his sister moved away."

Bonnie can't help herself—she starts laughing.

"Is there something else, worm?" Madelyn asks.

Thoroughly used and abused, Skunk points a finger at her as if he's about to give her the mother of all lectures, then he starts giggling and from where Bonnie's sitting, that's even worse. He giggles the way a pervert would when he gets some little kid in his car. Still chuckling to himself, he goes into the back room.

Oh, this isn't over, Bonnie thinks. *That sonofabitch is far from done.*

"That's enough, I'm leaving," Elaine announces. She looks at Madelyn and Lynn. "Are you coming with me or not? If we put some hustle in our bustle, the four-wheel drive on my Wrangler might just get us home."

She gets no arguments. They are leaving and that is that. Both Bonnie and Carpy try again to dissuade them, but it's strictly no-go. There's nothing they or anyone else can say to stop them. Skunk watches from the back room, still smiling that awful dead grin. He isn't going to try to stop them because, of course, they've insulted him, and he wants to thin the herd. Each and every one he can get out of the way is one more that will not get between him and Bonnie.

Bonnie knows this.

She need only look in his pig's eyes for validation. He's making very, very little attempt to hide his lust or his terrible desperation. He's a starving man and she's a juicy joint of meat. The shit Madelyn and the girls gave him drove him off for a time, but he's still over there biding his time and watching: a starving wolf in the darkness circling a campfire, waiting for a straggler to sink his teeth into.

And Bonnie knows who the straggler is.

57

She tries everything but begging to get the girls to stay, but Madelyn and particularly Elaine are adamant that it's time to go. They have broken no laws. They have committed no crimes. The sheriff cannot hold them.

"He can hold you as a material witness," Carpy says, quoting something he probably saw on an old movie.

Bonnie rather doubts there's any truth to it. Still, it stays the girls for a moment or two. They keep trying to call their husbands or boyfriends, refusing to accept that there is no cell service. They are thoroughly modern in this respect. Like most, they are as helpless as guppies out of water without instant communication. This is chaos. The end of times.

Madelyn keeps shaking her head back and forth. "I can't believe we can't get anything," she says, feeling her perceived social status crumbling around her.

"People survived for thousands of years without those things," Carpy points out. "I'm willing to bet you'll make it a few hours without Face-fuck-ing-Book."

Despite the tension that winds her in steel bands, Bonnie nearly bursts out laughing. It's one of the most intelligent things she's ever heard him say.

Madelyn says nothing. She looks hurt. She stares at her phone, teary-eyed, like a little girl with a broken toy.

Elaine, however, simply looks angry. "It doesn't make any sense and you know it. No bars, no reception, no nothing. It's crazy. It's like living in the Middle Ages."

Carpy chuckles. "Look on the bright side. Think of how happy them Facebook people are gonna be when they don't have to hear about what you had for supper tonight, what fucking movie you watched, or look at pictures of how cute your dog is when it's sleeping."

Madelyn looks like she's been slapped. It's as if something revelatory has just occurred to her. You trying to say people really don't care about these things? The very idea is staggering to her.

Her friend Lynn says, "This is worse than the Middle Ages. It's…it's like living in dinosaur times."

Bonnie tries not to let her mouth hang open too much, knowing full well that phones are much smarter than people these days. Did she really just say that? Dinosaur times? Bonnie is fairly certain there is no geological time period known as that.

"Wish they'd get back already," Carpy says.

Whether he means Nathan and Peanut or Teague and Clyde, he does not say. Probably all of the above.

"And what if they don't?" Lynn asks.

The question draws Skunk right in. "Then we stand together," he proclaims, staring at Bonnie. "We keep watch together and we keep each other company."

He practically drools as he says this.

Bonnie gets the drift all right and understands the innuendo just fine. She steps calmly behind the bar and draws herself a Coke on ice. As she sips it, she slides open a drawer and removes a paring knife used for slicing fruit and cheese during football games.

Try it, you piece of shit, she thinks, giving Skunk a hard look. Just try it and I'll slide this right in between yer balls.

Whether Skunk catches her ire or not is unknown; he just keeps staring at her as if his eyes are painted on. He's not the brightest guy in the world and subtlety is totally lost on him. He's never been any good with girls, at least the ones that matter. He stares, he ogles, he drools. He's like a twelve-year-old with his first real hard-on.

Bonnie doesn't bother trying to hold her death-stare. Skunk is too stupid. He probably thinks she's lusting after him. If he didn't disgust her so much, she would have laughed. In her experience, the ones that stare think they're real studs when just the opposite is true.

Only piece of ass he probably ever got was off some biker tramp or his own mother.

"Well, this has been fun and all," Madelyn says, pulling on her coat, "but if we're going to get going, then we need to move on that, or we'll be snowed in." She looked to Lynn and Elaine. "What say?"

They begin pulling on their coats, hats, and gloves. It's obvious what they want to do. This has gone far enough, and they've had more than their fill.

Carpy shakes his head. "Sheriff ain't going to like it. He ain't going to like it at all."

Madelyn rolls her eyes. "Yeah, and who died and made him God?"

"But we have wounded people here," Bonnie says, the look in Skunk's eyes making her feel very, very desperate for company.

"And we have families out there," Elaine tells her. "We can't contact them. We don't know what's going on. We don't even know if they're alive. So sorry, but we are leaving. That's just the way it is."

Skunk giggles. "You tell her, baby."

There's not a damn thing Bonnie can do about it and she knows it. It's soon going to be Carpy, her, and the wounded. And Skunk. She's going to have to deal with him whether she likes the idea of it or not. What that comes down to is that she will have to use the knife. Problem with that is that Skunk is no stranger to violence. If the stories that Bonnie has heard are true, then old Skunk has been in more than one knife fight. He knows how to handle himself, which means that unless she strikes fast and deadly, he will probably get the blade away from her. And if he does that—something which will probably turn him on—then he'll probably cut her a few times, then press it to her throat while he rapes her.

Sheriff…Clyde…Nathan…Peanut, she thinks, *please hurry back. Oh, please please please…*

As Madelyn and the others file out the door into the snow and the frozen blackness of night, Skunk watches them leave. Then he turns back and looks again at Bonnie.

And smiles.

58

As it turns out, Teague and Clyde are the first ones back. They come through the front door, dragging Stew between them who's like a living ice sculpture. Though they do not see it, the relief on Bonnie's face is a thing to behold, a positive angelic glow. They get Stew into one of the booths and Carpy swings into action, despite the fact that he's been hitting the Jim Beam pretty hard and he's about three bricks shy of a full load. He covers Stew with a blanket. Bonnie brings over a steaming mug of coffee.

Under the circumstances, it's the best they can do.

Bonnie looks into Sheriff Teague's eyes. "Brenda?" she asks in a low voice.

He shakes his head. As to whether that means they couldn't find her or she's dead, he does not say.

Stew thaws slowly.

He shivers uncontrollably, mumbling between sips of coffee but saying nothing really coherent. His teeth chatter like those of a Halloween skeleton.

Teague and Clyde sip coffee, too.

"No Peanut yet?" Teague asks.

Carpy shakes his head. "Not yet."

Teague doesn't like it. There's precious little he does like this night, but his deputy and Nathan Free not returning with Tony Russo is bad, real bad. Without a doubt, a cruel turn of events.

"Never seen a fucking storm like that," Clyde says, snow gone to water dripping from his heavy black mustache. "You can get lost in it, freeze to death in it. Storm of the fucking century. Swear to God, you get out in it, it's like it's plotting against you."

Carpy looks like he's going to say something, maybe comment on how crazy the very idea of that is, but he keeps his mouth shut. Clyde Taggert scares him as he scares a lot of people, so he keeps his opinions to himself.

Teague smiles. So that's what it takes to shut up Carpy. Noted. Then the smile fades from his lips. He looks around. "Where's Madelyn and her friends?"

Bonnie and Carpy look at each other.

"They left," Bonnie says.

"In this?" Teague snaps at her. "They'll die out there!"

Carpy looks panicked. "We tried to stop them, Will, both me and Bonnie did, but they wouldn't listen. They just wouldn't listen."

Teague wants badly to rail at both of them, but he knows that ultimately, it's not their fault. He suspected something like that would happen, but that doesn't make it any better.

Clyde gets to his feet and makes a beeline for Skunk. "I told you to watch things while I was gone. I trusted you to do that."

Skunk shivers in Clyde's shadow. He goes in at around 250 with a gut on him, but he's tough and ruthless by nature. But that's nothing in comparison to Clyde who's closer to 300, 6'5, with not a scrap of fat on him. He's made a career of intimidation with the physical skills to back it up. In prison, he beat several hardcore cons nearly to death, shanked several others, and killed another with a lead pipe... though all these offenses were witnessed by others, nobody dared rat him out.

"There was nothing I could do," Skunk says.

Which is about all he gets out before Clyde backhands him and puts him to his knees.

"All right!" Teague says. "That's enough."

It's only the intervention of the law that saves Skunk from a first-class beating.

Teague notices that Bonnie seems to enjoy Skunk's predicament a little too much and wonders what the hell that's about. Before any of it can be investigated further, Stew begins to talk.

"...out there...heard her... she screamed," he mumbles, but not so softly that the others can't hear him. "It was her... I know it was her, I know it."

"Just try to relax," Bonnie tells him, but it's like telling a man who just lost his arm that he'll feel better in the morning.

Stew shakes his head back and forth. "She was everything to me," he says. "I know how she could get, and I know a lot of you didn't like her because of her mouth… but she was the world to me."

Teague doesn't know what to say.

He feels badly about it. If there was any earthly way he could have found Brenda, he would have. But the storm was just beyond reason. A man—or woman—couldn't survive in it for long. He can only hope she found shelter.

"It called her, it called her out into the blizzard," Stew says. "And she answered."

"Who did?" Carpy asks.

But Teague knows—a clown, a goddamn clown called her out there. He knows this just as he knows he will never see her again or hear her vicious tongue. He looks at Stew and feels a lump in his throat. Stew won't survive long without her. The nature of their relationship has long baffled him. Stew was barely an individual under her yoke. He was part of her, an extra thumb, a vestigial limb, but certainly not an independent entity. Without her, he will not exist at all. That is the fact of the matter. He's already a ghost.

Though in Teague's opinion, Brenda Prechek is a hag of the first order, not just a motormouth but a goddamned chainsaw-mouth, he feels bad for Stew. The man is already lost, already afraid of being alone without his wife's guiding hand and razor-tongue. He's confused. Scared. Helpless.

And Teague's not feeling much better himself. Where the hell are Peanut and Nathan? The longer they're gone, the more desperate and worried he becomes. A voice in the back of his head keeps nagging at him——and justifiably so, he decides——that he needs to do something here, come up with a plan, do anything but take action because these people are counting on him and he has wounded here and he's the fucking sheriff. But the more it nags, the less he seems to be able to come up with a thing. He has no motivation. It seems that whichever way he turns, he runs into a wall.

We're trapped here, just like Clegg said. Can't get out. No one can get in. Stills and Wegley are out there, but they can't get to us. Peanut's fucking gone. This entire situation is going to shit, and it feels like I'm holding it together with spit and hope.

As Bonnie pushes in closer to him, a question on her mind, he pictures Craw Falls in his mind like one of those snow globes: pretty little town, you shake it, the snow falls and falls. Outside, the wind becomes a shrill scream that shrieks into the night.

"What are we going to do, Sheriff?" Bonnie says, airing her question.

Teague swallows, wondering the same thing himself.

The blizzard has this shithole locked up tight and the clowns have themselves a private hunting preserve. By morning, you'll have dozens dead. All those pretty little houses lined up out there and all of them nothing but meat lockers.

"Christ," Teague says out loud, remembering Clegg's words.

"Sheriff?"

Now they're all watching him.

He swallows again and says, "We're going to give Peanut and Nathan ten more minutes, then you and I, Clyde, are going over to the station house. There's someone there we're going to need."

Trapped in the belly of the monster that is Craw Falls, it's about the only thing they can do, he figures.

"Ten minutes," he reiterates, "then we go."

Bonnie looks at him with wide terrified eyes and behind his back, Skunk grins hungrily.

59

Tony Russo is liking this shit less and less by the moment. These two buffoons—Peanut and goddamn Nathan Free, cop and outlaw biker of all things—kick in his door, beat down his wife, and ever since, things have been going downhill. He keeps thinking of old man Peel hanging from the door, all this ranting about clowns.

Clowns for god sake.

Nathan and Peanut lead him back out into the storm. What sense does it make for him to be traipsing about on a night like this with killer clowns on the loose? Shouldn't he be home, trying to protect Midge?

The idea of that nearly makes him giggle because if there's one woman in the world that is no shrinking violet and definitely not in the need of protection, it's Midge. Still...

Soon as they're out of old man Peel's house—Oh, Jimbo, Jesus Christ, poor Jimbo—the storm reaches out for them, finds them, and pulls them into its body. The snow cycles around them in frosty white whirlwinds and the cold bites into them. It's no night to be out legging it, even if only to a waiting vehicle. Even mere feet ahead of him, Nathan and Peanut's forms become gray, shadowy masses that seem to lack substance. They are ghosts haunting the blizzard.

Tony forces that from his mind because if there's one thing he doesn't want to be thinking of on a wild, windblown night like this it's ghosts. Because whenever he thinks of ghosts, he thinks of the war, the first Gulf War, that is. He was a medic with the 24th Infantry Division. Outside Basra, a gunner named Keeland got wasted. Everybody liked Keeland. But nobody liked him better than Toby Woods, his best friend. Within hours following Keeland's death, Toby started getting funny. He started speaking with Keeland's slow Southern drawl, mimicking his somewhat crude sense of humor, and even smoking his cigarettes (Toby had never smoked in his life). It was weird. It was eerie. They took him away for psychiatric evaluation and that was the last anyone saw of Toby Woods. But by then, half the guys in the platoon were convinced that Toby was possessed by Keeland's ghost.

The memory of it still gives Tony a chill.

When they get over to Peanut's SUV, which is still running, they pile in and luxuriate in the warmth for a few seconds before they start rolling.

"I don't know what the hell Teague thinks I'm going to be able to do," Tony says.

Nathan looks over the seat at him. "Yer a medic, ain't you?"

"Was, Nathan. Was. That was a long time ago. If we don't have any medical supplies, there's not gonna be much I can do."

"Well, you got to try."

"Shit," Tony says.

Peanut stays out of it. He's having enough trouble just piloting the SUV through the storm. Even in four-wheel drive, it's fighting him, slipping and sliding, fishtailing and having a hell of a time punching through some of the drifts, many of which are higher now than a man's hip. And still the snow comes, driven by raw cycling winds, the headlights filled with spinning flakes. The wipers can barely keep the windshield clean.

Ain't natural, Tony thinks, *a storm like this. It just ain't natural.*

And it's as he thinks this that a voice drifts into his mind that he's never heard before, a very melodic fairy tale sort of voice that reminds him of his kindergarten teacher, Mrs. Bisbee, who always had such a fine, comforting voice. As a boy, her voice made him feel safe. She would always read them a story before nap time. Funny that he should be thinking of that now. The last thing he feels right now is safe. But in his head the voice keeps speaking and the more it speaks, the more it sounds like Mrs. Bisbee and the more Tony begins to relax.

"You talking to yourself back there?" Nathan asks him, but he does not answer because suddenly the SUV and who's in the front seat seem like they're a million miles away, phantoms from some other place, some other world.

Tony hears Nathan Free again and he tries to get his mouth to answer him, but it won't. It's as if someone else has commandeered his brain and he has no power over anything. The blizzard has wound him up in a soft white cocoon and all he has to do is accept it. Relax, Tony, you're not alone. We're here with you and we'll keep you safe. Just close your eyes and go with the flow, the voice tells him. He shakes his head back and forth because something inside him, perhaps survival instinct, tells him this is not right, that it is dangerous.

But try as he might, he cannot nullify the voice that speaks on and on.

"Jesus Christ," he whimpers, realizing that he can no longer hear anything but the voice, not even the sound of the storm. It's all gone as if it never was. He's in a vacuum with the voice. There's only the two of them and he's scared, even though Mrs. Bisbee assures him there's nothing to be scared of.

Just listen to me, Tony. Listen to my words. You know you can trust me because I always have the best interests of my pupils at heart.

Yes, yes, this is true. She was always so good, and he knows that she is good now. Much better than Peanut or that animal Nathan.

Once upon a time, the voice says in his mind, *there was a most terrible, awful storm, with fierce winds and blowing snow, and a poor little boy named Tony found himself lost in it. It was the most dreadful of situations. What was Tony to do? Where was he to go? Shaking in the cold, he looked all around him and there was nothing but the horrendous storm to all sides, closing in on him. He knew he must get home to his mother and sister who were waiting for him in the warm kitchen where a fine pot of hot soup simmered on the hearth and bread fresh from the oven waited to be sliced.*

But how to get there?

What must he do?

He knew he must not panic. He need only put one foot in front of the other. All journeys begin with a single step. Just a single step...

Tony's not sure where the voice is coming from, but he knows he can trust it. What he cannot trust is the men in the SUV. He's back with them again and Nathan is yelling at him, only his words make no sense and that's because they are vile, hateful words...lies. Yes, Nathan is spouting lies and he must not listen to such filth.

"Stop!" Tony shouts at Peanut. "Stop right now! Hurry! You have to stop! YOU HAVE TO STOP RIGHT NOW!"

Peanut looks back at him. "What the hell are you talking about?"

But Tony shakes his head back and forth. He must have a reason. A good reason. A reason they will accept. "I'm... I'm... I'm sick! Stop! Let me out! Hurry! I'm going to throw up!"

"Oh, what the fuck?" Nathan says.

Peanut slows the SUV because the last thing he wants is to have to clean vomit out of the back. He slows to a stop, the tires crunching through the snow.

Tony fumbles the door, gets it open, and falls out into the night. On his hands and knees in a drift, he looks up at the men that get out of the vehicle. They are bad men. He cannot remember their names.

"Just go away!" he says. "Just leave me alone!"

He tenses as they close in on him.

60

By the time Stan Barbacek makes it to the Sheriff's Office, he's nearly delirious—from the cold, the night, and what he has seen. Inside his head, it's all mixed up like voices trying to out-scream one another: the clown in the road, the empty plow truck, and what he saw at Taxi-a-Go-Go. He stands before Patti Wayland, blathering on about it all and what disturbs him most is that she does not seem to be as surprised as she should be.

"Now, Stan," she finally says, "just slow down. You're not making sense."

Snow melting off him, he breathes in and out really fast as if he's hyperventilating. "I'm telling you what happened. I'm telling you what I saw. I'm telling you I need help right goddamn now."

Patti is making a concerted effort to remain calm. That much is obvious. She is logging everything Stan says, regardless of how crazy it is.

Stan sits down across from her, then decides he doesn't like how close the chair is to the window. He gets back up, paces back and forth, tries to get control of himself. It's not easy.

"I don't have time for this," he finally says. "Where's the sheriff? I need to see him. I need to see him right now."

"He's out. He'll be back soon."

"You better call him."

Patti hesitates, wondering how she's going to do this, then she gets on the radio, trying again and again to get Teague. She gets nothing but static.

"It's this storm," she says.

Stan shakes his head from side to side. "We're in trouble. I think we're all in trouble."

"Go through it one more time," she tells him.

"Flo Hemminger is dead," he says. "That's all that matters. I saw her body. And I saw the thing that killed her." He takes the Apeman camera out of his parka. "I got it on video. I got it all."

Now Patti gives him a funny look, even funnier than the ones she's been giving him since he came in. "You filmed it?"

"I knew nobody would believe me! But this—" he held up the camera "—does not lie."

"A clown killed her?"

"Isn't that what I said?"

"It's just that... it's weird."

He utters a short bark of laughter. "Yeah, Patti, I know it's fucking weird. If you want weirder, I can let you see the video right now."

"No," she says.

That's how he knows she more or less believes him. The look on her face tells him that she'd rather peek into her own grave than look at what he's got on the camera. Anything but that.

She tries Teague again and again gets nothing.

"Do you know where he is?"

She gives him a cold, hard stare. "Stan, it's this storm. I don't know where anybody is. Jesus Christ, I'm not even sure I know where we are."

Which, in his way of thinking, is the first truly intelligent thing she has said. He looks around nervously, unable to relax. There are things happening out there, terrible things, and all they can do is wait. Jesus. What a situation. The panic inside him is sharp with rising spikes of adrenaline. He wants to move in every direction at once. He wants to run. He wants to hide.

Instead, he pulls out the camera and starts filming, panning around the office of the sheriff.

"What the hell are you doing?" Patti asks him.

"I'm making a documentary."

"About what?"

"About this night and what haunts it."

She shakes her head back and forth. "Listen, Stan, I don't know if Will would want you filming in here..."

But he ignores her, speaking right over her. "This is our situation: the blizzard has us locked in tight and there's no escape from it." He goes over near the window looking out into the night, hoping the mic will pick up that awful moaning sound of the wind. "The clowns are still out there. I'd like to fool myself into a false sense of security by saying they're just a bunch of nuts in face paint and silly costumes with harmless names like Bobo and Chuckles and Town Clown... but it's not true. What is out there, using the storm as camouflage, is not human. Even as I record this, they are stalking their human prey."

"Okay, that's enough," Patti tells him. "Just stop it. Please, Stan."

He steps away from her, filming out the front door into the street where the blizzard is dramatically illustrated by the streetlights that are filled with flying snowflakes. "There is death out there...death beyond human imagination. And tonight, I fear, it will come for each and every one of us in Craw Falls."

"Goddammit, Stan, you knock that off!"

This time, Patti is not asking him, she's ordering him. And from the look in her eyes, she expects compliance.

"It's just for my doc," he explains.

She squints her eyes shut and rubs her temples as if tonight has been more than she can hope to take. "So you're making a documentary about the clowns, eh? Like some kind of found-footage horror flick? Is that what you're doing?"

"In a way."

"That's sick, Stan. Really sick."

He doesn't care what she thinks. In his mind, he's the cameraman now. It's his job to document this. The camera is in his hand and he must use it, he must record what he sees which might be the only tangible record of this terrible night. What he has already captured, he believes, will be as important as the videos of U.S. Marines burning down the villages of poor Vietnamese farmers or the abuses at Abu Ghraib prison. Maybe even as important as the Zapruder film.

Some static comes in on the radio and it draws their attention. It comes in short bursts.

"Hey, maybe that's Teague," Stan says.

Patti does not think so. Her lips feel very dry and she licks them repeatedly. It takes her a few moments to find her voice. "Three, this is dispatch. Go ahead."

Another burst of static. There's nothing out there and she knows it. At least, nothing she wants to know about. Still, Stan looks desperate. About as desperate as anyone she's ever seen.

"Three," she says into the mic, "this is dispatch. Are you reading me? Three?"

Nothing but static.

Patti turns away from the radio. "There's no one out there. No one at all."

The radio crackles again and there is a beeping.

"The emergency channel," she says. "Channel Nine."

More static and then a weird whining sort of noise that is painful to hear.

Stan is filming again. He wants to capture that sound; somehow, he feels it's important. And maybe it is because it's rising now, becoming a piercing shrill that makes him want to cover his ears. Patti looks at him and her eyes are blank. She begins to tremble and shake, vibrating in her seat. Now she is convulsing, her eyes rolled back white. A trickle of bright red blood drips from her right nostril.

Stan moves quickly and shuts the radio off, killing that terrible sound that fills his skull with strange imperatives and his belly with the fluttering wings of birds.

"Patti? Are you all right?"

She blinks a few times. "I...yes... what happened?"

"That sound on the radio, it was doing something to you."

A look of terror mingled with understanding passes over her. "The signal," she says. "It must've been the signal."

61

As the storm sings a song of loss and loneliness outside the house, Midge Russo examines her blackened eye in the bathroom mirror. Her face is pale, and her eye is purple-black, closing up like a clamshell, but under the skin she is molten and hot, a searing mass of hate. An acid bath that could eat the flesh off Nathan Free's bones.

Hit me. He hit me. He goddamn well punched me right in the face, that dirty, stinking wagon-burner, that fucking bush nigger, that——

Midge turns from the mirror because she is no longer seeing herself; no, there is only Nathan's face and that makes her boil like hot molasses.

"You wait, Big Red, you just wait," she thinks, her teeth clenched so tightly her jaws ache. "The time will come. And when it does, God help you."

She walks into the bedroom and sits on the bed, listening to the storm, to the snow blowing against the window like fine sand. The town is going to be buried alive if this doesn't stop and Tony is out there in it with that dumb cop and Cochise. Thinking of Tony only makes her all that much angrier because when Tony discovered her on the floor, knowing that either Peanut or Nathan Free had assaulted her, he got that little smirk on his face which she knew meant he was amused as all hell.

"Little prick," Midge groans under her breath.

Why, a real husband, a real man, was supposed to protect his wife, not get that giggling schoolboy expression on his face when somebody assaulted her. But Tony's a little boy. He has always been a little boy that needs to be told when to eat, when to shit, and when to go to bed. That's the problem with men like him: they charm you with their little boy innocence and naivety, make you fall in love with them, wind you up tight, make you emotionally dependent on them, then... then, they reveal what's underneath, the manipulative, callous beasts they indeed are and have always been. But by then, of course, you're in too deep. And when a woman is in deep, when her feelings and well-being and sense of self-worth are inexorably tied to a man, she will allow herself to be dragged through the mud face-first.

And he has dragged me, she thinks, trying to fight back against the tears that want to come, the tears which are the curse of a proud, independent woman. *Through every stripe of shit he could find.*

A voice in her head whispers that she can leave anytime, but she shoos that away. If she leaves, that's accepting defeat, that she's not woman enough to face the challenge and best it. It's like shouting to the world that she's a quitter, a shriveling weak female, a loser, a nothing.

"A fucking zero," Midge says under her breath. "And I'll never be one of those."

She hears a sound downstairs...something that comes and goes so fast she can't identify what it is. But in her mind, it can only be one thing: Tony. He's come back out of the storm and he'll be full of excuses that she will not want to hear or tolerate. Just the sight of his boyish little pout will make her want to simultaneously take him into her arms and beat the stuffing out of him.

Midge gets to her feet.

Her heart is beginning to pound, her muscles bunching, her back up. Oh, that little sonofabitch is in for it but good this time. She moves slowly and resolutely down the hallway, pausing at the top of the stairs. She listens for him. He'll be in the kitchen getting a beer. Doesn't matter that he just came out of a blizzard, he'll still want a beer. He always wants a beer. That's the sort of man he is.

She waits, cocking her head.

Odd, but she hears nothing down there.

This makes her feel at once disappointed and uneasy. The former because she's gotten herself worked up for nothing and the latter because...well, because if Tony didn't make that sound down there, then what did?

Sighing mostly to calm herself, she starts down the stairs, realizing that she's becoming steadily unnerved by the sound of the storm outside and the eerie quality of the silence inside. The stairs seem to be endless. She hears a sound about halfway down and pauses again.

Jingle, jingle, jingle.

Of all the things she could have heard, this was possibly the worst. A harmless sound, yes, but one that seems charged with dread import. Bells. The sound of bells. But there are no little tinkling bells in the house. She hears it again and goes stiff with fear. It reminds her of the sound a dog might make if it had bells on its collar.

But like there are no bells, there are no dogs in the house.

There's just you, she tells herself, completely alone and completely helpless.

Which is bullshit. Midge fears no one, not really. She's a tough woman (at least on the outside) and she knows how to use her fists. Still, as much as she tries to toughen herself up, she realizes that inside she's trembling. Her mouth has gone so dry that she cannot even moisten her lips.

Jingle, jingle, jingle.

Before her nerve completely abandons her, she forces herself to climb down the rest of the stairs. At the bottom, there's only silence—heavy, pregnant with dread. That's crazy. She knows it's crazy, but that's the image that sticks in her head, roosts there, nests there: that the silence is pregnant. Like something from a book, something you must have read somewhere. But telling herself that does nothing to ease her terror which by that point is like some monstrous conjoined twin riding her back. She can almost feel its cold fingers winding around her throat.

"Tony?" she calls out in a weak little voice because she has to do something, anything, to break the fucking awful stillness. "Tony are you here?"

She knows he is not. One thing Tony is not is quiet or stealthy; when he's in the house, the TV's blaring, the microwave is beeping, cupboards and drawers are slammed, the house filled with his lumbering presence. He is not here.

Yet, a strain of optimism makes her try again: "Tony?"

The only response is that same noise again.

Jingle, jingle, jingle.

Midge nearly cries out at the sound of it. She does not believe in ghosts as such, but she is quite certain at that moment that there is something enormously unnatural in the house, something possibly even supernatural.

Breathing fast now, caught between the real need to run back upstairs and the desire to stand her ground and sort out whatever has dared invade her domicile, she stands there quaking with fear. She tries to explain it away and send it packing, but it clings to her. It is huge and irrational, even omnipotent.

Do something, do anything.

She tries to tell herself that she's Midge Russo. That she's taken down men twice her size, that once it took two cops to drag her out of the Whistle Stop when she had a good package on and got into a fist fight with not only that whore Sherri McClean, but her piss-mouthed ex-con boyfriend. That's the person she is, and she takes no shit.

This actually works for a moment or two until she hears that damn jingle, jingle, jingle again and a vein of white fear opens up inside her, making her heart seize momentarily and a blaze of heat expand in her chest.

By then, she has stepped into the living room and there's something on the floor, something which might be perfectly harmless were it somewhere else besides the floor next to Tony's recliner.

She sees it, trembles, takes a step back, perhaps hoping it might go away as ice-cold sweat runs from her pores.

62

As the bad men come for him, Tony scrambles to his feet in the snow and runs. He knows what they want, and he knows what they are. He must not let them get him.

"TONY!" he hears Nathan Free shout. "TONY! WHAT THE FUCK ARE YOU DOING?"

Tony keeps running, stumbling through the snow deeper into the blizzard. *Don't listen! Don't listen! They just want to get you in their car!*

"TONY!" This time it's Peanut.

Tony keeps charging, plowing through drifts, slipping, sliding, falling over and getting up again. And when his boots can't get a grip, he crawls. Forward momentum is the thing and he knows it. Whatever else might happen this dreadful night, he must keep going so the bad men do not get him.

"GODDAMMIT, TONY!" Nathan Free's voice wails off in the storm, seeming to come from some distant, windblown world. But the words he actually hears are quite different: "GET BACK HERE, BOYYYYYYY! WE GOT TREATS FOR YOU! WE'LL GIVE YOU CANDY! LOTS AND LOTS OF CANDY!"

As Tony scampers through the snow, covered in it like some frightened hare, he knows what the bad men will do to him. Candy. Lots and lots of candy. That's what they always promise. Tony saw it in a safety film at school—they offer candy to get you in their long black cars where they do awful things to you, terrible, terrible things that will warp you forever. Perverts. Perverts. Tony knows very well. When they get you in there—the other kids told him—they make you touch their wieners and sometimes, sometimes, they make you put their wieners in your mouth because that's what perverts do.

Don't let 'em get you, Tony! the voice in his head warns him. *You need to get home where it's safe! Where they can't touch you!*

He keeps going because he must keep going. That's the thing. In fact, it's the only thing. Nothing else matters and nothing else exists in the cramped, distorted little world of Tony Russo where a grown man has suddenly acquired the mind he had when he was seven years old. How this could be, he does not question because he has no idea that it has even happened.

What is, is what is.

There's nothing but now.

The voices of the bad men are still calling from the storm; they will not give up easily. They are wolves that come in the night for meat. And now that they have smelled it, they will stop at nothing to get it.

Tony cuts down an alley, crawls beneath a truck on the other side of the street and waits there, buried in snow. They will not find him. They will not know where he is. If they want him, they will have to dig him out and he will escape.

Now the voices are gone.

Tony is alone.

There is only the howling, blowing voice of the storm. It manages to sound both lonesome and hungry at the same time. He knows if he hides here he will freeze. Carefully, he digs his way out. There is no sign of the bad men. The world is pure devastation. Snow is cycling down from the sky, piling up, drifting in white waves. The wind seems to have a voice. In fact, it has many voices and the longer he stands there, the more he can hear them calling out to him.

No!

He must get home. Home to his mom and his sister and the hot soup and warm bread. Home where things are safe, and he will not have to worry about the bad men. He knows the way. Despite the blizzard, he knows exactly how to get there, and he will let nothing stop him.

"I'm coming, Mom. I'm coming."

That's a good, good boy, Mrs. Bisbee's voice says in his mind. *She'll be waiting for you with wonderful surprises. Hurry! Hurry now!*

Tony needs no further prompting. He moves off into the storm, Mrs. Bisbee's voice guiding the way.

With something akin to pure terror, Midge blinks her eyes, the spit dried up in her mouth.

She cannot speak.

She can only stare at what is on the floor: a gangly limbed clown puppet, sprawled as if it was dropped from high above. It is dressed in a red costume nearly faded to the pink of butcher's paper with age, water-stained and dirty, set with white polka dots that have gone nearly yellow. There are ragged ruffles at the wrists and collar, a choker of tiny bells at its throat.

Midge shakes her head back and forth because this cannot be, it just cannot be.

But it is. The clown puppet's face is the mottled white of a new moon, its nose long and jutting like a carrot, its chin pointy as that of a hag. Its eyes are shiny yellow ovum lacking pupils set in black vertical slashes. Tufts of bushy green hair sprout from the sides of its skull and atop its head there is a witch-like cone hat with orange pom-poms glued to it. It grins with a blackened mouth from which sprout gnarled, overhanging teeth.

Midge stands there, seemingly welded in place. A terror that is hot and sharp moves up from her belly in waves. It runs down her arms and up the back of her neck. It tightens her chest, squeezing her heart.

It can't be here, a voice informs her. *There's no way something like this could be here.*

Yet, it is. But it's just a puppet—she can plainly see the strings attached to the back of its head, its arms and legs, its rump—and it cannot move itself. But she did hear bells and that means someone must have been playing with it or shaking it.

Her skin crawling with gooseflesh, Midge spins around, nearly certain she sensed some malefic hulking shape right behind her. But there is nothing. Nothing at all. Her heart hammering, her scalp feeling suddenly too tight for her skull, she looks this way and that with rising panic, her hair greasy with fear-sweat.

She turns back.

The clown puppet is not on the floor. It is not anywhere. The rocking chair across the room moves back and forth slowly as if someone has just bumped into it. Midge scampers over to the fireplace and grabs a poker, behind her she hears the jingling sound of tiny bells.

"Who's here?" she demands, her voice nearly hysterical in tone. "Who's in my goddamn house?"

Jingle, jingle, jingle.

This time it comes from the dining room. Terrified, panicking, but angry, very angry at her own fear, she dashes in there, clicking on the light. But there's no one to be seen.

A squeaking sound.

She looks up. The flame-shaped bulbs on the chandelier are unscrewing, one after the other. And as they do so, each of them goes out until the dining room is plunged in darkness. With a cry, Midge retreats into the living room. She hears the jingling of bells, then tiny scampering footsteps.

She grabs the cordless off the end table, knocking its base to the floor. She punches in 9-1-1 with a trembling finger and hears only static. "Hello?" she says. "Oh God, is someone there?"

There is a field of static crackling, then a voice, a high-pitched, scratching elfin sort of voice: "Once there was a big fat cunt who was tormented by a little runt! She cried, she screamed, she ran for cover, but the little runt was still above her—"

Midge screamed. "GET OFF THIS LINE! GODDAMN YOU, GET OFF THIS LINE!"

But the little elfin voice carried on and on: "...dangled and dangled by his strings, eager to show her his pretty things! Bend her over, sayeth the runt, make her squeal, make her grunt!"

Midge throws the phone against the wall, backpedaling and falling over the arm of the recliner, her bathrobe opening and exposing her mountainous breasts. In the corner, she can still hear the shrilling voice on the phone. Whimpering, her bare feet sliding on the carpet, she gets to her knees and right away she hears the jingling bells.

The clown puppet is sitting in the rocking chair, rocking back and forth with a slow mechanical sort of cadence. Its mouth is grinning, its hideous teeth even larger. Its cone hat seems to be set atop its head at a rakish angle.

The bells at its throat jingle merrily though nothing whatsoever touches them.

"STOP IT!" Midge cries. "YOU STOP IT RIGHT NOW!"

But the bells continue to jingle.

Filled with a manic, demented rage, she charges the clown, reaching out for it, wanting to get it in her hands where she can crush it and tear it into pieces. Her fingers grasp its body which is soft and boneless, quivering beneath her touch. It makes a guttural noise in its throat.

Then it is yanked away and up.

Held taut by strings which seem to fade into the ceiling tiles, it dances away through the air into the darkness of the dining room. A strident laughter echoes out of the shadows, "Tee-hee, tee-hee, tee-hee…"

Full blown hysteria breaks open inside Midge. She screams at what she has felt, seen, and heard. Drooling and delusional, she goes after the clown puppet, swinging her fireplace poker back and forth in devastating arcs. She knocks a painting off the wall. She shatters an arm of the chandelier. She smashes in the etched glass doors of the china cabinet, sending her grand-mother's herringbone china crashing to the floor along with her collection of depression glass.

But none of this matters.

The only thing that concerns her is the clown puppet, the evil little runt. She has to snap its wires and beat it down, tear it open and yank the stuffing out of it. She swings and swings, out of her mind with rage and horror, bashing and crashing into things, tripping over her own feet and colliding with the dining room table.

And it's at that moment she feels something like a dozen burning hot needles pierce her left ankle right to the bone. The agony makes her fold right up, the poker falling from her hand and rattling on the table.

Making a strained whining sound in her throat, her ankle burning from the bite of the clown puppet, she scrambles about in the dark seeking the poker. She must have it. She needs it or that hellish little moppet will get her, do terrible things to her. It has gone beyond horror now into the realms of pure survival.

Her hand brushes the poker.

Grasps it.

Then the clown puppet lands on her back. It feels much heavier than she could have imagined. She feels its sharp little fingers scraping over the back of her neck. One of its hands tangles in her hair, yanking out strands by the roots. She screams again and it's not so much from the pain but from something phallic and stiff that prods her in the back. She knows what it is because it can only be one thing. As she tries to throw the clown, fighting to her knees, it jabs her repeatedly in the back with it, all the while jabbering that piercing little laugh, "Tee-hee, tee-hee, tee-hee…"

"GET OFF ME!" she shrieks. "GET THE HELL OFF ME!"

Trying to get to her feet, her ankle twisting with agony, she feels the little monster climb her. It jabs her now in the back of the neck with its member which is just as cold and wet as the tongue of a dog.

She screams yet again, contorting and tossing the clown aside, hearing it bounce off the wall. It makes a sort of chittering noise like a raccoon which rises into a squeal of deranged triumph.

Midge crawls out of the dining room with her poker. Her ankle is blazing, but the pain of it seems secondary to the pure terror that envelops her. In the back of her mind, she is aware that she might be insane, that reality as she has always known it has been subverted in the most appalling way.

Ass on the living room rug, she examines her ankle. It has been laid open, blood smeared right up her bare leg. There is a feeling like cold jelly moving in her veins as if the clown's bite is venomous.

Help, she thinks, *I have to get help. I have to get out of here and get some help.*

But here comes the clown puppet again. Like a jester, it performs a joyous and oddly perverse little dance as it moves through the air in her direction, its strings taut and manipulated by hands she cannot see and a mind she cannot know. It glides through the air five feet off the floor with exaggerated steps, gaining on her, ever gaining on her. Its pale mouth is grinning. Overlapping, gnarled teeth jut like those of a rodent. They are yellow and glistening, ropes of drool hanging from its mouth. As it approaches, a black and hairy tongue pokes in and out of its lipless mouth in an obscene imitation of cunnilingus.

Its intentions are quite clear.

Midge knows she cannot let the puppet touch her. If it gets its tongue in her or does worse things, all that is left of her mind will go to a greasy warm suet. She must fight now not just for life but for sanity.

When the clown is four feet away, it launches itself at her like a jumping spider, white hands held out in claws to grip and tear at her.

With a cry, she swings the poker like a baseball bat. The clown makes no attempt to avoid it. It lets out a perfectly awful screeching as the poker hits it, knocking it against the wall. It lands on the end table, then slides down to the floor. It lays there, inert, head bent on its neck, limbs sprawled. As she stares down at it, it is nothing but a toy, a silly stuffed toy.

Midge stands her ground.

She will not be fooled.

She will not be baited in by the little monster.

Her instinct, fully tuned now, will not allow it. She stands there uneasily, her left ankle throbbing painfully. She breathes in and out, practically gasping. Her heart pounds in her chest.

The clown puppet does not move.

Whatever diabolic sort of life there was in it seems to be gone now. There is nothing, no indication that it ever could have moved. She knows if the police—or anyone else for that matter—were to show, her story would sound like pure delirium.

If it wasn't for her ankle, maybe she would even believe it herself.

"Move," she says. "Don't play games with me. I know you can move."

Tangled in its cobweb-like strings, the clown puppet does nothing.

Still Midge waits.

Three minutes that become four and finally five.

It twitched! Didn't you see it? It just twitched!

But she cannot be sure. *Did it move? Did it really move?* Breathing deeply, she limps over to it carefully, quietly, then jabs it with the poker, pressing it to the wall. Still, it does not move. The fireplace, she thinks, the gas fireplace.

Yes, one flick and it will be roaring. The clown caught on the poker's hook, she carries it over to the fireplace. She flicks the switch. The flames rise up.

And the clown puppet moves.

It leaps free of the poker hook with amazing dexterity. Now it is not a harmless toy; it is pure cunning, pure evil. A shrill cry suffocating in her throat, Midge swings at it again as it jumps in her direction...and misses.

It slashes her face, tears at her throat.

The poker is dropped. She seizes the clown puppet and it wriggles in her grip. Its mouth opens wide and she sees a second set of needle-like teeth beyond those that protrude from its mouth. It snarls and spits at her. The grotesque enlarged phallus between its legs pokes her in the ribs.

Now I've got you! Now I've got you!

She will push it into the flames. She will hold it there and watch it burn. The clown puppet, perhaps sensing her intentions, writhes with reptilian gyrations in her hands. It squirms free. But it does not try to escape. It attacks. It bites her knee. Her thigh. Then her hand as she falls over, trying to fend it away. It tears two of her fingers off at the roots.

Midge screams and contorts.

There is no time to search out the poker. It attacks faster and faster, striking like a rattlesnake, nipping and puncturing her, each time ripping out a chunk of flesh. Then it hits her. It is a soft, plush sort of thing. There is no way it can hit her with such impact, but it does. It punches her in the face again and again. Somewhere during the process, she falls to the floor, her other eye blackened, her nose gushing blood, lips split open. Two of her teeth come out in a bloody froth.

She hangs on the edge of consciousness, beaten and bitten, pain-wracked and mindless, sobbing and trying to curl into a ball.

It pushes its lewd face into her own. Its tongue licks her with a stabbing motion, the fine hairs on it abrading her cheeks and lips. At her ear, she feels its hot breath, then it whispers in its wicked, nymph-like voice, "The runt will suck her blood and chew her cherries, stuff her like a goose and make her merry! Up her ass, in it goes! Bury it deep and where it stops, no one knows!"

She is only vaguely aware of what comes next, the horror, the defilement. She sees her world through a haze of blood, her body bunched and agonized.

She is barely even conscious when something like an icicle slides between her ass cheeks and the runt begins its merry romping.

The world of Craw Falls is a white oblivion sculpted by the storm. It is the end of all things and the beginning of others too horrible to contemplate. A howling maelstrom of pure elemental wrath where death is not a metaphor nor an abstraction, but something with form and volume. An organic sentience that stalks you, plots your end, and grins with the bared teeth of a wolf.

Though Peanut feels in his gut that it's a really bad idea to go chasing after Tony, he has little choice as Nathan Free leads the charge.

He stumbles through the merciless innards of the blizzard, calling out for Tony, shivering white inside as the wind seems to yank his voice off into the night and throw it back at him from a dozen disparate locations.

"Tony!" he calls. "Oh, Jesus Christ, Tony, come back!"

He stops every ten hard-fought feet and repeats this, though each time his voice sounds weaker and his determination to go on evaporates a bit more.

The same cannot be said of Nathan Free, the sergeant-at-arms of the Dead Skulls, a legendary head-cracker, ass-kicker, and all-around bad boy in that part of the state. As the storm tries to push him back, he pushes that much harder into it, shouting for Tony that much louder. It's hard to say who is the stronger force of nature, the storm or Nathan.

But he's moving too fast.

"Nathan!" Peanut cries.

One second, Nathan is just ahead of him, a gray and blurring shape against the blowing snow, and the next, he is swallowed by it.

"Nathan!" Peanut shouts. "Nathan! Wait!"

But Nathan is gone and Peanut, in the back of his mind, is certain that the storm has separated them on purpose. This is exactly the scenario he fears the most: not clowns from hell so much as being alone in this godawful blizzard. There is something weird and otherworldly about it. It's filled with wild flying shapes and darting shadows. It throws snow in your face and sends subzero fingers up your spine. It howls like a pack of slavering dogs and moans like the spirits of the dead haunting an empty house.

"NATHAN! GODDAMMIT, NATHAN!"

But it's pointless; Nathan is gone and maybe, just maybe, the storm wants it this way. Still, to his credit, Peanut fights forward, all the time wondering if he'll ever be able to find the county SUV again. He pushes on and on until he's tripped up by a four-foot drift and planted on his face. He fights to his knees, brushing snow from his face. As it melts from his body heat, the cold crystallizes it on his eyebrows and mustache. He tries to get to his feet and the wind knocks him on his ass.

He feels like sobbing.

There's no strength left in his limbs, no willpower in his soul. He's done, used up. This goddamn blizzard has sucked the blood from his veins. What is left behind is a man who is weak and unsure.

Which is why you'll never be like Nathan or Clyde, a taunting voice tells him. *You have no real fortitude, no inner reservoir of strength. You lack self-confidence and self-esteem. You're passive and spineless. All your life you've wanted things, but you've been afraid to take them. Guys like you will always be sucking mud on the bottom instead of swimming the clear waters at the top.*

The voice drones on and on, tapping him, draining him dry until there is nothing left. He sits there in the drift, failing on every conceivable level. Borderline hypothermic, nothing makes sense. Everything is confused, muddled. He knows if he does not get up now, it's all over with——he'll die out here.

Though there is no strength in his core, he rises on trembling legs, weak as a colt, teetering in the wind.

Just lay down, the voice says. *Lay in the soft white blanket of the snow. It'll be easy. The end will be gentle and peaceful like going to sleep.*

"No," he mutters. "No."

Trust me. I know best.

But he will not lay down and he will not give up. He doesn't know what keeps fighting on inside him, but it pushes him forward into the storm relentlessly.

The voice fades in his mind, then rises up into a screech of cheated hatred.

Peanut calls out weakly for Nathan, for Tony, for anybody. He tries to think of what Will Teague would do (as he does quite often when he's in a tight spot). Teague once told him flat out that he was no good as a cop. And when Peanut asked him why he kept him on, Teague simply said, "Because, son, sometimes in the weakest of men, there is the strongest of hearts." It was said with a sort of quiet admiration and Peanut has never forgotten it. When he's feeling low—like now—he remembers it.

He has faith in you. Don't let him down.

Now Peanut moves faster, his stride determined, his voice so loud when he calls out that it nearly shatters icicles hanging from roof lines. "NATHAN! NATHAN, WHERE THE HELL ARE YOU?"

He trudges on, thinking for a moment he hears a voice, but the storm is so loud it will not register. He pushes forward through a curtain of snow and this time he does hear a voice.

In fact, it calls his name: "Peanut."

65

He turns and there is someone standing ten feet away right between two parking meters where the snow swirls and flies, obscuring everything. The form blurs, becomes indistinct, then solidifies.

It's a clown.

It stands there in a baggy jumper of red and green diamonds that flap in the wind like a flag. Its huge white hands are held out, fingers twitching. Orange wiry hair grows from its pale, balding cranium. Huge yellow eyes set in black ovals watch Peanut. It grins with a mouthful of long sharp teeth. They are silvery and glistening like galvanized nails. As its grin widens, trails of brilliant red blood seep from the corners of its lips.

"Tonight, Peanut," it says with a hollow, reverberating voice like a whisper echoing down a pipe, "we'll kill you all. We'll kill you in your beds and in the streets and in your houses. By the time we're done, there will not be one living soul left in this shithole. Do you believe that, Peanut? Do you?"

As an inescapable sense of doom settles over him, Peanut believes what the clown says. The only other thing he believes in on this terrible night is the 9mm that he has deftly drawn from its holster without even really thinking of doing so. But there it is, in his hand, filling it. He grips it tightly, raises it swiftly, and pops three rounds directly into the clown.

At that range, he can hardly miss, and he doesn't.

Two of the slugs drill through the clown's chest, making it jump with each impact, but it's the third that really causes damage: the clown leaps up, shrieking with the awful metallic sound of a grinder biting into aluminum plating. It's the sound of agony and rage. It cycles up into a shrill whining that breaks apart in the wind.

By then, the clown is down in the snow, shuddering as blood black as waste oil gushes from the hole in its throat and splashes from its mouth as it tries to speak or growl.

Although the sight of it is enough to turn his stomach over and over again, Peanut feels a sense of satisfaction that he has mortally wounded this fucking monster, put it down in the way it needed putting down.

He carefully approaches it. Couple in the head, he tells himself. That will finish it.

But as he gets closer, the clown begins to change, not into something more horrible, but into something that makes Peanut feel weak in the pit of his belly.

"Oh no... oh no," he mutters. "Oh Christ..."

Lying in the snow is not some demon clown, but a woman that he recognizes: Bonnie Faust from the Broken Bottle. Like many men in town, he has admired her for years, seductive but distant, attractive but unapproachable. Now she lays in the snow bleeding out. There's so much blood. She looks like a French fry dipped in ketchup. Her body jerks with convulsions, fingers scratching in the red snow.

"Oh, Bonnie," Peanut whimpers. "I'm so sorry... I thought... I thought..."

She breathes with a horrible gurgling sound, opening and closing her mouth like a gulping fish, blood bubbling out. It's at this point that Peanut, in his distress, realizes that she's wearing the same outfit she had on at the Broken Bottle: jeans and a hoodie. Hardly the sort of thing you'd brave a blizzard with.

"Peanut," she says, holding out a hand to him. "Help me..."

Absolutely broken by the idea that he has just shot down an innocent woman, his thought processes are confused and random. The inconsistencies of what he is seeing do not occur to him. There is only dreadful self-realization that he has murdered Bonnie.

He stumbles over to her and seconds before he would have gripped her outstretched hand, a form leaps out of the storm and knocks him aside.

"PEANUT!" it cries. "GET THE FUCK AWAY FROM IT!"

The voice belongs to Nathan Free who has the riot gun from the SUV in his hands. He's aiming it right at Bonnie of all things. Except, it isn't Bonnie, of course. What it really is, is hard to say. Not a clown any more than it was a woman in a hoodie and jeans out in the storm of the century. It is a flaccid, flowing thing, rubbery and melting like hot wax. It begins to shriek with that metallic unearthly wailing again, the Bonnie mask it wears elongated into a fright mask with gaping eye sockets, a fissured face, and a ragged, howling mouth that opens wide as a soup bowl.

Peanut, down in the snow, shakes his head from side to side, completely overwhelmed by what he is seeing. A sound comes from his mouth that is partly a scream and partly mad laughter.

As the thing that was Bonnie begins moving with a boneless sort of spiraling/corkscrewing, Nathan Free fires on it with the riot gun. He puts a hole bigger than a dinner plate through it and the effect of that is instantaneous: the Bonnie-clown horror begins changing. As burning plumes of rancid steam blow from it like hot geysers, it shifts and moves, bends and sways, becoming many things but nothing in particular. And all of this within a matter of seconds.

Nathan Free is certain it is splitting like a cell.

Peanut thinks what he sees is only a shell; that there is something far worse beneath.

Regardless, it stands up on a dozen rubbery B-movie monster legs—pink and warty stalks—and begins to slash out at Nathan with a curious collection of thrashing limbs. Some look like sickles and others like the Grim Reaper's scythe.

Nathan does not back down.

He sights in on what he figures is the thing's head, a bifurcated swelling mass at its top that writhes with wormy growths. He jerks the trigger and it vanishes in a pink-and-gray meat spray that paints the drifts in multicolored hues. Then the monster drops into the snow, it shakes and shudders, goes still. It begins to blacken like a dead insect, curling up, becoming something else which must be its natural form.

But whatever that is, Peanut does not see because Nathan yanks him to his feet and drags him away into the night.

Over at the Broken Bottle, things are tense. Clyde wants to get going. He does not like waiting like this. He keeps baiting Sheriff Teague about how they're sitting around and doing nothing while the clowns lay waste to the town. And this is eating at the sheriff.

He's goading him into leaving, Bonnie thinks. *And I'll be left alone here with Carpy, Stew, and the injured...and Skunk.*

And that's unacceptable, really unacceptable.

"Give them a few more minutes," she says because she feels she's got to say something, anything, to stay them.

"We don't have a few more minutes," Clyde says.

"And what are we supposed to do while you're gone? We're not medics. We don't know crap."

"Do your best," Clyde says.

Which is a stupid thing people say when they can't think of anything else and Bonnie knows it. If Clyde wasn't so damn intimidating, she would have told him so, too. But she doesn't. No, she waits there behind the bar, blank-faced, lower lip trembling slightly as Stew makes sobbing sounds deep in his throat and Carpy avails himself of all the liquor, pouring shot after shot down his throat. If Brenda were here, she would have raised holy hell. No matter. Brenda is not there, but Skunk is. He's a predator and he has, of course, already sized up the situation as any good predator will do. Carpy is wasted. Stew destroyed by the loss of Brenda. The others are wounded. That leaves him alone with his prey.

This makes him grin.

Bonnie sees that grin on his face, and it makes her stomach roll over. By God, it's the sort of salivating, hungry look a dog gets when you offer it the remains of your T-bone. She's willing to bet that he has to keep swallowing so the drool will not run down his chin.

Then, nearly without a thought, she says, "Take Skunk with you."

She says this to Clyde who glares at her, thinking one of his Skulls are being disrespected.

"Why?"

"Because I don't like the way he keeps looking at me and I don't trust him not to try something."

As Clyde turns toward him, Skunk suddenly looks very innocent. A stupid what, me? look on his face that's not remotely convincing.

"You bothering her?" Clyde asks him.

"No way, man."

You lying little sonofabitch, Bonnie thinks.

"You keep away from her and keep your hands off her," Clyde warns him. As if to emphasize this, he stabs a finger at Skunk's chest, driving him backwards. "I'm not fucking around. You cause trouble with her, I'll take it out of your hide."

"It's cool, Clyde. It's cool."

Clyde does not look convinced. He towers over Skunk. He is pure menace and certainly not a man to cross. The look he gives Skunk is pure acid and Bonnie is certain that he has beaten Skunk down before and perhaps more than once.

"That goes double for me," Sheriff Teague says. "You got a sheet long as my left arm, boy. You lay a hand on this girl, I'll see you do twenty fucking years. Get me?"

Skunk nods. His eyes shine brightly behind the lenses of his glasses. He smiles with a mouthful of bad teeth. "Got it, Sheriff. No trouble, no trouble."

As soon as the sheriff turns away from him and Clyde does the same, Skunk puts his eyes back on Bonnie. They smolder like hot marbles. His Coke bottle glasses only enhance the effect. Lots of people wear them these days, especially women who want to look sexy... but they do not look sexy on Skunk. In fact, they make him look like a slavering child molester.

Bonnie figures that's not too far from the truth.

"We can't wait any longer," Teague says. "We'll be back soon as we can."

Little more is said as they don their parkas, hats, and gloves. Neither of them look at Bonnie as they leave as if they've got bigger fish to fry than her virtue.

Then they're gone and the tension in the bar increases. Bonnie starts brewing coffee. No more booze for Carpy. Maybe if she gets some into him and Stew, they can put up a united front against Skunk. She doesn't believe it, but she has to cling to something.

Anything.

"Well, now we wait," Skunk says, staring at her bosom. "And see what happens."

67

Nathan's starting to think that Peanut is the weak link in his chain. He doesn't like weak links—they have a tendency to snap. And he can't have that. Not with the current situation. It's only Peanut and him out here. They need to be able to count on one another.

These are the sort of thoughts playing through his head as he drags Peanut away from the clown thing. Right now, cool heads and clear thinking is needed and Peanut lacks both.

"But, Nathan," he says, yanking on his arm, "it was Bonnie... I know it was Bonnie. It was a clown, I mean, and then it was Bonnie."

Nathan lets go of him because he's really starting to bug him, but Peanut clings that much tighter to him. It's like they're going to prom together or something. Finally, Nathan shoves him away.

"Listen you idiot," he says. "It wasn't Bonnie. It wasn't anybody. That's all. You didn't shoot a human being. It was one of those clowns. It made you think it was Bonnie same way that other one at the bar wanted us to think it was Leo."

"But... but what are they?"

Nathan shakes his head. "I don't know, man. I just don't know."

It's a question he keeps asking himself. One that doesn't have any good answers. Shape-shifters? Monsters from outer space? Demons? Mutations? Who in the hell knows?

You just better keep your eye on the road ahead, he tells himself, *and worry about that shit later.*

"They got to be something," Peanut declares. "Got to be."

Nathan shrugs.

Peanut looks around fearfully, the snow still falling, curtains of it whipping around them. "They could be all around us."

"Stop that."

"Might be right behind us. Following us."

"Enough," Nathan tells him. "We got to find that SUV. That's first. There's nothing else."

Good thinking. Rational thinking.

Even though he's sergeant-at-arms of the Dead Skulls—which means he keeps the other Skulls in line, handles discipline and infractions of club rules, and is the guy who metes out justice to other clubs and individuals that mess with the Almighty Dead Skull Nation—he's also known by many as the reasonable one of the bunch. The cool head. The thinker. He's the guy you can talk to whether you're just a citizen or a patched member of the club. He's helped people in lots of ways. He's steered his brothers through troubles with the law, their old ladies, even drugs and alcohol.

He takes pride in helping his boys through the hurdles of the outlaw biker lifestyle and has settled countless beefs with the law and the John Qs. He's not the sort to fly off the handle and crack your head for no good reason.

Yet, if Peanut doesn't get his shit together and shut his yap, stop acting like a frightened schoolboy, Nathan is going to hurt him. He's going bitch slap him for starters and kick his teeth out for closers.

And Peanut being a cop...well, that's just not reasonable thinking at all.

The thing is, Nathan's scared, too.

Scared like he's never been before. He's been through the shit—blood wars with other clubs, dope burns, prison rumbles, trouble with the law—but all of those things were known quantities with known limitations. Not like this. This was right off the map. So, he's scared, too. He might not be flaunting it like Peanut, but he is.

Right now, though, the thing is to find that SUV and get back to the Broken Bottle. Clyde isn't going to be happy about them losing Tony. As club president, when he sends you out to do something, he expects it done. Teague's not going to like it much either.

"Shouldn't we have found it by now?" Peanut says.

He's right. When Tony jumped out, they were on 6th Street and that's where they are now. They left the SUV quite near First United Credit Union and now they've passed that particular landmark. So, where is it?

Nathan does not like this at all.

"Maybe someone swiped it," Peanut says.

"Maybe."

They stand there, squinting in the blow, the wind nipping at them. The only thing they can do is make for Central Avenue and leg it over to the Broken Bottle.

"Oh, shit," Peanut moans. "Will is going to be pissed. If I lost another one of his cruisers, he's going to go batshit."

"Another?"

"It's a long story."

Nathan sighs. "It's gone, man. We left it running, lights on. It should have been easy to find. It's gone."

Peanut looks around desperately, probably wondering how he's going to explain this one. Nathan expects him to start whining, but he doesn't. Instead, he says, "Listen."

Nathan only hears the wind. He can't seem to remember a time when he wasn't hearing it.

"Car coming," Nathan tells him.

Yes...except it's more like a truck: a heavy rumbling. But in this? Who the hell would be out driving in this?

"Maybe it's the plow," Peanut suggests.

Now they can see headlights coming down 6th. They're like the luminous eyes of a prehistoric beast coming through fog in some cheap movie. The snow blows and whips in frozen sheets, the wind cutting through them. The lights are closer, closer.

"We'll try and flag 'em down," Nathan suggests.

It's a good idea. Maybe their luck is finally going to change. They step to the side of the street where they'll still be visible but out of harm's way.

"It's coming," Peanut says, noticeably brightening.

It's coming, all right, seeming to pick up speed as it gets closer. Now the lights—high beams—are blazing bright and the driver pours it on, moving faster and faster, way too fast for conditions. The vehicle is fishtailing, sliding this way and that, vaulting through drifts, going out of control then regaining it at the last possible moment.

Now it's going into a slide.

Peanut stares open-mouthed at it. "It's... it's the SUV," he says, dumbfounded by the possibility.

"GET OUT OF THE WAY!" Nathan shouts, yanking him out of the vehicle's path.

They both slip and fall down, crawling and stumbling over the snowbank as the SUV bounces off the bank, spins, bangs off a parked car, and continues on into the storm.

Brushing snow from himself, Peanut says, "You saw who was driving it?"

"Yeah," Nathan says.

A clown.

68

"What is it this time?" Patti Wayland asks as she stands outside Clegg's cell. She feigns annoyance, though in reality she's happy over any diversion from the radio and any excuse for company.

Clegg stares at her. He does not smile—he has one of those stern, immobile faces that seem incapable of such a thing—he just eyeballs her. Despite his gruff and somewhat menacing appearance, his eyes are oddly sympathetic, as if he not only senses her anxiety, but feels it himself.

"Any luck on the radio?" he asks.

And being that she is a woman not without pride, Patti thinks, *lie, lie, lie! Don't tell him what he wants to hear. Don't give him the satisfaction.* But her own weakness betrays her. "None. It's dead out there. Completely dead."

He nods. He seems to get no satisfaction from her admission. "I thought not."

Though regs specify that she should get back to the radio, she does not. Sitting out there alone is more than she can take. The dead radio scares her in ways she cannot fathom.

Again, her mouth betrays her. "What is this about? Clowns and all that. What is it really about?"

Clegg takes his time in answering. "It's about evil. An ancient evil that stalks the human race. An evil that not only feeds on our flesh and blood, but our minds. This evil likes to scare us to death before making a meal of us. The fear is important. Very important. To the evil it's like...seasoning. It likes its food well-seasoned as we do. And fear, pure terror, provides that necessary seasoning.

Patti supposes that some rational part of her wanted denial of it all, but there is none; only confirmation of her darkest fears.

"And you hunt these things?"

"Yes."

"You kill them?"

"Yes."

She feels weak in the knees, dizzy with fright. She lowers herself to the bench outside the cells, breathing deeply to calm herself.

"Patti."

She chews her lower lip, her eyes growing misty. The night, the storm, and what's in it has her more frightened than she's been since she was eight years old.

"Patti, look at me."

She does not want to, she's nearly ashamed to admit her fear, but there is something rather fatherly in Clegg's tone.

"I want you to listen to me," he says. "I want you to listen very carefully. I came here to Craw Falls to stop what's happening out there right now. I may be the only one who can. That's why I need you to let me out of here."

"No."

"Yes." He keeps his eyes fixed on her. "Many people have died out there tonight. And many of them have been your friends and neighbors. I need to get out there and do my job before any others die. Do you understand that?"

She shakes her head, but hears herself say, "Yes."

"Good. Let's waste no more time. Now let me out so I can stop this evil. It's the right thing to do, Patti."

She keeps shaking her head, thinking, *that's crazy! It's insane! You'll lose your job! You'll be brought up on charges for aiding and abetting!* But inside, she knows it's beyond all that now. She throws the switch and opens the cell.

"You're doing the right thing," Clegg tells her. "Now, I have a lot of work to do. What you need to do, Patti, is go home. Lock the doors. Let no one in regardless of what they say or what they promise. They might look like your friends, but they're not. They're evil. Lock yourself in and you just might survive this night."

With that, he gathers up what Peanut took from him and steps out into the storm. The business of killing clowns has begun.

By the time Tony gets home, he's numb from the cold. His thinking is topsy-turvy. He's confused and unsure and terrified of things he cannot put a name to. He stands outside the house he knows is home, yet it doesn't seem right. Something's wrong. Had he been seeing it through an adult eye, he would have known this is not the house he grew up in but the house he lives in as an adult. But he does not see this. Whatever has happened to his mind, whatever arcane force has turned back the clock, everything is now filtered through the mind of Tony Russo at seven years old.

Oh, now now, says Mrs. Bisbee's voice. *There's no reason to be alarmed! This is your house. You must trust me on this. Teacher knows best, Tony. Teacher always knows best. Now get out of the cold before you freeze to death. All you have to do is remember how it felt all those long years ago when you came in out of the cold and your mother was waiting for you.*

Do you remember?

Can you remember?

Will you remember?

Yes, yes! Tony can remember and it's this that propels him up the snow-covered walk to the front door. Cold deep inside now, he opens the door and steps into the warmth. Oh, it's so much better. So very much better. He falls to his knees, wanting to weep that he is finally home. He unzips his parka with stiffened fingers, pulling off his hat and gloves, trying to work heat into his hands.

For a moment, just one moment, he smells something foul that does not belong... then it's gone. Now there are only good odors he remembers from boyhood: the smell of fresh-baked bread and hot soup. God, is there anything better than that when you come in out of the storm?

"Sit down, Tony," his mother says, busy at the stove, stirring the pot of soup with a practiced hand.

Tony does. He slides into his usual seat at the table and for a moment, that uncertainty again takes hold of him. In fact, it more than takes hold of him—it seizes him and shakes him as if it's trying to wake him up. But he senses danger there, a dark and endless danger, a bottomless pit from which he will never escape. No, no, no. He does not want that.

He wants what he sees in front of him.

He wants what is...is...is offered.

Yes, oh yes, oh most certainly yes, says the voice of Mrs. Bisbee, so warm, so comforting like a cozy, well-worn sweater. *We must always take what is offered. It would be rude to do otherwise. You do see that, don't you, Tony? Good, good. I cannot abide rude little boys. They make me quite cross and you do not want to make me cross, Mr. Tony Russo. No, you certainly do not want that.*

There's a tone to her voice that he does not care for. Something terrible being implied that his young mind immediately rejects. There's only here and only now. Oh, the soup smells wonderful! He wonders what kind it will be. Chicken noodle? Beef barley? Tomato? Maybe the kind with the little meatballs in it.

For the first time, he seems to realize that his sister is sitting across from him. *Charlotte?* he wants to say. *What are you doing?* She's acting a bit off. Part of him thinks that's hardly surprising, while another part of him is greatly disturbed. She is sitting there, limp and lifeless, her head resting on one shoulder like her neck is broken. Her arms dangle at her sides. Her face hangs forward, a long string of drool connecting her mouth to the tabletop. He finds it hard to believe that his mother is not snapping at her about proper posture at the dinner table.

His mother sings as she stirs.

Again, that uncertainty haunts him. His memories tell him that this is not his house, not the house he grew up in but a different house, a house where an adult Tony lives. He knows he must fight against such thinking or Mrs. Bisbee will get mad and far worse things might happen.

"Oh yes, they will," his mother says in that voice you never dare argue with. He recalls that he used to call it the voice of doom. "Awful things happen to awful little boys who do not do what they are told."

As she turns and steps towards the table, her image wavers and bends as if he's looking at it through a candle flame. She becomes oily and fluid…but only for a second. Then she is standing over him, holding the soup pot in one hand and the ladle in the other. The soup is steaming. The pot must be burning hot, yet it doesn't seem to bother her in the slightest.

For a moment, the hot vapor of the soup blows into his face and he can smell the perfect awfulness of what's in the pot, a Mulligan stew of festering meat and suppurating sores and sour milk. He cringes from the stink of it. Then the foul odor is gone and it's just the yummy smell of hot chicken soup again. Mom ladles it into his bowl and he notices that her hand is scaly like the belly of a reptile, her nails yellow and splintered.

"Eat the soup like a good boy," she says.

As she returns the pot to the stove, strands of blistered skin from her palm cling to it, then break like cobwebs.

Everything is wavering around him now and Tony is feeling scared beyond anything he has ever known. In his bowl, a chunk of chicken that bobs on the surface of the soup is speckled black. It trembles, then splits open, disgorging a particularly fat white maggot.

He looks over at his mother who waits by the stove. Her face is pallid and flaking, cracking open like drying plaster. Where her eyes should be there are two perfectly round, ragged holes, a simmering liquid blackness in the sockets. She has no nose. Her mouth is a lipless slash, lopsided and grinning.

Tony lets out a cry even though he knows it will bring the most awful trouble. This…woman is not his mother. No, no, no, this is Midge. This is his wife. Or something that once was his wife.

She steps over towards the table. "Oh, what's wrong, Tony? What's the problem, my little man? What's eating you, little fella?"

Now Tony sees that Charlotte has been replaced by some sort of clown doll. He blinks and blinks again, but the image persists. She is a clown doll. She wears a dull red jumper with faded white polka dots that is stained with what might be blood and other drainage. Her face is bleached white, scarred and cratered, eyes glowing a phosphorescent yellow.

She cocks her head at an unpleasant angle. "What's a matter, Tony?" she asks in a hideous squeaking voice. "Don't you like the soup? Isn't it tasty? Isn't it grand?"

Things like greasy brown flukes swim in the soup now. Charlotte—moving with unnatural jerking motions because of the strings that work her—scoops a spoonful and sucks the flukes like noodles between her flaking, narrow lips. "Mmm-mmm good!" she says as she chews them up. One of them tries to escape from the left nare of her long pointy nose and she sucks it back in like a slimy booger.

Humming under her breath, Mom brings the bread over: a crusty loaf of the sort she made when Tony was a boy... only this one stinks like something long dead. Plumes of nauseating, foul steam rise from it.

"There you are, my little man," says his mother. "Now break bread with your sister."

Charlotte the clown doll grins with a jagged smile, tiny cracks fanning out from her lips and splitting her face open like fissures in ice. "I loves me that bread!" she declares, reaching out for it with claw-like hands. Tony notices that she wears a tall pointy hat like a dunce cap set with orange pom-poms. Shaggy green hair sprouts out to either side of her skull in wiry bunches. Lice hop in it.

Tony wants to run, to do anything but be where he is now, but his mother seems to know that and places a firm hand like an owl's claw down on his shoulder.

"No leaving the table," she says in the voice of Mrs. Bisbee, soft but with a menacing undertone.

Tony can smell her hot, sour breath blowing down him. It smells like she has been chewing on gassy, green carcasses acrawl with maggots.

Charlotte's clawing hands move with the spasmodic twitching of an automaton. Great ropes of gray drool hang from her mouth. Her needling fingers tear into the steaming loaf of bread, ripping it open and releasing a perfectly awful stench of death. The interior of the loaf is the blue-green of mold. Glistening red worms are threaded through it like especially swollen, oily strings of licorice. Charlotte's hands stuff hunks of bread into her mouth. Her discolored gnarled teeth bite and chomp, severing worms and spilling their juice down her chin. It looks like the blood from thawing hamburger—pink and watery.

She keeps eating and slurping and slobbering. Tony needs to be sick. His gorge rises like a gas bubble in his throat as Charlotte watches him, her mangled gray teeth forever gnashing. Her luminous yellow eyes stare into his own and he begins to shake his head frantically back and forth.

"THIS ISN'T REAL!" he cries out. "NONE OF THS IS REAL!"

His disbelief breaks the evil spell, and everything seems to stop. His mother no longer moves. The soup ladle clatters to the floor. Food drops from Charlotte's mouth. The tiny cracks in her face widen and she begins to flake apart. Her strings go limp and she dangles there like a corpse, mouth hanging open and the light in her eyes fading until there is only a terrible sucking blackness in the sockets. The loaf of bread, what remains of it, speckles with black dots of mold. It turns green and fuzzy and then cracks open like a shell with a puff of dust.

Charlotte is gone and so is Mom.

Charlotte's soup spoon is dropped into the bowl.

And a voice in the back of Tony's mind, the voice of Mrs. Bisbee, says, *"Oh, you naughty naughty little boy! Look at what you've gone and done! Just look! It could have been gentle and cozy and painless, but now it's going to be harsh and dark and agonizing! Now you'll scream, you'll scream—"*

And she's right, horribly right, because Tony does scream. He screams and falls right out of his chair. The floor is covered in dust. There's nothing else down there but dust, blackened food scraps, and a mildewing shift that must have been his mother's dress, something she wore many decades before.

70

Tony scrambles across the floor on all fours until he reaches the living room and then the entry. He sees the stairs leading to the second floor. They shimmer like a mirage. The house seems to spin around him as if it's caught between fantasy and reality, the past and the present, what is and what can never be. Sweat runs down his face and his mouth makes a gasping sound as he climbs the stairs, knowing he must find Midge. She'll know what to do; she always knows what to do.

Finally, out of his head, Tony reaches the upstairs landing, pulling himself down the hall over the russet shag carpeting.

Just outside the bedroom door, his head begins to clear, and he hears. ..sounds. A married man knows the sounds of his wife's rising passion, her orgasms, as well as he knows the rhythms of his own heart.

And that's what Tony's hearing now—Midge squealing with carnal delight as she gets off...and with volume. Her cries echo through the house as the bedsprings creak violently.

Tony throws the door open and rushes in.

What he sees is far worse than what he imagined. Midge is spread-eagled on the bed and on top of her is the clown puppet that pretended to be Charlotte. It is, quite literally, fucking the hell out of his wife. Its skinny wooden flanks hammer against her meaty white thighs and her fingers tear at its dirty red jumper.

"STOP THIS! STOP IT!" Tony cries, confused, disoriented, dreaming but awake.

The clown doll dismounts Midge's flayed, bloodless corpse. It moves off the bed with that same jerky, convulsive motion as its strings are worked from above.

"You'll excuse me, kind sir! But any port in a storm, as they say! Gotta drill for oil while the sun shines!" says the clown doll, bowing and tipping his hat to Tony. Its voice is cracking and dry, nearly an airless squeal like rusting gears. "Runty McBean, the jester with the sores that fester, tit-twister and ass-fister extraordinaire, at your service!"

As Tony backs from the room in absolute horror, he notices that the clown doll has an enormous larval-white penis that is engorged like a grub. Flaccid yet firm, it is pointing right at him, the meatus not a slit but the puckered black mouth of a bloodsucking worm.

"Tonight is your lucky night, my friend," says Runty McBean, gliding towards him. "Because tonight old Toneee is going to get the boneee."

The clown begins to laugh with the shrill noise of shattering glass that soon becomes a manic, deranged scream that fills the air, a swarm of buzzing hornets that get inside Tony's head until he cannot think.

He stumbles away, finding the hallway, bashing into the wall and tripping down the stairs. The laughter gets louder and louder as if the clown is just behind him or in front of him or off to the left or the right.

On his hands and knees, his ankle twisted, a pained sobbing coming from his throat, Tony nearly makes it to the door before the clown descends on him in a most randy mood.

71

In the fenced-off impound yard behind the sheriff's office, the black van with its jacked-up frame and big off-road tires waits. Already, it's caked with snow. Right away, Clegg hears his dog barking.

"That's my girl," he says. "You been waiting for me."

Key in hand, he brushes snow from the back door and opens it. Inside, amongst some very dangerous looking military hardware, a Rottweiler bitch waits. Her teeth are bared. Easily 150 plus pounds of muscle and bravado, she is ready to leap to protect the van and its contents. She is about as fierce of a beast as can be imagined. But when she sees Clegg, she softens and offers a friendly bark and a submissive whine. He pets her and she clings to him.

"Who's the good girl? Who's the good girl?" he says, hugging her. "You are. That's who. Trixie!"

Trixie yelps excitedly.

Clegg closes the back door and piles into the front, turning over the van. It starts right away. The engine rumbles like it wants meat.

"Let's warm it up in here," he tells Trixie. "Goddamn yokels. They would have let me rot in that cell and you freeze to death. Well, we'll help 'em despite their stupidity."

Sitting in the passenger seat, Trixie barks.

Clegg lights a cigarette. "I ain't got no plan here, girl. We're gonna let your nose guide us to the clowns. We'll take 'em out one by one because that's what we do. Am I right?"

Trixie barks.

The van is beginning to warm up and Trixie's liking it. She's been shivering for some time and this is making her feel good again.

Clegg gives her a pat and a jerky treat. "All right then, let's go bag us some clowns."

72

Over at the Whistle Stop, Brick Zutema has his hands full. As things most malicious and certainly wicked run wild in Craw Falls, he waits patiently for 2:30 so he can close up and sweep the drunks out the door like the day's dirt. What worries him is that the tensions between Winn McCoy and Jaylene Thone are escalating. Winn is still smarting from his exchange with her and every time she laughs from the other side of the bar, Winn gives her the evil eye. He makes it plainly known (as he does every night) that he does not take shit from women. He's a firm believer that it's a man's world and that a woman's place is in the kitchen or the bedroom.

"Listen to that cackling cunt," he says as he drains his Pabst in a single swallow. "Thinks she can laugh at me. I could show her a thing or two."

"C'mon, Winn. She's just having a good time," Brick tells him. "It has nothing to do with you."

Winn grunts. "Fucking twat."

"Enough," Brick says.

Not that it does much good, because once Winn has his dander up he's like a gas leak looking for a good spark. Sooner or later, Bricks knows, he's going to find it and if he can't find it, he'll create it. Winn has always been that way—pissy, angry, and fast with his fists—and much of that is because of his old man who was known as Chub McCoy. He routinely beat men once he had some alcohol in him and routinely did time in the county lockup. And when he wasn't raising hell out on the town, he was raising hell at home, abusing his wife and kids.

It was a terrible situation, and everyone knew it. At least, those old enough to remember Chubb who had been dead twenty-three years by that point.

Even all the beer Winn is swallowing or his favorite songs on the juke—"North to Alaska" by Johnny Horton or "Big Bad John" by Jimmy Dean—are calming him tonight. The demons are loose inside him and they want blood. And that's a bad enough situation when a guy is twenty, but Winn's pushing sixty and he's too damn old to be playing the game anymore.

"HEY BRICK!" Jaylene shouts over the din. "DRYING UP OVER HERE!"

Winn flinches and slams his bottle down on the bar.

Brick sighs and goes over to Jaylene and her friend Karen, mixing them fresh drinks, a Jack and Coke for the former and a Slow Screw for the latter.

When Jaylene gets her drink, she raises it high. "Here's to WADD! Everyone drink up! Women Against Drunken Dicks is buying!"

The laughter booms and everyone is having a good laugh at Winn's expense...except for Winn. He's visibly trembling, and Brick knows something ugly is about to happen just as he knows that there's not much he can say to stop it. About all he can do is throw them out and for that he better have just cause.

"Hey, Karen!" Winn calls out. "What do you like best about your boyfriend? The hair on her chest or the bulge in her pants?"

That misfires. Karen looks miffed, but being the mousy type, she just ignores it. Not Jaylene. She bursts out into hoarse laughter, so loud you can barely hear Faron Young singing "Hello Walls." Everyone else thinks it's hilarious, too. If Jaylene isn't offended, why, there's no reason they should be either.

"That's okay, Winn!" Jaylene calls back to him. "You're just jealous because my dick is bigger than yours!"

More laughter. It's really rolling now. Brick tells everyone to calm down, but nobody's paying him much mind by that point; there's far better entertainment to be had.

Jaylene is singing along with Faron Young and Winn is gritting his teeth, because that goddamn bitch made fun of him again and his brain doesn't work fast enough for him to hurl a better insult back in her direction.

"GOTTA LOVE THIS SONG!" Jaylene shouts at the top of her lungs. "IT'S LIKE A THEME SONG FOR WINN FUCKING MCCOY! HELLO BALLS! I SURE MISS YA SINCE YOU UUUUUUP AND WALKED AWAAAAAAY!"

"Fucking fish-licker, that's it!" Winn cries out.

Before Brick can do a damn thing, Winn is going right at her, the insults flying back and forth. Then they're shoving each other as their respective groups try to keep them apart.

"ENOUGH!" Brick yells. "YOU WANT TO DO THAT SHIT, DO IT OUTSIDE! GET THE HELL OUT OF HERE!"

Both of them head towards the door, only pausing briefly to don hats and coats and gloves. It's on. There's no doubt in anyone's mind that it is most certainly on. A blast of icy wind and the door slams shut. There's only four people in the bar by that point. Lots of half-drained beers and drinks, but that's it.

"You better go break that up," Maggie LaCross says, "before they kill each other."

But Brick is way ahead of her. He gets nothing on his cell or the landline. They've both gone belly-up like the cable. No cops, no help. Whatever happens, he'll have to do it himself.

"Shit, shit, shit," he says under his breath as he pulls on his wool coat and gloves.

Like goddamn high school all over again.

He steps out into the blow, wind shrieking and snow flying. A dozen people are out there, shivering, egging Jaylene and Winn on. But they don't need any help. Already, they're grappling. Pushing and shoving, slipping and sliding on the ice. Winn's best days are far behind him. He's a professional drunk that maybe eats something every other day. But despite weighing only 130 pounds soaking wet, he's wiry and mean. Jaylene goes in at an easy 200. She's taller than Winn and has been in lots of fights through the years.

"BOTH OF YOU! STOP THIS SHIT!" Brick cries.

He's ignored. Jaylene hits Winn in the face with a glancing blow and he staggers back, nearly losing his footing. She presses her attack, swings again and misses. Winn, despite his age, ducks under her blow and drills her in the belly. She lets out a gasp of air and doubles over. Winn grabs her in a headlock with one arm and rapidly punches her in the face with his free fist. Not to be done in and unable to throw him, Jaylene reaches back and grabs him by the crotch of his pants, giving what she finds there a nasty twist.

Winn lets go with a shriek of pain and drops into the snow and Jaylene falls backwards, still doubled over, trying to catch her breath.

"ENOUGH!" Brick says, getting between them. "I WANT YOU BOTH OUT OF HERE!"

The onlookers grumble about the fight being broken up just when it was getting good and filter back into the bar, leaving Brick standing there in the fierce wind, staring down at the crippled combatants. He does not leave until Jaylene gets to her feet and joins Karen, both of them walking off. He helps Winn to his feet.

"That fucking slitty-licker's going to get it," he says. "See if she don't."

"Go home and sober up," Brick tells him.

"Yeah, fuck you," Winn says and limps awkwardly away into the night.

Brick stands there a few more moments and he's not even sure why. The snow is really flying. Visibility is so bad, he can barely see across the street. He watches Winn's form fade into the storm and then notices that someone is following him. Without really knowing why, he hurries into the Whistle Stop.

73

By the time she hears it, Patti Wayland knows it's too late. She should have left as Clegg said, but she didn't. And now she's going to pay for it.

The signal comes through the emergency channel in a shrilling whine and fear seizes her. She shuts off the radio but it's too late: it keeps coming. It no longer requires the radio to broadcast itself. At first, there is no real pain, just shock and surprise like being slapped or even shot. A tingling spreads through her limbs followed by a localized paralysis in her trunk... then agony as it feels like white-hot needles are jabbed into her extremities, a million volts coursing through her. Her body jerks and contorts, her eyes roll back white and her teeth clench. She grunts and groans, pink saliva running from her mouth, blood trickling from her nostrils.

What happens then is purely subjective.

Wherever her mind is, whatever has been done to it, she sees herself as a raw, decaying piece of meat. It feels as if there are thousands of fly eggs inside her, each one ripening and bursting, releasing a carrion tide of squirming maggots that infest and feed and hatch into a multitude of buzzing corpse flies that fill her belly, her throat, and finally her head with a reverberating cacophony of buzzing until she can no longer form a single rational thought. And by then, she is convulsing, limbs whipsawing, head jerking back and forth as her brain short-circuits and her neural pathways are overloaded, consumed, and ultimately reconfigured.

It all happens very quickly and by the time it's done, she is no longer Patti Wayland. She is, in fact, something quite different. And her priorities have completely changed.

74

When Teague and Clyde Taggert get to the sheriff's office, Stan Barbacek is waiting outside for them. Teague sees him and inwardly sighs. Oh Christ, what now. Stan waits there with a camera in his hands. He looks from Teague to Clyde, as if wondering what in the hell they are doing together.

"What's going on now?" Teague asks.

"Clowns," Stan says. "They're everywhere."

"Tell me something I don't know," he says.

They step inside and Patti is not there. Teague feels fear worm into him right away. He and the others search the station, even knock at the door of the ladies' room, but Patti Wayland is not to be found.

"She was here before," Stan says. "I was here a half an hour ago and she was sitting right at that radio."

"Well, she ain't there now," Clyde says.

Teague checks the cells in the back. He is not surprised to find Clegg missing. He figured something like this would happen. Patti was probably scared, and she did what Clegg asked. He finds it hard to believe that she would have gone with him, though.

"What now?" Clyde asks.

Teague sighs. "Hell if I know."

Stan says, "You ain't gonna believe this, but..."

He begins reeling out his night's adventures, which are all pretty wild, right out of a horror story, but he tells them calmly and with abundant details. On any other night, Teague might have thrown him in the clink to dry out, but this is sure not any other night.

"Clowns," Teague says as he lowers himself into a chair. "Goddamn clowns."

"They got to be everywhere by this point," Clyde says.

Teague nods. "I want to see your footage, Stan."

"Long as I get it back."

"You'll get it back."

Stan pops out the SD card and hands it to him. Teague leads Stan and Clyde back into his office. They use Teague's laptop to watch Stan's footage. Clyde rolls his eyes at Stan's narration, but he doesn't roll his eyes at the empty city plow and what Stan captured at Taxi-A-Go-Go. Teague watches it again and again.

Finally, he sighs. "This is madness, just madness," he says.

"Took some real balls to do what you did," Clyde admits.

Stan practically beams. Clyde is all about balls and guts and initiative. He's legendary for all three. When he says you've got balls, it's really saying something. Particularly when you realize that yesterday, he wouldn't have wiped his ass with a guy like Stan Barbacek.

"What are we gonna do?" Stan asks them after he gets his SD card back.

"That's the problem," Teague admits.

Clyde sketches out the situation, the thing that happened over at the Broken Bottle. And from the look on Stan's face, it's obvious that it's much worse than even he imagined.

Finally, Stan says, "How does this Clegg figure into things?"

Teague explains who Clegg is and what he claims to be, which is no crazier than anything else this night. Stan listens to it all, more intrigued by this situation all the time. If things weren't interesting enough before, they sure as hell are now.

"So what's our plan?" Stan asks.

They follow Teague into the other room and he hopelessly tries the radio again. In his way of thinking, there's nothing worse than being cut off this way. Modern law enforcement is a network. Without that, hell, you might as well be back in the Wild West.

Clyde is beginning to look pissy. "C'mon, Sheriff, what's it gonna be?"

Stan watches him, too.

They're waiting for him to come up with something, but he doesn't have a damn thing. In its broadest possible sense this entire situation might be considered a civil disturbance and possibly even an act of terrorism. But knowing this does him no good. He needs to act. He needs to do the job before it's too late if it isn't already.

"All right," he says, thinking about old westerns he watched on TV. "We're on our own. Let's arm ourselves and get as many people in on this as we can."

75

For thirty minutes after the sheriff and Clyde left, things were pretty calm at the Broken Bottle, but Bonnie knows it won't last. Skunk is still eying her like a nice juicy slab of sirloin, but he has yet to slake his appetite. Maybe Clyde threatening him and Teague promising him hard time has done some good. Bonnie hopes so, but she doesn't necessarily believe it.

She uses the bathroom—locking the door so that pervert doesn't get in—and when she comes out, she's struck by the stillness. Everything is silent. Even the juke is quiet. All you can hear is the moaning of the wind and the snow against the windows. It's unsettling.

"Where's Stew?" she asks.

"Stew?"

"Yes, Skunk. Stew. Where the hell is he?"

Skunk shrugs. "I think he went to use the head."

Bonnie doesn't feel comfortable with the answer. "He's not in his right mind. You should go check on him."

Skunk swallows a shot of Jim Beam. "Sure."

He walks into the backroom and she can hear the squeaking of the swinging door as he checks out the men's room. He comes back, calm and unperturbed as when he left.

"He ain't there."

"Well, where could he be?"

Bonnie doesn't like this at all. She quickly checks the kitchen and then the storeroom. He's in neither.

"This place got a basement?" Skunk asks.

"Yes," Bonnie says.

"Maybe he's down there or..." and he grins salaciously "...maybe he went upstairs. Let's go look for him together."

"Forget it."

Stew's gone, probably to look for Brenda, and despite Bonnie's best efforts, Carpy has now passed out, his head down on the bar.

"Some people just can't handle their liquor," Skunk says.

Watch him now, Bonnie thinks with a chill. *He's going to try something, so watch him real close.*

The paring knife is in her back pocket. She's terrified of the idea of using it. Pulling it on Skunk might be a bad idea. It might excite him. It's just the sort of thing that would turn on a guy like him. He might find the idea of taking it away from her akin to foreplay. She's not sure if she can stick it in his belly even if it comes to that. He's an experienced fighter, so he might disarm her very quickly... and if he doesn't, the idea of plunging cold steel into someone makes her belly jump.

As she thinks over these things, Skunk has edged in a little closer.

Sneaky little shit.

Carpy's no help. Even if he were sober, he's no match for Skunk who's a predator by nature. A guy completely lacking in any morals or ethics, a perfect example of survival of the fittest. The wounded are not even moaning anymore. They're out of it. What happens now will strictly be between Skunk and his victim.

"I like your eyes," he says. "I like how they shine in the light. They're like...like emeralds. I always liked emeralds." He stops his advance just as her hand is reaching for the paring knife. "One time down in Chi, me and some boys from another club I was in took down a jewelry store. We went in there at night and took all the rocks we could find. Nice ones, too. Diamonds, rubies, sapphires, and...emeralds. Bright green emeralds. I still got a couple. Your eyes are the same color. I'll give 'em to you if you want."

The spit dries in her mouth. She knows she cannot be a shrinking violet now. She must stand up to him. Psychologically, it's very important.

She takes a swig off her Diet Coke. "Yeah? And what do I have to give you?" she asks with some derision, adopting the same tone she uses on the drunks that are always hitting on her.

Skunk chuckles and lights a cigarette. He takes a swallow off Carpy's drink. "Only what I'm going to take anyway." He shrugs, blows smoke out through his nostrils. "But if you give it, it can be nicer. I'll be easy with you. I'll give you the emeralds when I'm done tapping you."

The way he says this makes her skin literally crawl. It's obvious that he does not see women as human beings; they're just holes to be filled. Things to use and then discard once you've dirtied them up. He thinks offering the emeralds is being romantic. A simple barter. Like, hey, kid, I'll give you a buck if you get me another beer. Bonnie tries to keep her tough barmaid act intact, but Skunk is not like the guys who hit on her every night. They're only half-serious; his intent is deadly. He's probably raped lots of girls and maybe even guys when he was in prison.

"You better watch it," she says to him. "Clyde will kill you if you touch me. The sheriff will put you away."

Skunk pulls slowly off his cigarette. "They ain't coming back," he tells her. "Clowns got 'em by now. It'll take a real badass clown to get Clyde, but I saw how that one was, the one that got Mongol. You can't fight something like that. They ain't coming back and neither is Nathan or Peanut." This makes him smile. "Only a matter of time before the clowns come for us. We might as well die with a smile on our faces."

"Fuck you," Bonnie snaps at him.

His smile grows broader. "That's it, baby. That's it exactly. I'm going to fuck you and that's just the way it is. You make it easy, I'll be gentle on you. You don't... I'll fucking hurt you real bad."

He's moving towards her again.

She can see twin images of herself in his Coke-bottle glasses. She looks like the victim she's about to become: a frightened woman off a paperback cover or one of those old true detective magazines.

"You better keep away from me."

He stares at her with his toad's eyes behind the glasses. They are flat, dead things. There's no mercy or compassion in them. They're reptilian. Bonnie knows right then that the only thing that has kept him from going on a serial raping spree across the county is his fear of Clyde Taggert.

Skunk moves closer now. He's rubbing his crotch and Bonnie can see that he's hard.

She pulls the paring knife. "You get any closer and I'll cut you."

Skunk stops, looking from the blade to her, back and forth. "Takes guts to ram a blade into someone," he tells her. "You got that kind of guts?"

She holds the knife out before her, her eyes steely. That says it all.

Skunk giggles. He reaches inside his leather jacket and produces a lock-blade. It's spring-loaded and greased, the blade snapping into place with a deft flick of his wrist. It's double-edged and easily six inches long.

"Looks like we got ourselves a showdown, Bonnie. Winner take all." His grin widens and she can see all his bad teeth. "You win and you're free. I win... well, you know what happens then."

As much as she expected this Bonnie still can't believe it's happening. This is not how things are supposed to work. There're only two choices: she can make a wild run for the door or she can go down fighting. There's no doubt in her mind that Skunk is going to cut her. And when he's done, he will kill her.

"Show me your tits," he says.

He lunges for her and Bonnie cries out, slashing at him with the knife. She's amazed at how fast she moves and so is he because he falls back, but not quick enough to avoid getting slashed across the cheek.

He's morphed into full predator mode now.

The knife in his hand, he moves in for the kill. Bonnie slashes at him, but never even gets close. It's as if he anticipates her every move. Maybe he was playing before, but he's not playing now. The most disturbing thing to her is that she can see how hard he has grown. He's getting off on this. She's definitely on the defensive now, trying to keep away from his blade. Her attempts at cutting him are impotent. He jumps at her and she jabs. He slashes her wrist and she reflexively drops the knife.

That's it.

She's done.

Skunk moves in to claim his prize. His dead eyes are huge behind his glasses. He's drooling.

"Now," he says, "let's take a look at those tits..."

76

Although Winn McCoy lives only a scant three blocks from the Whistle Stop, it takes him nearly thirty minutes to make it home. But in that storm, three blocks is a long country mile. Of course, he's not in the best shape—he's drunk, hurting, and his balls are throbbing from the death twist Jaylene Thone gave them. Christ, she worked them like oranges on a juicer.

"Gonna get that snatch," he keeps whispering under his breath. "Gonna get her and hurt her bad."

The blizzard is coming on strong. He can barely keep his eyes open more than a squint. The wind has turned his face to slack rubber. It punches into him with such ferocity that his hobbling, painful gait is little more than a seesawing, drunken lumbering. The world is desolation, utter desolation. Everything is draped in white like furniture in an empty house.

By the time he fights his way up the walk to his porch, he's numb all over, his beard frosted into white spikes and his eyesight is blurry. There's over two feet of snow on the porch and the driveway is locked in by cresting white dunes. He hasn't seen anything like this in years.

As he begins his ascent of the steps like a climber fighting his way up the Himalayas, he looks up and sees something that had not been there moments before: lights. Not just any lights, but colored lights. In fact, each window that faces out to the street has a different color glowing in it—red, green, and yellow like a freaking stoplight.

Hell is this about?

He wonders if its hypothermia, if he's hallucinating the entire thing. But as he blinks and then blinks again, the image does not change. It does not even waver. It makes no sense. Winn lives alone. He doesn't have so much as a dog for company. He was married once, but Bev left him seventeen years before. Sometimes he can barely remember her face. Other times, he can remember nothing else. But even if she came home (which was patently ridiculous), Christmas was near on two months gone.

Which can mean only one thing: somebody is fucking with him.

Well, now that's something Winn understands and knows how to deal with. Inside, he begins to boil and, truth be told, most days he's at a low simmer. This is how he survives day by day, by knocking the shit out of anything that gets in his way. It gives him a certain level of satisfaction. It's how he vents his pent-up frustrations and burning hostility towards the world in general. Yes sir, he knows how to handle things like this just fine.

He fights his way to the storm door, kicking snow free until he can get it open two feet. He squeezes through, opening the inside door and stumbling into the warmth. By then, his balls are no longer hurting so badly. He tosses his hat and coat aside and marches up the stairs, turning on lights as he goes.

But once he gets up there, he stops in the hallway because there are no glowing colored lights up there. He checks all the rooms that front the street. Nothing. And no apparatus evident to create such lights in the first place. He goes from bedroom to bedroom, then back again.

Crazy.

Deflating at the idea of not being able to bust somebody's chops, he steps into the bathroom and relieves himself. It's when he's done, that he hears something else. Something high and squeaky. It's coming from outside, muffled by the walls and the ever-present drone of the storm, but he can still make it out—*creak, creak, creak*. Well, then, there's still a possibility of a good beatdown.

Down the stairs Winn goes, deflating again because he knows what the sound is. It's just that goddamn porch swing in the back that Bev insisted he put in. Wind makes it creak at night. The storm must be playing hell with it.

Sighing, Winn steps into the kitchen and skids to a halt.

Through the windows, he can see the swing in the snowstorm. Its white with snow like everything else.

And somebody is sitting in it.

That's bad enough, but the insane thing is that it's a fucking clown of all things. Winn blinks his eyes a couple times because he's got to be seeing things.

But, no, it's still there. A clown in some kind of satiny suit rocking back and forth. It has a bushy Ronald McDonald hairdo and big black eyes, a crooked black hole for a mouth with something equally as dark leaking from it.

A clown. Out in the storm.

Though a certain apprehension weaves through him, he thinks, one of those goddamned punk kids that think it's funny to scare people at night. Well, he's in for a rude awakening now because Winn is going to beat the hell out of him on general principles.

Winn goes to the back door and flings it open. The wind hits him right away, unbearably cold, snow flying into the kitchen. There's a funny smell on it, a wild sort of smell that reminds him of the den of a bear. Then he's outside.

But there's no clown.

He fights through drifts on the back deck and sees only the swing rocking back and forth. The unnerving part is that there are no footprints out in the yard, either coming or going. What's maybe even worse is that the snow on the swing is undisturbed.

Winn stands there, shaking not with rage now but fear and uncertainty. The wind blows and moans and he is not sure what to do. He makes to go back inside, looking up again as if his eyes are drawn by a force he does not understand.

A clown stands in the window on the second story.

The window of the spare bedroom.

Shit!

He rushes inside not thinking, not trying to make sense of how this goddamned clown could sneak past him and get in the house. He only knows that it has. Inside, there are snowy footprints leading from the kitchen into the living room and going right up the stairs.

Enough.

That's enough of this madness.

Winn stops long enough to retrieve his .410 from the closet. He keeps it loaded with number four buckshot year around. Now, he figures, things are going to get interesting.

He moves up the stairs, ready to kill. He's never shot a man before, but he finds the idea more than a little exciting. Besides, this is a home invader dressed like a fucking killer clown. He'll be in his rights to kill the sonofabitch.

At the top of the stairs, he pauses.

There are no sounds, only that smell again. But in the confines of the house, it's concentrated, a thick, unpleasant odor of wild things, of blood and urine and raw meat. He moves slowly up the hallway.

"You want to live another day, shithead," he says, "you better come on out, otherwise this four-ten'll be the last thing you see."

Winn figures that sounds good, like one of them cool kind of things Lee Van Cleef might say in a spaghetti western. He's got the little prick now. There's no way he can get away. Sweating now, filled with dread, Winn moves to the bedroom at the end. The smell is stronger. In fact, it's nauseating. He kicks the door open and turns on the light.

The bedroom is empty.

How the hell could this be?

He checks under the bed. Behind the dresser. Then he opens the closet, bringing up the .410 real fast. At first, he sees nothing but a grainy darkness in there... then there's a clown standing inches away, its eyes like black greasy holes staring out at him.

Winn pulls the trigger.

The hammer clicks on empty chambers. He pulls it again and again. And it's at this moment that the clown drops shells at his feet.

No, no, can't be...just can't be...

The clown's mouth is an immense bloody hole from which a black, serpentine tongue dangles. There are teeth in there, jagged like the blade of a saw. Winn knows that this is no costumed hooligan, no rubber mask he is staring at but the real thing. Then the clown strikes. Too fast to be seen, it slashes out with lethal claws and splits open his face. He sees his own blood spatter against the pale peach walls. The .410 drops uselessly from his hands.

Then he stumbles back, bleeding profusely. He presses his hands to his face and blood that is impossibly red oozes between his fingers. He screams and runs from the room. If he can make the stairs... but no, the clown is there. It opens its mouth even wider, making a terrible gurgling sound, and lashes out again, seizing his left arm in a crushing grip. Still crying out, Winn tries to wrestle his way free and the clown twists his arm out of its socket with a grinding, gristly sort of noise.

Then it tears it free in an eruption of gore.

The agony is unbelievable. Winn almost goes out cold, but something in him refuses to die. Weak and dizzy, he makes it to the stairs, splashing the walls with his blood. The clown is there again. It shoves him and he tumbles down, splitting open his head on the hardwood steps. He sprawls at the bottom, twisted and broken. His eyes are still open, his chest rising and falling frantically.

Through blurred vision, he sees the clown come calmly down the stairs. When it reaches him, it kneels next to him, studying him dispassionately as some sort of black drainage hangs from its mouth in glistening ropes.

Winn is beyond fighting.

The clown brings its puffy, scarified visage in closer to his own, the jaws opening wider and wider like those of an egg-eating snake he saw in a nature doc once. Its teeth impale his jaw and forehead, its blubbery lips sealing against his skin, engulfing his face, and then with a relentless, unbelievable suction, it sucks his eyes from their sockets. Then the ring of teeth begins chewing and chewing, scraping the flesh from his skull and sucking it down its throat.

77

Clegg drives the van slowly down the main drag of Craw Falls, keeping an eye out. He's been hunting clowns a long time and he knows the signs. If it wasn't for the storm, all of this would have been a lot easier.

As he passes Taxi-A-Go-Go, Trixie clearly gets excited. She begins to bark and then to whine low in her throat. There's absolutely no doubt in Clegg's mind that she has the scent. Once she gets a whiff of clown, that old girl just will not let go, not until she runs her quarry to ground. And when she does that, that's when Clegg does his thing.

"You smelling one?"

Trixie barks, wags her tail, then puts her muzzle down low and growls.

Yep, Clegg thinks, *she's got one.*

He pulls the van over and lets Trixie out. Oh, yeah, she's got the scent all right. She's barking and snarling, wanting to mangle some clownmeat. Nothing the old girl likes better than taking care of business.

Clegg opens the back and gets some gear. "Okay, girl," he says to Trixie. "Find me a clown."

78

The world is bleached white and blowing. It's vanilla ice cream and whipped topping and meringue. This is how Stew Prechek sees it as he stumbles through the storm, searching for his wife. When he was in the bar, he thought he heard her voice calling to him.

"Did you hear her?" he asked Skunk.

Skunk shrugged. "Nah."

"I know it was her. I should go look for her."

"Sure," Skunk said. "I think you should."

And now Stew is doing just that. Though he's wrapped in a thin coat and gloves, he does not feel the cold. He knows it's winter, yes, and a real storm is blowing, but that's all he knows.

Other than his wife's voice.

"BRENDA!" he calls into the howling wind which has already made his face stiff and numb. "BRENDA! CAN YOU HEAR ME?"

The wind blows and the snow falls, whipping over the drifts and working itself into spinning devils, but there is no response. Yet, now and again, Stew sees a vague form just ahead. As soon as he nears it, it retreats into the blizzard. It's her. He knows it's her. She's playing a game, drawing him in.

I'm coming, dear. You know I would never leave you out here alone. You know how I feel about you.

Just thinking these thoughts makes him feel warm at his core. He follows the retreating shape deeper and deeper into the storm until it feels as if he's been transported to some white-iced fairyland.

"BRENDA!" he shouts. "PLEASE WAIT FOR ME!"

And then, miraculously, the shape pauses, allowing him to catch up. His heart begins to beat faster. It pounds and drums rat-a-tat-tat inside his chest, growing larger, swelling, filling him to bursting and he has never, ever felt so much love for his wife. It is a Valentine river and he is swimming in its sweetness.

Brenda, smiling happily, holds her arms out and he is drawn to her, magnetized and pulled closer and closer, only noticing at the last terrible moment that she is splattered with blood and carries a hatchet in one hand.

But forward momentum has him and he stumbles closer and closer yet. Despite the gore and the hatchet whose blade is dyed red, bits of tissue and hair sticking to it, he is in love with his wife and thank God, thank God, he has found her at last.

It's only when he's mere feet from her that the wonderful warm bloom of love inside him turns to a chill fear that freezes the blood in his veins and turns his heart into a block of ice.

Because this isn't Brenda at all.

It's a goddamned clown.

It stands there with the hatchet, a large, very large, clown in a silver-white suit of funeral satin that billows in the wind. A hot stink of decomposition wafts from it despite the cold. And why not, for as it steps closer he sees that it is not a clown, but a ghoul, a haunter of graveyards and war zones, something that gnaws on corpses in cold boxes and picks at the dead strewn across the gutted plains of battlefields.

Its face is white as fresh bone, a gruesome death's-head visage of seamed papier-mâché plastered to a yawning skull. With a huge grinning black mouth, a triangular cavity for a nose, and deep black pits for eyes, it is the worst possible thing to encounter in a blizzard. It's a monster, a skull-headed, deranged monster that has come out of the storm to harvest souls.

Stew, his mind blanked by horror, slips on the snow-covered ice, and simply does not have the strength to right himself. He goes down to one knee like a sacrifice at the foot of some dark pagan god.

His mouth moves, but no sounds come out.

The clown accepts him, splitting the crown of his head wide with the hatchet. Blood and gray matter steam in the snow like hot porridge. Stew tips over face-first. His corpse writhes momentarily as his brain short circuits with random bursts of electrical activity.

When he stops moving, the clown seizes him by the ankle and drags him off to be fed upon in private.

79

By the time they reach the Broken Bottle, Peanut feels like an Eskimo Pie. To his untrained eye, the Bottle looks no different than it did when they left. The lights are still burning, and the snow is still falling, the wind groaning about the eaves.

God, it's a hell of a storm. They'll be many days digging out from this one. But that, of course, is not what seeds the anxiety deep within him. As he and Nathan Free stumble out of the cold and through the front door, he feels a subtle sense of terror worm through him. And when he gets inside, it begins to escalate.

The warmth feels good after being out in the storm, but inside he still feels cold because of what he sees, namely Skunk holding a knife on Bonnie.

"What the hell are you doing?" he says.

He's not a guy who flies off the handle, but he does not and never has trusted Skunk. Numb as he is, he races across the bar, pulling his 9mm and pointing it at the biker. At that moment, he knows he will kill him. He knows he will not hesitate.

"It's cool," Skunk says, putting the knife away. "Everything's cool. Sheriff and Clyde went to the station. I'm keeping an eye on shit."

But saying that does not diffuse Nathan Free who charges right past Peanut and before Skunk can even think of defending himself, he's already on the floor, Nathan having hit him twice.

"FUCK DO YOU THINK YOU'RE DOING?" Nathan cries out. "DON'T YOU EVER LEARN, YOU USELESS MOTHER-FUCKER? HOW MANY TIMES WE GOT TO GO THROUGH THIS SHIT?"

Skunk does not bother getting up. There's blood on his face from a split lip and a livid purple bruise is swelling on his cheek. He's been caught and he knows he's been caught. And by the sergeant-at-arms of the Dead Skulls which means he's really and truly in the shit.

"It's not how it looks, man," he says.

"The hell it isn't!" Bonnie tells them. "He was threatening to rape me! If you hadn't come in, that's exactly what he would have done!"

She's close to tears but will not give in to them. She stands there proudly, angrily. Peanut looks from her to Skunk to Nathan as he holsters his sidearm.

"Will's gonna hear about this," he says. "And for a guy like you, it'll mean going back inside where you belong."

Skunk ignores him because such threats are idle, and he knows it. What he does not ignore is Nathan who keeps staring at him.

Nathan bends down and whispers, "I wouldn't want to be in your skin when Clyde finds out. Way I'm thinking, I'll be digging a hole out in the woods."

Skunk is scared because Nathan does not make idle threats. What he has done in the past is something Peanut and Bonnie know nothing about, but Skunk knows exactly what Clyde and Nathan are capable of, how easily they kill when crossed or when club rules are breached. And one of Clyde's standing rules is that you do not interfere with citizens unless it cannot be helped. It's safer for the club and it's safer for them. Most 1%er organizations operate this way.

Skunk is in deep trouble with the Skulls now. The law is the least of his worries and he knows it.

"Are you okay?" Peanut asks Bonnie.

"Course she's okay," Skunk says, and Nathan kicks him.

"I'm all right. But if you hadn't come back…" She lets that trail off; no more needed to be said. She looks over at Nathan. "Don't leave me alone with him. If you have to go, take him with you."

"We're not going anywhere," he promises her.

"Why did they go to the station?" Peanut asks.

Bonnie sits next to Carpy who's still sleeping, facedown on the bar. She wraps some gauze around her slashed wrist. "To get some guy named Clegg."

"Oh, boy," Peanut says. "Now it's gonna get good."

He doesn't wait for them to ask; he just starts telling his story of Clegg that began at the schoolyard. Maybe any other night they would have laughed at it, but not tonight.

246

80

Sometime after she leaves Karen Baylen's house, deciding against spending the night, Jaylene Thone realizes she's being followed. She can clearly hear footsteps crunching through the snow behind her. And every time she stops, they stop a split second later.

The big problem is the storm. The snow is blowing around in heavy, whipping sheets. There's just no way to see who's back there.

More than once, she stopped and called out, "Hey! Is someone there? If you are, then you better goddamn well answer me!"

But there is never any reply. After she stops for like the third time, she begins to wonder if it isn't all in her mind or if maybe it's just her own footsteps bouncing back at her.

If it had been high summer, well, she would have probably backtracked to see what this was all about, but the cold is like pins and needles against her face, her breath chugging out in great white clouds of vapor.

She pushes forward, telling herself that if she keeps pouring it on, she'll be home in fifteen minutes. Down Third Avenue, across the Canal Creek bridge, then just a hop, skip, and jump and she'll be at her place.

But, God, that wind, that insufferable wind. It keeps battering her from the back, from the front, sometimes (it seems) from both directions at once. Even in her parka and snowpants, the scarf around her head and the wool hat pulled down over her ears, it isn't enough. The wind manages to get inside her coat and blow right up her spine.

The town is deserted tonight, snowed in, buried in the white stuff. Huge drifts are blown right across streets, more than one car abandoned in them.

What a mess. She tries to move faster, but the wind will not have it. Trying to step over a drift, she skids on the ice beneath and hits the ground.

Dammit!

She lays there, drunk and sleepy, knowing she had better get up and moving if she doesn't want to freeze to death. In those precious seconds before she does, she hears the sound of someone coming again, heavy boots crunching through the crust of snow. She pauses, balanced on one elbow. For a moment, all she can hear is the wind and falling snow, tree branches scraping together… then, yes, there it is again.

Okay, this is bullshit.

In the back of her mind, she wonders if it's Winn McCoy, coming to finish things up. She hopes it will be. That sonofabitch gave her a good pounding. She will return the favor without Brick interfering.

But even as she thinks this, she doesn't really believe it will be Winn. He's home licking his wounds until next time.

Jaylene stands up, breathing hard, shivering in the cold, brushing snow from her eyes. If someone is following her, then she'll just wait for them and get this over with. She stands there while the snow covers her, and it isn't long before a lone figure appears.

It steps out of the curtain of snow maybe twenty feet away and waits there. It's Winn, all right. No denying that twisted-up little pug-nosed face. Liquored up and stupid.

"Better get out of my sight, asshole," she says into the wind. "I won't tell you twice."

She turns and starts walking away, knowing she's being the better person even though she really, really wants to beat his ass. But she will give him this chance. She makes it to the iron rungs of the Canal Creek bridge, hoping that idiot will just go away. And, for a time, it seems like he will. That's perfectly fine with her by that point; she only wants to get somewhere warm and get a hot drink in her hand.

Then, halfway across the bridge where the wind's really screaming, she hears that dumb shit coming. And, yup, there he is. He stops again, waiting, not saying a thing, just stalking her like a fucking animal.

Okay, fuckface, you wanted it and now you'll get it.

"NOT A FUCKING BRAIN IN YOUR HEAD, IS THERE?" she cries out to him as she trudges in his direction. "I GIVE YOU A FUCKING CHANCE TO ACT LIKE AN ADULT AND YOU STILL GOTTA BE A BRATTY LITTLE PRICK! ALL RIGHT! OKAY!"

By the time she reaches him—more than a little amazed that he does not even attempt to move or defend himself—he still has said nothing. He simply stands there, an ice statue, a snowman, and that really pisses her off... it's so defiant. His face is frosted white, the mouth open and grinning. All those teeth, those glittery silvery-white teeth. Raging, she swings at him, connects with a straight-arm punch that he takes dead-on. Even if it doesn't put him down, it should knock him back or make him wobble at the knee. It does neither. His face absorbs the blow, rippling like some sort of gelatin.

Jaylene shakes her head back and forth.

It can't be! It just can't be!

For the first time, she's really afraid because this is not only fucked up, it's unnatural. The fear inspires anger and she hits him two more times. He does not absorb these blows—no, worse, he bobbles from side to side but does not go down. He bobs back and forth just like one of those inflatable punching bags from the 1970s. When she was a little kid, her brother had one. It was called a Bop Bag. Basically, a large balloon with a weighted bottom.

The character on her brother's Bop Bag was Bozo the Clown... and that's near to what she's seeing in front of her now.

It is not Winn McCoy, not really.

It's a rubber Bop Bag, a Winn-McCoy-as-Bozo-Bop Bag. Same dour monkey face, but with a huge grinning red mouth, a bright red orb for a nose, and wings of scarlet hair jutting from each side of his skull. He/it bounces in the wind, smiling at her. One of the painted-on eyes winks at her.

Jaylene takes two or three fumbling steps backward, the wind off the creek cutting through her like surgical knives. She's staying on her feet through sheer force of will as a mad, swooning terror tries to kick the legs out from under her.

A cloying, gagging sweetness blows off the clown in waves of rising heat. It makes her stomach roll and her head spin. She falls back against the bridge railing. As she does so, there's a loud *skreeeeeeek!* sort of noise, the sound of stretching rubber as the clown inflates to the bursting point as if it's being pumped full of helium. It becomes a gigantic, swollen mass that bops in the wind, towering over her by many feet. Then it splits open with a spattering of greasy pink pulp and out comes an eruptive mountain of writhing flesh and boiling dark blood that rains over her, nearly burying her in a bubbling sea of gore. Another clown is born from it. It reaches for her with fingers like gnarled black roots, gluing her to it with snotty webs of tissue, welding its form to her own. Dozens of demonic clown heads rise hydra-like from it on strings like circus balloons, agonized mouths screeching at her. Licking, glutinous blue-green tongues set with thorns like rose stems lay her open, exposing the bleeding succulent fruit beneath her skin. Now the heads pop one by one, vermiform expulsions of decomposition squirming free like desert sidewinders.

Jaylene—disemboweled and slashed open—fights against the pulpous clown mass that she is now a part of. She sees another clown face emerge from a pulsing, hissing womb of anti-creation and...just for a moment...something far worse hiding behind it, an obscured, striated countenance with multiple glossy eyes, then it is gone, engulfed by a mammoth clown head that protrudes on a fleshy, wrinkled trunk. Out of its mouth and empty eye sockets great blunt worms slither. They are corpse-pallid, corkscrewing and segmented. They spiral in the air before her, then punch through her face like spinning drill bits, connecting her to it, then drawing her forward until she melts into the central clown mass.

Joined forever with it, it leaps over the railing, blazing hot and roiling, striking the snow-covered ice of the creek below with hot plumes of steam, burning its way down, down until it reaches the coveting black waters which bubble and hiss before going calm and freezing back over with a skin of ice.

81

After Teague outfits Clyde with a riot gun and Stan with a 9mm Colt, they go back out and hop into the SUV. As they drive slowly through the storm, the four-wheel drive barely punching them through drifts, ass end fishtailing, Stan begins his narration again: "We're going out into the storm again. What will we find? Will we survive an encounter with what haunts it? We drive on, perhaps to our own deaths, but certainly to an appointment with mute fate."

"Okay," Clyde says. "Shut him up or I will."

Teague sighs. "Stan, enough okay? You can do your voiceover later."

Stan shrugs.

He's pretty sure that neither of them, and particularly Clyde, can appreciate how important this documentary is and will be in the future.

82

Over at the Whistle Stop, it's nearly closing time and things are winding down as they do every night. Tonight is more downhill than ever because after the Winn McCoy/Jaylene Thone battle, everything is anticlimactic. There are about five regulars left, most staring forlornly into their beers because they know that, although they don't have to go home, they can't stay here. The preprogrammed music on the juke has kicked in and added to the forlorn sense that something has been lost which will never be found again—John Denver has finished "Take me Home, Country Roads" and the great Patsy Cline's "Walkin' After Midnight" sounds terribly melancholy.

Brick hasn't seen a night like this in years. God knows, when you're a bartender, you get your fill, but tonight... shit, it's like there's something in the air. Something unreasoning and chaotic. Even though the excitement is done for the evening (he hopes), he can still feel something building in the bar and maybe the town in general and he does not like it. What it is exactly, he cannot put a finger on. But it's not just imagination, it's there.

Wanna roust these people out of here, he thinks, *and get them damn doors closed and locked. Then I'll feel better.*

This is what he keeps telling himself. He knows if he can just get this damn night over with, things'll be okay. His digs are upstairs. All he wants is to get up there, put in a DVD, and lay on the couch.

That's all.

He's easy to please.

His nerves are really acting up tonight. He's fumble-fingered and agitated. As he sets a beer glass atop a stack of the same, he nearly collapses the entire stack with his shaking fingers.

"Easy there, cowboy," Maggie LaCross tells him, finishing off her last vodka martini of the night.

"Long night," he says over the music.

"Ain't it, though?"

Old Maggie has been a regular at the Whistle Stop for more years than Brick has been alive. Her last husband—that would be number three—died twelve years before and she likes to talk about how she drank each of them under the table and into the ground one after the other. Which is what she's doing now, only Brick is not listening. He's absently studying some of the others in the bar mirror—Bill Wiecek and his wife Pearl, a trio of younger people who are familiar but nameless to him—noticing how they look frightened, as if they're afraid to leave tonight. And it's as he does this, going through the till at the same time, that a vague sense of terror sweeps through him. Something in his chest seems to clutch as if he's on the edge of a panic attack.

That's when he sees someone sitting between Pearl Wiecek and the young trio of drinkers, right there where seconds before he swore there had been no one.

He turns around and sure enough, Midge Russo is sitting there, staring at him with bloodshot eyes, a lopsided grin on her face.

Brick's mouth goes dry at the sight of her. "Where'd you come from?" he asks her.

"I came in out of the storm," she says.

Which is insane because he knows the door has not opened. Yet, here she sits. He hasn't seen her in the Whistle Stop in many months since he threw both her and her husband out for causing trouble. Now she's back. Alone. She looks decidedly pale, her eyes glassy and bulging.

Though he does not want her kind in the bar, Brick suddenly lacks the courage to tell her to take her business elsewhere. There's something about her that gets his heart pounding and makes him feel weak in the belly.

"Last call," he says automatically.

"It's death out there," Midge says to no one in particular. "Tonight, people are dying in the storm. By morning, there's gonna be a lot of corpses out there, lot of people who ain't people any longer."

Maggie shakes her head. "Well, that's a hell of a thing to say."

"Those that leave this bar tonight will not make it home safely. They will be hunted like animals and put to death. Stalked and killed, their carcasses hung up to dry."

"Hell is she going on about?" Bill Wiecek asks.

"You need to stow it with talk like that," Brick tells her, knowing, somehow, that it will not be that simple. "Now what do you want to drink?"

Midge considers this a moment or two, tapping a long and scaly looking finger to the tip of her nose. "Ah," she says, nodding. "I'm very thirsty. Very, very, very thirsty. How about a Manhattan. I always did have a taste for them."

Brick goes to it, happy to be away from those glaring, blood-seeped eyeballs. He goes through the motions—rye whiskey, sweet vermouth, bitters. He mixes it, pours it over ice, tops it with a maraschino cherry.

Midge takes it from him and swallows it in one gulp.

"There's a thirsty girl," Maggie says, appreciating a hard drinker.

"Another," Midge says.

Brick is going to tell her she has to pay but then he sees a fifty laying on the bar. He makes change, recharges her drink. Again, one gulp and it's gone.

"Another," she says.

"Closing time," Brick tells her.

"Another."

He wants to tell her to leave, but he finds that he cannot any more than he can bring himself to turn the lights up, signaling closing time. The jukebox is supposed to wind down after Roger Miller's "Chug-a-lug" but now it's cranking again with "Whiskey Bent and Hellbound" by Hank Williams Jr. Brick isn't sure what's going on any more than he knows why he's knocking out another Manhattan for Midge. His hands seem to be moving independently of his brain.

She takes this one down just as quickly. "Another," she tells him. "And another and another and another and another."

"You better take it easy," Maggie warns her. "Maybe you don't feel it yet, but you will. You're sitting on a powder keg, hon."

"Yeah, you better go easy on that," Bill Wiecek tells her.

"BUT I'M STILL THIRSTY!" Midge shouts. "THIRSTY! THIRSTY! THIRSTY! CAN'T YOOOOOOUUUU SEEEEEEEE HOWWW THI-IIIIIRSTY I AMMMM???"

Brick knows this is out of control and he snaps out of whatever held him. He's cutting her off and getting her out that goddamned door if it's the last thing he does. She's scaring him and she's scaring the others. The crazy thing is, they do not abandon their stools and head out. They do not move. They just stare at her, transfixed, eyes empty, drinks forgotten, minds completely blanked. Even as she begins to cackle and screech like an old witch, shuddering and quaking, seeming to change as they watch. Even when her head pops up on a long serpentine neck like a Jack in the Box, they do not scream as they should—they just wait as a mouse in a snake's cage waits for death.

Brick waits, too, rooted in place behind the bar.

Her face is yellow and waxen, eyes like gelid clusters, her mouth a suckering hole of shining needles. Her head swings back and forth on a tube-like neck made of oily segments, finding first Maggie, then Pearl, fixing its mouth to them and draining the blood from them with a gurgling, slurping noise. When it drops them, they look like empty plastic bags, dirty, well-used, shriveled in upon themselves.

Brick still has not moved; he is unable to.

He is a puppet and she holds his strings taut. His nervous system has been compromised. As she comes for him, his bladder lets go. He feels hot urine run down his leg, but he does not flinch. Midge no longer looks anything like Midge—she is a crawling mass of crab-like legs that scuttle forward, dragging a heaving, bloated mass, her head darting forward on a wrinkled accordion-like neck.

As she prepares to feed upon Bill Wiecek, she releases her grip on his mind so that he can scream. But that is all he does as she comes for Bill, swollen with blood, endlessly parched, thirsty beyond reason. As she sucks his life away, the juke plays one last song—The Warm Red Wine" by Ernest Tubbs.

And Brick begins to whimper.

83

Trixie is clearly excited, bristling and barking, tensing and ready to leap. She senses clowns and she wants them dead.

"Easy," Clegg says, and she calms down but is no less alert and ready for battle.

She follows the scent into Taxi-A-Go-Go. As soon as they get inside, she starts growling. But she's well-trained and does not kick up a fuss. There's a wild stink in the air like piss-stained straw and animal remains. Clegg knows that odor very well. It's a telltale sign of what he hunts.

"Let's see what we can see," he says.

Trixie in the lead, he tours the cabstand. He sees everything that Stan did earlier—the blood in the corridor, the black footprints, the inky stained mess on the bathroom floor.

Trixie is nearly driven into a fit, particularly by the footprints and the stains on the floor. Clegg lets her check it all out, getting the scent and getting it good. With the pervading sewer smell in the bathroom, it's a wonder she can pick up anything. But she does. And the first place she leads him is to the cellar door.

He opens it, flicking the light switch. The bulb below provides scant illumination. Clegg takes a deep breath and looks down at Trixie. "Go slow, girl, but get it done."

The dog, almost calmly, goes down the steps with Clegg right behind her. She pauses at the bottom, cocking her head as if she's listening for something. Then she puts her nose to the floor and instantly shudders. She's got the scent. There's no doubt.

She casually follows it, turning this way and then that, but always zeroing in on the spoor. She follows it right to the brick partition at the far end.

She growls in that characteristic way of hers. Clegg understands. He puts his light on the nest that Stan discovered, the collection of rags and bones and scraps that the clown had been resting on. Much of it is saturated with blood now.

"Get back," he tells Trixie.

He points the gun assembly of the flamethrower at the nest. He squeezes the trigger briefly and the nest is burning with orange-yellow flames, crisping and popping. The burning stink is nauseating.

Then Trixie barks.

A clown stands there. Clegg appraises his old enemy—black satin clown suit with the red polka dots, the green hair, the pallid face and dead eyes set in greasy black ovals. The clown breathes rapidly, its chest rising and falling. It looks at him with scarlet, malevolent eyes that bleed red tears. Its lips pull back from hooked yellow teeth.

Then it screams with a high-decibel blast of maniacal hatred, gouts of yellow foam dripping from its jaws which now look oddly sickle-shaped.

Clegg squeezes the trigger of the flamethrower and a gout of fire hits the clown, knocking it back in a loose semicircle, engulfing it with flame. It squeals and screeches, throwing itself against the wall and then forward, flaming bits raining from it. It fights against the flames, tearing and clawing at itself, ripping out smoldering chunks and burning clots of tissue in a lunatic whirlwind of motion.

And a voice in the back of Clegg's mind says, *wait... wait now. It's going to show itself. It's going to show what it really is. It has no choice now.*

And it doesn't.

So it does what comes natural to it: it escapes.

Lit up like a melting candle, it literally explodes from its skin.

The burning clown hide splits open and hits the floor in a pall of greasy smoke, crackling and popping, a pink gushing protoplasmic form emerging and becoming something alive and skittering and completely alien. It is a large, quivering brown-gray mass of withering shrouds and folds of creeping flesh. A dozen jointed, crab-like legs, spurred and scrambling, sprout from it along with a snapping, coiling tail that looks like an undulant spinal column. The entire thing is sizzling and sputtering. It is damaged, burnt and still blazing in places. A bone-like webbing rises from its arched back and looks oddly like it might have supported wings.

"You ain't going anywhere," Clegg tells it.

It squeals and mewls, glaring out at him with a sort of face which sprouts eight or ten globular eyeballs, and a proboscis-like snout with a suckering mouth and bunches of wiry yellow tendrils.

Then he squeezes the trigger and the beast is once again engulfed in flame. It rages and screeches, smashing into the walls, flaying out with crisping black appendages, finally crumpling into itself and curling up on the floor like a dead spider. As it burns, it makes crackling, popping sounds like green, sap-filled wood.

By then, the cellar is filled with rolling clouds of black pungent smoke. Clegg watches it burn a moment longer, then gets out of there.

"Well, girl," he says to Trixie as they climb the steps. "That's one."

84

For whatever reason, Midge does not feed on Brick. She turns away and slips into the back of the Whistle Stop where the pool tables are, scuttling away on her many clicking legs. He waits for her to return, but she does not. He stands there, drained corpses sprawled about him like deflated balloons. Inside his head, he is bleeding out. There is an ugly, gaping wound up there, the blood not just running, but gushing out of him, emptying him much as Midge emptied the others.

He stands there uneasily for about ten minutes, then he starts to move. It does not seem to be a conscious decision. Like an automaton, he marches towards the back room with a lumbering, mechanical tread.

NO! NO! NO! PLEASE OH GOD NO! a voice in his head screams at the force that holds it, compels it. LET ME GO! LET ME GO! PLEASE PLEASE LET ME GO!

He fights desperately for control, but he is weak, weaker than he has ever been in his life. His feet carry him along through the back room. There are, realistically, only three places he can be going, and he knows it—the banquet room in the rear, the back exit, or down to the basement. He knows it will be the third option and it makes him shiver white with terror.

Not there, not there...

But, yes, that's exactly where he's going. The crazy, unsettling thing is that all night long he has been thinking about the basement. Maybe not in the front of his mind, but surely in the back or underneath in the dark pit of his subconscious. Regardless, it has been there ever since he came on, an unnatural sort of magnetism drawing him to the basement as if there's something there he simply must see. The only thing that's stopped him from going down there thus far, was something like common sense tempered by fear.

I don't know what's down there, he thought beneath his thoughts many hours before, but I don't like it. I don't like it at all.

Now he's thinking it again as he's compelled to go down there and face what terrifies him the most. Something which is formless in his mind, but no less destructive in its monolithic terror.

He stands before the basement door, his guts shriveling in his belly. His hand reaches out and touches the knob, grips it, turns it, and slowly pulls the door open. A hot stench of dry-rot, age, and something like rotting pelts comes up from the cellar darkness. He breathes it in, repelled at some primary level. The terror inside him rises to dangerous levels. His heart pounds and fear-sweat trickles down his temples.

He descends into the darkness, down, down, taking each worn wooden step slowly and carefully. At the bottom, his hand reflexively reaches for the light switch. He flicks it. The light comes on for less than a second before the bulb crackles and goes out. But it's long enough for him to see that there are things down there which do not belong. Insane and impossible things that make the flesh at his spine crawl.

Please, oh please, no further!

But, of course, he does go further. Because that's part of it. He wasn't directed down there by that unknown, omnipotent force just to catch a fleeting, split-second glance of what waits for him, but to know it on a very private, intimate level, to have his face rubbed in its obscene awfulness.

He walks across the floor, nearly drenched in freezing sweat, and things bump into him, hanging things. They brush him and thump into him and he knows that's because he has upset them, that they are swinging back and forth now like laundry sacks. Whatever they are, they have an oily, reptilian sort of feel to them like snakeskins.

Before his heart completely seizes with fright, the bulb overhead flickers dully to life. Not completely but providing a dim and flickering illumination. Enough so that he can see those things that dangle from the rafters like the chrysalises of butterflies.

Clown costumes.

This is what hangs from the rafters: clown costumes. Dozens of them hanging from hooks. The amazing thing is that they are not just the satiny suits themselves, but the floppy shoes and gloves and the horrendous grinning clown masks. They are less like suits or costumes and more like empty clowns. There is darkness in their eye sockets and beyond their mouths. They are flaccid things, seemingly waiting for wearers, for life, their heads sagging to their shoulders as if their necks have been snapped by hangman's nooses.

The terror that owns Brick is feverish and dreamlike—it is unreal and nightmarish, yet perhaps more real than anything he has ever known in his life. It is at that moment that he becomes painfully aware that his very presence has agitated the clown suits. They're not only swinging back and forth around him but making hissing noises that he recognizes as respiration.

Now there are slithering noises around him, followed by rustling sounds, a creaking and a popping. He soon sees why. The clown suits are activating, they are inflating, they are coming alive around him. A terrible face looks down at him, its mouth rotted into a black, cancerous hole. It has one bulging green eye; the other is a yellow suppurating crevice. Other faces, white as bone, press in like balloons, watching him with bleary, mucus-filled eyes and smiling with sagging mouths of blackened teeth.

They are all coming alive.

This is what he feared all day and was brought here to see. As they are born around him, it's like watching some mass hatching of snakes. They swing back and forth on their hooks, slithering and squirming, filling with meat and blood and evil intent.

Inside his head, Brick screams but he does not run. He waits and soon enough the clowns drop from their hooks, crowding around him. He begins to whimper as they put their white puffy hands on him and then their mouths.

Last call at the Whistle Stop and the lights go out.

85

Within ten minutes, Teague has heard it all. All that he wants to. All that he can stomach. As Peanut fills him in on the Bonnie-Skunk situation, he feels something in his belly begin to do a slow crawl. He wants to go over to Skunk and beat his face in. It would give him immense satisfaction to do so, but he cannot give into such things. The situation is bad enough without making it worse. Due process of law, due process of law.

"It's my fault," he says as he stands there, the last of the ice dropping from him. "I should have known better than to leave this biker trash here with you, Bonnie. I apologize for that. For my lack of concern for your safety."

"It's not your fault, Sheriff," Bonnie says.

"In the morning, we'll sort this out and bring up charges of attempted rape on this piece of shit," Teague tells her.

Peanut nods with satisfaction at how Teague is handling things: properly, legally, with great calm. Nathan watches Skunk very carefully. Whether he is angry or not, is anyone's guess. He looks as he always does—determined, capable. The man that Stan finds the most interesting is Clyde. He does not rant or rave, he just watches Skunk with narrowed eyes, giving him the sort of look that makes Skunk wither.

If I was him, Stan thinks, *I wouldn't buy any green bananas.*

While Teague and Peanut chat it out with Bonnie and Carpy, Clyde steps over near Nathan and whispers something to him. Whatever it is, Stan figures it must be something dire and final. Then they both watch Skunk carefully. He does not meet their eyes.

God, if I could just get this on video!

But Stan doesn't dare because he has the feeling that he's on Clyde's last nerve and he doesn't want to push things. He knows enough about the leader of the Dead Skulls to realize that you do not push him.

Now Teague turns toward Skunk after giving Clyde a hard look that plainly says, I trusted you. Just this once I trusted you and you let me down. He steps nearer to him, hands on his hips.

"You didn't think we had enough shit to deal with tonight? You thought you'd throw in some rape to spice things up, eh?"

Skunk's bruised and bloodied face does not emote. "I didn't rape anybody."

"You were going to!" Bonnie snaps.

"Yes, you were," Peanut says. "You had a knife on her."

"I was defending myself. She pulled a knife on me first."

Bonnie's face reddens. "It was a paring knife! I was trying to protect myself!"

"And you had every right," Teague tells her. "Every right."

"Shit," Skunk says.

"You need to shut your mouth now," Nathan says as he steps in between Skunk and Clyde.

Stan watches it all. Amazing. It looked like Clyde was going to go for Skunk. That's a beat down you wouldn't want to miss. Nathan is trying to diffuse the situation. That's obvious. Stan does not doubt that if Skunk evades Teague's law, that he will not evade Clyde's.

"Everybody's making a big stink over nothing," Skunk says, trying hard to look like the cool, rational one. "She's been teasing me all night. I was just going for it was all and she pulled the knife. Shit, I got needs. We all got needs, don't we? Bitch was just pulling my chain."

What might have happened then was anyone's guess, but something intervenes. The front door opens and Clegg steps inside with a mean-looking Rottweiler. It's like something from a movie because everyone stops what they were doing, forgetting what they were saying, and just stares. In his long fur coat and flat-brimmed hat Clegg looks like a bounty hunter from a western. And maybe that's not too far from the truth.

"Evening," he says, promptly locking the door behind him.

Teague is the first one to snap out of it. "Where the hell is my dispatcher? Where is Patti?"

Clegg nonchalantly produces a cigarette and lights it. His dog is growling low in its throat. It's either ready to protect its master or there's someone in the room it does not like.

"When she let me out, she was fine," Clegg explains. "I told her to go home and stay there. Lock herself in."

Teague has a riot gun in his hands, and it looks as if he's thinking of bringing it up, but he doesn't. And whether that's because of the dog or the military-grade weapons Clegg is carrying, it's hard to say.

"If anything has happened to her—"

Exhaling a cloud of smoke, Clegg says, "If anything has happened to her, it has nothing to do with me. I'm not what's killing people out there and I think you damn well know that."

"But... but you can't break out of jail! It's not legal!" Peanut stammers.

This brings a sort of half-smile to Clegg's face. "Son, I did not break out. Patti kindly let me out so I could kill these damn clowns."

Stan has his camera up and he's shooting it all. This is good. This is just too good to miss.

"Somebody should probably explain what's going on here," Carpy says, still groggy from sleep and too much booze.

Peanut explains it as quick as he can.

"So you're here to save us?" Clyde says. "Well, ain't we lucky."

Clegg does not bother commenting on that. He takes in the club vests that Clyde and Nathan and Skunk wear. On the backs of each, there is a jawless human skull impaled by a dagger. Above, it reads: DEAD SKULLS, mc. And below, VERMILLION SD. That's all he really needs to know; he can put the rest together pretty easily.

"He's got that flamethrower on his back," Peanut says, something which is patently obvious.

He does. He's also wearing the chromed-up .44 Magnum on his hip and has a Remington 879 12-gauge pump with a pistol grip in his left hand. He is most certainly loaded for bear. Stan is videoing it all. He's not about to miss out on a confrontation like this.

Teague says, "I suppose it wouldn't do me any good to tell you to drop your weapons."

"None. And there's no reason to since I'm no threat to you or any other human being."

Teague sighs.

Clyde being Clyde has brought up his riot gun. "I think I can take you out before you can bring that shotgun up."

"Put it down, Clyde," Teague orders him.

"You might be able to do that, my friend. But you're forgetting about one thing."

"Yeah?"

Now, slowly, Clegg opens his fur duster the rest of the way. Before, all they could see was the .44 Mag at his hip, now everyone sees something of a much more disturbing variety: he wears a camouflage vest with six blocks of some yellow material wired together.

"It's a goddamn bomb belt like a terrorist!" Peanut says.

"And it's wired to my wrist. I hit the button, this place is flattened," Clegg explains.

"What is that stuff?"

"Semtex," Clyde says as if he's very familiar with it. "Plastic explosive."

He lowers his gun and steps back now.

"What the hell is it you want with us?" Teague finally asks him. "The clowns are out there."

Clegg utters a low unpleasant laugh. "Not all of 'em, Sheriff. Sees that's why my dog led me here—because you got clowns among you. Some of you ain't quite what you appear to be. And now we're going to find out who is who."

With that, he brings up the spout of his flamethrower. Which, of course, is threatening enough. But it's not this that makes the others step away from each other and cast suspicious eyes at one another. Any one of them might be a clown and they know it.

"Nobody leaves," Clegg says and he's not fooling around. "Not until we find out who the clowns are."

86

Something has changed in the bar. Something has shifted or been altered. The atmosphere feels heavier, brooding, and threatening. Clegg no longer seems to be the enemy nor does Skunk. Now everyone is suspect. The paranoia spreads from person to person.

The Rottweiler is watching everyone with a blank, killing stare, her hackles up. She is growling and looks ready to leap.

Clegg pets her and lets her lick his hand. "Boys, I want to introduce you to Trixie. She's one-hundred percent clown hound. If they're around, you can bet this girl will find them."

Stan says, "Trixie is a heck of a name for a beast like that," he says.

The dog watches him with steely eyes, suspicious of the camera and him in general.

"No offense, pooch," Stan offers by way of apology.

Clegg pets Trixie, rubbing her behind her ears. "She don't take no offense, mister. She's smart and loyal and she'll defend me to the death. You, too, once she trusts you."

"Why don't you shitcan that camera, Stan," Clyde says.

"Because I'm documenting this. If it's not documented, who'll believe us...right, Sheriff?"

Teague shrugs. "I don't give a damn. Keep it rolling. Why not?"

Clegg pulls off his cigarette. "What we're going to do now might get ugly. In fact, I can assure you that it will get ugly, but there's no other way. The killing of clowns is serious business."

Stan grins. He actually got that on camera. The killing of clowns is serious business. That's a good one. That's more than he could have hoped for.

"So you're just going to start killing innocent people because your dog says they're clowns?" Bonnie asks.

"No, darling. I have no intention of killing innocents. Trixie is always right. She can smell things you or I can't. And until we separate the clowns from the people, you're all suspect." He gives his full attention to Bonnie. "You, for example. How do I know you're not one of them?"

"Because I'm not!"

"So you say. The signal could have gotten to you or one of them might have grabbed you when you were alone."

"This is stupid," Peanut says.

But no one else seems to think so. They are watching the proceedings very carefully, even Teague.

"But I haven't been alone!" Bonnie informs them.

"Yes, you have," Skunk says, grinning. "You went off to the kitchen by yourself more than once. You were in the shitter by yourself two or three times. I know. I was watching."

"So you went to the bathroom by yourself?" Clegg says, pointing his shotgun at her.

She gives him a dirty look. "I've been going pee by myself for many years now."

Carpy giggles at that.

Clegg, however, sees no humor in it. "One of them could have gotten to you in there. It might be wearing your skin and talking to me right now."

All eyes are on Bonnie now. She expects someone to intervene on her behalf and point out how silly all this is, but no one does. No one at all. She begins to feel threatened. Her green eyes dart helplessly about.

"Maybe we ought to slow down," Nathan says, holding up one hand. "Let's not go crazy here."

For a moment or two, no one says anything. They listen to the dismal, forlorn sound of the wind outside as it howls around the Broken Bottle. Snow hits the outer walls like sand. Rafters groan and outside, a loose board rattles.

Skunk seems to be enjoying it all. "No, you're right, Mr. Clegg, she might be one. I wouldn't trust her." His smile widens. "And for that matter, I been to the shitter by myself quite a few times. Even been outside a couple times. I might be one, too."

"Then maybe I ought to kill you right now," Nathan says, pointing his gun at him. "Save me some work later."

Skunk keeps grinning. "And if I'm one of them clowns, it'll be the last you do." He enjoys the unease and paranoia, the outright suspicion and the willingness of people to turn on one another. "You and Peanut were out in that storm for a long time. Who knows what might have happened out there?"

"Shut the hell up," Nathan tells him.

"Were you two together out there all the time?" Clegg asks them. "Did you leave each other's side for even a few minutes?"

Peanut swears under his breath. "Tony got out of the cruiser, said he had to throw up. Then he ran. We went after him. We got separated for a couple minutes... I saw a clown. But it was Nathan who killed it. If he was a clown, why would he kill one of his own?"

"So you'd be thinking he wasn't one," Carpy says.

"Yeah, he's got a point," Bonnie agrees.

Nathan glares at her, wondering if maybe he should have let Skunk have his fun with her. Bitch sure turned on him fast.

"Bullshit," Peanut says, standing closer to Nathan as if they're old pals. "Besides, when I saw that clown, I shot it. When it went down, it looked just like you, Bonnie. I thought I killed you. Now why would it take on your appearance?"

"How the hell should I know!" Bonnie says, clearly agitated.

Skunk giggles. "Only two reasons, Peanut. Either you got yourself a hard-on for Miss Perky Tits and the clown knew it...or because she's one of them."

"I am not!"

"Everyone settle down," Teague finally says.

Clyde shakes his head. "This... this is just crazy. It's a mindfuck. A big goddamned mindfuck."

And that's exactly what it is. The confusion and uncertainty were deepening. Even club brothers like Clyde and Nathan were keeping their distance from one another.

Although Stan keeps filming it all with the Apeman, he's getting scared by all this. His heart is pounding, his nerves jangling. Like the others, he very badly wants to run from the bar, get away from everyone.

They might all be clowns... who knows? he finds himself thinking. But this does not make him feel better. He feels very paranoid, as if they all might jump out of their skins at any moment and attack him.

Clyde, clearly needing a diversion, says, "So tell us about this signal."

"It's how they get places," Clegg explains.

"They broadcast themselves?"

"In a way."

"That's nuts."

"How did you think they got here? On the bus?"

Clyde bristles a bit at that, but he holds in his anger. He has a feeling that Clegg is as much of a wicked ass-kicker as he himself. And there's the bomb belt to be considered, too.

"They send themselves like radio waves?" Teague asks.

Clegg shrugs. "Not exactly. I'm not a hundred percent sure how they do it or what form of energy they take, but I do know that they send themselves places using infrastructure that's already in place—telecom towers, radio dishes, cellular networks. They need a receiver and they always manage to find one. There's a tower about three miles outside town. That's the one they're using, I'd bet."

"That's the old WKKY tower," Teague tells him. "It hasn't been used in twenty years."

"Doesn't matter. It's still capable of receiving and transmitting. At least for them."

Stan jumps in. "Okay, this is probably crazy but what about taking out that tower? Dynamiting it or what not?"

"I was thinking the same thing," Clyde says.

"A little too late. They're already here. Among us."

But Stan's not buying that, not completely. "But they're still broadcasting that signal. It almost got Patti. I was there. I recorded it. Maybe we should knock that tower out."

Clegg shakes his head. "They're here. We need to destroy them. That's the black and white of things, people. And we have to do that one by one, same way they got here."

Which brings them full circle, everyone realizes.

Clegg explains that the signal works like any other sound—your ear picks it up, the eardrums and associated bones vibrate, the vibrations are transferred to the inner ear via fluid where the hair cells of the cochlea change them into chemical signals for the nerves that send them as electrical impulses to the brain for instantaneous interpretation.

"And that's where the trouble starts—those impulses have something coded mathematically in them that will crush your willpower and personality and begin a horrible mutation, making you into one of them."

"But what are they?" Stan asks.

Clegg shakes his head. "A life-form. Where it comes from, we don't know. It can broadcast itself anywhere and replicate itself with available biological materials."

Stan is loving it. Even though Clyde gets annoyed every time he starts shooting with the Apeman, he keeps doing it. His video documentation is the most important testament they have. But in his mind, he keeps thinking, the sound, the signal, the sound. It's all tied up in that. If you couldn't necessarily shut it off, maybe you could disrupt it somehow. He's not sure how it would work, but there's something there and he knows it. Something important.

"All right," Clegg says. "Enough bullshitting around. All of you line up against the bar. And put those weapons you carry on the floor."

"Fuck that," Clyde says.

"You'll get 'em back when I know you're human," Clegg tells him.

"Just do it," Teague says.

You don't argue with a guy wearing a bomb belt.

Riot guns and handguns are set on the floor and they all begrudgingly line up as Clegg asked.

"You want me next to you?" Skunk asks Bonnie.

"Fuck you," she says.

"Hey, the night's still young."

"You better shut your mouth," Teague warns him.

Skunk giggles. Nothing seems to have an effect on him now. He's not intimidated by Clyde and Nathan, nor remotely impressed by Teague.

"Okay, let's do this then," Clegg says. "Let's find out who is who."

87

This is great, this is just fucking wonderful, Nathan thinks as everyone stands there, waiting for it. Nobody dares get close to anyone else because no one trusts anyone. That's what it has come down to. Although his rational mind understands the reasons for this all too well, deep inside he is sickened.

"When this is over with, my brother," Clyde tells him, "we're going to straighten out some shit."

Which is the sort of thing Clyde often says to him being that he is the club president's right-hand man. But Nathan can see beyond his words and he knows that Clyde is as paranoid as the rest now. Through all the fighting and bleeding and turf wars they have stood together; now these clowns threaten to tear them apart.

Clegg comes over with Trixie and she's as mean-looking as any bitch Nathan has ever seen. Drool hangs from her jaws. She is heavy-bodied, well-muscled, yet quick for her size. And (he fears) goddamned smart as her breed tend to be. She studies the crew assembled there, then steps lightly toward Teague and begins to growl.

"Now wait a minute," he says.

Then all hell breaks loose.

88

Bullshit," Peanut says. "There's no goddamn way Will is a fucking clown!"

The sound of his voice is jarring in the silence. It seems to echo through the bar, bouncing around and coming right back at him. He steps from the line and Clegg puts the business end of the flamethrower on him.

Trixie barks.

"Peanut! Get back here!" Teague orders.

You better listen to him," Clegg says in a ragged whisper. "Or I'll light your ass up.

The sound of his voice makes Peanut ill. He wants to throttle him, stomp him, shoot his guts out. God, he's sick to his stomach—something crawls inside him like a parasitic infestation. Whatever malefic unknown quantity poisons the very atmosphere of the Bottle, it's inside him now. God, it's in his blood and marrow, gestating in his cells, filling him with a formless darkness.

Clegg and his dog pull back.

"Just wait!" Teague says.

"Peanut?" Nathan says in a subdued voice that is not quite a whisper. "Peanut?"

But Peanut cannot hear what he is saying and if he does, it makes no sense. Not over that other noise that seems to be inside him and outside of him at the same time. It's a squealing drone like the feedback from an amplifier and it cycles up louder and louder as he listens and tries not to. The noise tears his thoughts to fragments. He shakes and shudders, the room spinning around him

And from somewhere very far away and far too close he hears a voice that just might be his own screaming: "STOP IT! STOP IT! MAKE THAT

GODDAMN RACKET STOP! I CAN'T THINK! I CAN'T I CAN'T I CAN'T..."

Teague steps in and slaps Peanut across the face. It has no effect. Peanut is still shouting only now his words are nonsensical gibberish:

"...INAHOUSEINAMINDINACRAZYPLACEWHERELAUGH-LAUGHALLTHECRAZYFACESLAUGHANDTHEANGLESS-CREAMLITTLEBUNNYFOOFOOIDON'TWANTTOSEEY-OUINACRAZYHAZYPLACEPICKINGUPPICKINGUPTHES-IGNALTHESIGNALTHESIGNALWHAT'SYOURFREQUENCYKEN-NETH—"

Teague slaps him again and again and again, more now out of fear and confusion rather than anger. Peanut is convulsing, limbs whipsawing in every which direction, his body gyrating and his head snapping back and forth, shoulder to shoulder. It's like he's being electrocuted.

And then he hits the floor.

By this time, everyone has pulled way away from him.

He's on his knees, still trembling, an occasional abdominal spasm running through him as if he's got the dry heaves.

"Peanut?" Teague says, his voice edged with panic. "Oh, Jesus, Peanut... what the hell is going on?"

But if he doesn't know, everyone else does.

"CLOWN!" Carpy cries out. "HE'S A FUCKING CLOWN!"

Peanut begins to giggle with a low, evil laughter. Slowly he lifts his head and, of course, he's no longer Peanut. He is something else now. The signal has gotten inside of him and converted him, and he is no longer good old lovable guitar-playing Peanut who wouldn't hurt a fly.

"*Peeeeyaaanit,*" he says in a particularly dry and scraping voice, blowing out coffin dust from his lungs. "*Jeeeezizzpeeee... yaaanitjeeeezizzpeeeeyaaani tjeeeezizzpeeeeyaaanit... waadahellllllllllizzzgoinonnnnnnnn...*"

Teague stumbles back out of shock and terror because what Peanut is saying is bad enough, but his face...it has changed. It has gone milk-white, the nose hawkish and hooked like that of an old crone. His mouth is a black, flayed oval big around as a fist, eyes pressed into narrow sockets painted black. The eyeballs spin, one clockwise and the other counterclockwise.

He lets out a screeching sort of sound and begins to tear the hair from his scalp with white talons. He leaves only a few wiry bunches at the top. Now his hands claw at his skull, tearing grooves in it. Rivers of gore run down the whiteness of his face. Blood spatters his cheeks.

"Not you, Peanut... oh Christ, not you," Teague says.

The clown opens its mouth of silver needles and lets out the roar of a beast. It is so loud that it actually rattles beer glasses on the bar top.

Trixie is barking and snapping at him. Clegg orders her back and the clown advances on him. Maybe it was Peanut once, but not anymore. Even clown does not completely encapsulate what they are seeing—a pallid-faced white, gelatinous monstrosity that bulges from Peanut's uniform like Pillsbury dough from a biscuit tube. His eyes are huge, glassy, and purple-red, rolling in their sockets, his face a pulpous, membranous mass threaded with brilliant red veins. He reaches out with hands like flaccid tentacles, the fingers of which corkscrew like worms exposed to sunlight.

"DO IT FOR CHRISSAKE!" Clyde shouts. "BURN HIM!"

The clown hisses as Clegg shoots a brilliant tongue of flame at he/it. The burning fluid covers him, and he screeches with manic fury and agony as he's reduced to a fighting, dying, melting shape that crackles and pops, finally bouncing off the bar and landing on the floor in a black, sizzling mass.

Stan nearly falls over his own feet as he watches the clown that was Peanut turned into a blazing pyre that shrieks and carbonizes and falls to pieces. He bumps into Teague who shoves him out of the way because things are suddenly happening on every front now. The entire bar begins to rattle and shake, the lights flickering.

He hears Bonnie scream.

Clyde is gripping the sides of his head and shouting something about his brain exploding and there's no doubt that the signal has found him, too, and is inside him. He clenches his teeth as blood foams from his mouth and his head snaps back and forth. Things pop and snap inside of him as he contorts and convulses. It seems as if his body is not a body at all but a writhing nest of alien worms that move beneath his flesh like corded muscle and explode from his mouth and eyes in coiling, twisting, segmented pink ropes. He boils and oozes, becoming clown-like and then wears a dozen faces that melt into one another as spurred limbs and rubbery tendrils and clusters of eyes emerge.

Teague dives to the floor, grabs a 9mm handgun that once belonged to Peanut, and empties the clip into the Clyde-thing with little result save that it jerks with each slug. Nathan, still bound by his blood oath to the club, dives on Teague and begins pounding the hell out of him with a wild flurry of rights and lefts until Bonnie shatters a bottle of Skyy vodka over his head. He does not go out, but as he tries to stand, he trips over his own feet.

Stan is still filming as the Broken Bottle shakes again as if something immense has bumped into it. He falls back against the bar and quickly brings his camera up once again and sees... he does not know what he sees—something hiding inside of Clyde and the living, metamorphosing, undulant column of flesh and feelers and globular eyes he has become. For a second, the mass opens, and he sees something else in there, something eldritch and impossible and geometrically deranged that must be the true form of the clown that transmits itself as electrical energy, then it's gone, pillowed in a convulsive, bubbling stew of clown-flesh and rippling tissue.

Clegg tries to get a clear shot at the Clyde-thing, screaming, "OUT OF THE WAY! GET THE FUCK OUT OF THE WAY!" but it's sheer pandemonium in the smoking, gore-strewn bar.

Just as he thinks he's got a clear corridor for firing, Trixie goes shit-crazy and launches herself at Clyde with manic hatred. She vaults up and seizes one of his many spiraling, scaly tentacles in her mouth...and squeals immediately. It's like biting into a high-tension line or a white-hot stalk of pig iron—her mouth is seared and smoking, the jaws welded together by secreted acids or intense heat or both. The tentacle—pulsating and pink and knobby with warts—lifts the agonized animal up into the air, swinging her back and forth, smashing her into Teague who takes Carpy down with him.

As Clegg cries out, Trixie is blown up like a helium balloon and then pops as what look like dozens of worming entrails explode out of her.

The Clyde-thing, wailing and squirming, has now become something like a clicking crustacean from hell—a wriggling, soft-bodied thing encased in shell-like plates from which rise bony, conical protuberances like horns. It balances itself on a thorny tail, rising up like an attacking millipede with dozens of tiny quivering legs hanging from its belly. It slithers and hisses, creaks and squeals and makes the most horrendous grinding, chitinous noises. Clear, oily jelly exudes from beneath its plates and its head—if it is a head—is glossy and speckled brown, a dozen black gelid eyes arranged in a semi-circle.

Then its jaws open, revealing shard-like teeth and three blue-green tongues set with suckers... and then, as awful as all that is, the creature kicks it up a notch by vomiting out what looks like the mucid embryonic head and upper body of a clown, bulbous and rubbery-lipped, formed of some vibrating thread-like tissue. From the holes of the clown's eyes and mouth, finely segmented worming shapes emerge to lick the air.

Clegg squeezes the trigger on the flamethrower, then squeezes it again, and the unearthly thing before them explodes with fire, shrilling and wailing...

90

Well, isn't that how the old wheel of chance spins? Skunk thinks to himself as he watches the absolute chaos unravel around him. *You're all set to nibble some blue-ribbon tee-tahs and tap the mystery of the Juicy Lucy and look what the fucking cat drags in.*

Goddamn Peanut and Nathan.

Then Teague and Clyde.

And what a fucking mess it is now.

These thoughts pass through his mind quickly as he's hit by a perfectly rancid stench of mossy corpses. It makes him recoil and gag. The contents of his stomach—mostly greasy pizza from the Broken Bottle's old pizza oven—jump around in his belly and try to leap up the back of his throat. He has not smelled anything so bad since that time he and Mongol opened Big Tuna's (Mike Murchowsky's) grave out in the woods after he'd been in it a month to get the keys to his Chrysler Imperial.

Jesus.

Now there is a clown and Skunk figures it's just for him.

It stands there, wearing a yellow sort of Ronald McDonald jumper and silly red shoes and Skunk is pretty certain it's of the female variety. It waits with a limp stance, arms hanging, head tipped sideways. It does not even look real. The face is long and narrow, white as corpse flesh. It looks like a rubber mask—mouth sprung open in a toothless grin, eyes empty black sockets. Blood has run from them in garish red streaks and gouts of it stain the mouth crimson. A lemon-yellow scalp lock hangs from the top of its head and dangles over its shoulder.

It looks, in whole, like some kind of horror show mannequin waiting there.

Skunk is not given to fear.

It's generally thought in the Dead Skulls that he's simply too stupid to be afraid. Maybe there's something to that, but for one moment, horror floods through him, leaving him feeling chilled and helpless.

But it passes.

In Skunk's experience, all things do one way or another.

When Carpy tunes in on the signal, his change (like Peanut's and Clyde's) happens very quickly and seemingly without provocation. Being the sort of guy he is, he's trying to make his way towards the door when it happens.

Nathan sees it coming and goes right after him as does Teague. Maybe they were pounding the tar out of each other not moments before, but now they're unified in killing what Carpy has become.

They cut off his advance and he turns towards Stan and Bonnie, showing them what has erupted from his skin—a quivering collection of egg-like eyes and slashing tendrils. The eyes are red with black pupils that dart in every which direction. The tendrils whip back and forth, trying to strike at anything that gets too near.

Nathan blasts away with one of the riot guns, pulverizing eyes and squirming ropes and snapping tendrils. The creature bleeds a brown ichor. But despite being wounded and taking another three rounds from Teague it is surprisingly agile and healthy. It leaps from the floor up onto the bar top as more rounds punch into it, popping eyeballs and splattering gore that is sometimes brown as dried blood or green as antifreeze.

A snaking limb whips out with blurring speed and nearly takes Nathan's head off. He stands there momentarily, too surprised to die, then hits the floor, limbs shaking before going still.

"Shit," Teague says under his breath.

Clegg fires the flamethrower at the creature until it and the bar top itself are awash in fire. The Carpy-thing howls and screeches and hisses angrily, finally dropping to the floor, burning and withering, blackening to a shuddering husk. Two scythe-shaped talons rise from it but lack the strength to fight and collapse into the bubbling, smoldering tar pit of the creature itself.

92

The clown still has not moved.

And although he knows better, Skunk cannot get past the idea that it's fake. The eye sockets look into an empty black void. There are no teeth in the mouth, only darkness. He's nearly certain that if he kicks it, it'll fall right over.

But if it's fake, man, then who put it there? And how did they do it without you noticing?

Skunk moves forward carefully. The knife is still in his hand. He has stabbed over a dozen men in his life. He knows how to do it. How to strike, how to jab, and how to finish it with a quick slash across the throat.

He steps lightly.

His hand tightens on the knife.

He expects the clown to wake up at the last possible moment the way such things do in fright flicks, but it merely stands there like a spook house dummy. Skunk licks his lips and then rams the knife into the clown's belly. He moves very fast and it's doubtful that the clown could have stopped him even if it wanted to. The knife goes in and Skunk follows it with a flurry of jabs that would have easily incapacitated the toughest of men, making them fold up and bleed out.

Blood that is black as dirty brake fluid runs from the wounds and stains the clown's jumper. It trickles to the floor and forms an oily pool.

Behind Skunk, Bonnie gasps.

He likes that gasping.

It excites him.

The clown moves. It lifts its head and looks into his face with its hollow eyes, a single trickle of blood coming from its corpse-grinning mouth.

Skunk buries the knife in its chest.

It has no effect.

Even though the face remains stiff and immobile like a rubber mask, he can hear the clown breathing. It's as if its outer shell is dead, but its core is very much alive.

Skunk feels fear, the first real fear he has felt in years. It's incapacitating. In the mere seconds from the time he slammed the knife into the clown's chest until he's overwhelmed by pure terror, the clown takes hold of him. It moves fast. It has claws like a panther and with one devastating swipe, it opens up his belly. Viscera and blood explode out of him and splash across the top of a table, knocking over several beer glasses.

Bonnie screams.

Skunk, making a wet gobbling sort of sound, falls into the clown's arms. It takes its time with him. Perhaps it senses the romance and passion in his soul, the need for shared intimacy. As he bleeds out, the clown holds him up, shaking him like a doll, his entrails swinging back and forth like blood blooms and moist, peeled snakes. It rocks him like a baby, splashing itself with his fluids.

Maybe this is foreplay.

If so, next comes consummation, the act itself: the clown's mouth splits wide and out of it comes a mass of viscid pink eyeballs with darting pupils like a cluster of grapes. They emerge with a convulsive collection of yellow, snake-like tendrils that suction themselves to his face with nickel-sized suckers. And then from the squirming nest of these, something else, something possibly worse—an orifice like a toothed vulva that bites into him and peels his face from the skull beneath with a busy tearing/slurping/scraping noise.

Once his skull is crushed and the seed of his gray matter loosened, the clown bites into his throat, sucking the blood out of him with a juicy suctioning noise. This lasts but seconds. Then the clown takes hold of his head and twists it around on his neck. The sound is like that of a leg being torn from a Thanksgiving turkey—grinding and gristly, followed by a wet popping. The latter being Skunk's vertebrae letting go as his head is ripped free.

The clown turns towards Bonnie.

Blood-spattered and grinning, carrying the trophy of Skunk's head in one hand, it begins to move in her direction stepping over his corpse.

Then Teague shouts, "BONNIE!" and yanks her out of the way just as the clown is engulfed in fire courtesy of Clegg.

283

93

Now all that's left is Teague and Clegg, Bonnie and Stan. The Broken Bottle rumbles and shakes. They fall against one another, trying to stay on their feet. Something is happening. Something beyond anything they have known as yet. That it will be terrible, they do not doubt, and possibly awful beyond description.

The bar is burning. The smoke is thick, and flames lick up the walls. They need to get out of there, yet, they do not move. Survival instinct should send them running out into the night but after so much loss, it does not seem to exist within them any longer. They stand there next to each other, Stan and Bonnie holding hands, but all of them pressed in tightly together. Save Clegg, they all unconsciously reflect on what a perfectly mundane night it started as and how impossibly insane it has now become. Clegg knows it had to come to this. One of these times, it had to come to this.

In each of their minds, they think private thoughts which they do not share.

Stan clutches the Apeman camera to his chest, thinking, *even when they see this, they won't believe it. They just won't believe it. That's why they're never going to see it.*

Bonnie squeezes his hand and thinks about her bed of all things. *I want to pull the shades and crawl into bed and feel warm and safe. That's all I want. I just want to go to sleep.*

Teague does not think of himself, but of Peanut who was, in many ways, like a son to him. *Sometimes you were the worst cop I knew and sometimes you were the best one I could imagine. I don't plan on getting out of this, so see ya soon.*

And Clegg, secretive and unknowable, a mystical and mysterious figure by all accounts, thinks, *well, come on already. I know it's not over and you know it's not over, so play your final hand and I'll play mine. You took my dog and now I'm gonna take your life.*

The Broken Bottle rumbles one last time, then the entire front of the building collapses, pulled out into the street. The entire structure creaks and groans, moving in the wind. Snow cycles in followed by something that no one expects but something they do not shrink from: a great pulsating mass of flesh that pushes into the bar, steaming and simmering and pestiferous, a mutant assemblage of clown flesh composed of thrashing clown limbs and suckering clown faces and thousands of bubble-like eyes. Worming appendages slither and creep. Mouths mewl and squeak. It's a great bubbling, hissing, effervescent mass of gore and distorted anatomy and clown meat that has come to drown them in its sluicing seepage.

Clegg and the others do not run.

There are no theatrics. No screaming or crying out or mad rushes to safety. There is only acceptance. And a communal, psychic hatred for what has destroyed Craw Falls.

Stan and Bonnie grip each other's hands that much tighter. Teague steels himself until it feels like he's wound immobile in iron bands. And Clegg, thinking of Trixie, reaches for the button at his wrist.

He presses it.

The Broken Bottle explodes with a mushrooming orange-yellow cloud of fire and flaming debris that shoots up nearly four-hundred feet in the sky and then comes back down in a rain of blazing wreckage. Whatever was in the bar is atomized. Whatever secrets it contained, burn throughout the remainder of the night until there is nothing left but blackened beams and rafters and a curling funnel of greasy black smoke that dissipates in the blizzard.

Just before dawn, the storm blows itself out.

THE END?

Not if you want to dive into more of Crystal Lake Publishing's Tales from the Darkest Depths!

Check out our amazing website and online store or download our latest catalog here.
https://geni.us/CLPCatalog

We always have great new projects and content on the website to dive into, as well as a newsletter, behind the scenes options, social media platforms, our own dark fiction shared-world series and our very own webstore. Our webstore even has categories specifically for KU books, non-fiction, anthologies, and of course more novels and novellas.

About the Author

Tim Curran is the author of *Skin Medicine, Hive, Dead Sea, The Devil Next Door, Blooding Night, Bioterror,* and *Bad Girl in the Box,* among others. His short stories have been collected in *Alien Horrors, The Horrors of War,* and *The Brain Leeches.* His novellas include *The Underdwelling, The Corpse King, Puppet Graveyard, Worm,* and *The Sunken City.* His fiction has been translated into German, Russian, Japanese, Spanish, and Italian. Find him at facebook.com/tim.curran.77.

MISSION STATEMENT

Since its founding in August 2012, Crystal Lake has quickly become one of the world's leading publishers of Dark Fiction and Horror books. In 2023, Crystal Lake officially transitioned into an entertainment company, joining several other divisions, genres, and imprints, including Torrid Waters, Crystal Lake Comics, Crystal Lake Games, Crystal Lake Kids, and many more.

While we strive to present only the highest quality fiction and entertainment, we also endeavour to support authors along their writing journey. We offer our time and experience in non-fiction projects, as well as author mentoring and services, at competitive prices.

With several Bram Stoker Award wins and many other wins and nominations (including the HWA's Specialty Press Award), Crystal Lake Publishing puts integrity, honor, and respect at the forefront of our publishing operations.

We strive for each book and outreach program we spearhead to not only entertain and touch or comment on issues that affect our readers, but also to strengthen and support the Dark Fiction field and its authors.

Not only do we find and publish authors we believe are destined for greatness, but we strive to work with men and women who endeavour to be decent human beings who care more for others than themselves, while still being hard working, driven, and passionate artists and storytellers.

Crystal Lake Publishing is and will always be a beacon of what passion and dedication, combined with overwhelming teamwork and respect, can accomplish. We endeavour to know each and every one of our readers, while building personal relationships with our authors, reviewers, bloggers, podcasters, bookstores, and libraries.

We will be as trustworthy, forthright, and transparent as any business can be, while also keeping most of the headaches away from our authors, since it's our job to solve the problems so they can stay in a creative mind. Which of course also means paying our authors.

We do not just publish books, we present to you worlds within your world, doors within your mind, from talented authors who sacrifice so much for a moment of your time.

There are some amazing small presses out there, and through collaboration and open forums we will continue to support other presses in the goal of helping authors and showing the world what quality small presses are capable of accomplishing. No one wins when a small press goes down, so we will always be there to support hardworking, legitimate presses and their authors. We don't see Crystal Lake as the best press out there, but we will always strive to be the best, strive to be the most interactive and grateful, and even blessed press around. No matter what happens over time, we will also take our mission very seriously while appreciating where we are and enjoying the journey.

What do we offer our authors that they can't do for themselves through self-publishing?

We are big supporters of self-publishing (especially hybrid publishing), if done with care, patience, and planning. However, not every author has the time or inclination to do market research, advertise, and set up book launch strategies. Although a lot of authors are successful in doing it all, strong small presses will always be there for the authors who just want to do what they do best: write.

What we offer is experience, industry knowledge, contacts and trust built up over years. And due to our strong brand and trusting fanbase, every Crystal Lake Publishing book comes with weight of respect. In time our fans begin to trust our judgment and will try a new author purely based on our support of said author.

With each launch we strive to fine-tune our approach, learn from our mistakes, and increase our reach. We continue to assure our authors that we're here for them and that we'll carry the weight of the launch and dealing with third parties while they focus on their strengths—be it writing, interviews, blogs, signings, etc.

We also offer several mentoring packages to authors that include knowledge and skills they can use in both traditional and self-publishing endeavours.

We look forward to launching many new careers.

This is what we believe in. What we stand for. This will be our legacy.

Welcome to Crystal Lake Publishing—Where Stories Come Alive!